Pirate's Desire

Being a tale of a Lady's Adventure at Sea

by Andreya Stuart

Find More Books by Andreya Stuart on
Amazon
&
www.MobileLoveStories.com

PROLOGUE

LONDON 1717

Corwyn Tyler Chase, dressed in a warm, brown woolen gown and a white molly cap, arrived at the London docks to board the Albatross precisely at four. With her she had five trunks, her new lady's maid, and a letter from the ship's owner promising her passage to Virginia.

As she made her way up the narrow gangplank, staring down at the roiling water that filled the gap between boat and dock, she found herself abruptly toe to toe with a hawk-faced first mate. He was tall, dirty, bare footed, ill-shaven and his narrow grey eyes regarded her with both irritation and suspicion.

"And what do ye think ye'll be about?" he asked.

Corwyn took an unsteady step back. Why, she wondered, was the plank so narrow? Why was there no net between the thin rope rail and sodden wood?

"If you will allow me to board, I have a letter from the owner-"

The man did not budge, eyeing the maid and the luggage that still waited on the dock. "We'll be having no women aboard this ship-"

"But, I have a letter from the owner promising me passage to Virginia-"

"The master will have no truck wi' it," he said. "Now get you on down, little miss-"

"I have passage-"

"Nay," he said.

Corwyn, exhausted by the horror and scandal of the last weeks, considered just letting herself drop into oblivion. It must be fifty feet to the water, and if she went below and the ship crushed her-

She began again.

"I have a letter from the ship's owner. I have paid for passage. Let me board or I shall send for him to come. I daresay-"

"We carry no women without men. Have ye a husband or a brother-"

"My brother is Captain of Her Majesty's Ship the Trident. Twas he that spoke to the owner and paid my fare-"

"And where is he?"

"He sets sail with the tide-"

"Your husband?"

"Where is your Captain?" demanded Corwyn. "Get him or I swear I shall send for the owner and see you both sacked."

"Let me see the order," the mate said.

"Let me board and you shall see it," she said.

When he made no move to obey, she began to turn so she could go down the shakey bridge back to shore.

"Twill be for the captain to decide," the mate said.

Then he rabbited up to the deck leaving her shaken by the sudden movement of gangplank. Corwyn wearily turned to follow him back up on to the boat.

When the Captain came to the deck he was dressed hardly better than his man. He had a greatcoat on and he was arguably cleaner. But still his feet were bare, and his wide flat toes gripped the deck like fat fingers.

He took Corwyn's note, stared at it blearily, then handed it back. He looked her up and down and said, "I've no truck with women at sea. They make the water rise-"

Corwyn interrupted him, violating everything her brother had ever told her about a Captain being like to a god on his own ship. She was past having patience with men, and there was only one man on earth she feared at this point, and it was for this reason she was leaving England.

"Let me have my cabin so we can get underway, or let me send for your master to have you and your mate cast off this ship. I have paid for passage and you have no right to bar me."

She might have said more but the Captain was already ordering the first mate to take up quarters with the second so she and her maid could have a cabin for the crossing.

As the trunks were taken away, Corwyn looked back toward shore. At last, for once, reason had prevailed. Perhaps she would be permitted to escape her motherland with her life. Surely it was almost all she had left.

The ship set sail as the day died, making its slow way through the other deep sea vessels that crowded the Thames. Corwn saw the ever shifting masts reach upward like the trees of a winter forest, long spars like stark branches dark against a sooty sky.

She saw night overtake the banks of the river as they made for the open sea, looming buildings illuminated only sporadically by the glow of lamp or candle. Wind chilling her face, cloak billowing about her, Corwyn felt like she was sailing off the end of the world.

Once she had longed to see foreign lands, had prayed she might visit the New World with Ben. Why, she had wondered, could a man become a Captain, an adventurer, but a woman could only become a wife, confined to a house, sentenced to care for a family? Was there really no higher aspiration? Was that all the world offered her? To go from daughter to mother with nothing in between?

Now she wished for nothing more than her bed at Chase Manor and the peace she had known before she ever came to London.

Corwyn turned to find Margaret, the maid that had been found for her this morning, had also come up to watch London slide past. Her broad, round, features were reddened by the wind, and she looked entirely at ease. She had family in Virginia, two brothers and a cousin. Corwyn envied her. Marget was starting a new life and a grand adventure, Corwyn was fleeing for her life.

It had all begun badly enough. Corwyn, the beloved and unexpected daughter of elderly parents had been born fifteen years after her two older brothers. There had been many children born and lost between them. Sons, she had been told, all gray, pale and thin.

When Corwyn had come into the world, strong, pink and bright-eyed, there had been some hope that she might survive. Still she had been christened without fanfare just hours after birth, and she had slept in her mother's bed for a full five years before anyone could trust the miracle that she wouldn't be carried off by a sore throat or a bad cough.

A merry, happy, raven-haired little girl with bright green eyes, a ready wit and frequently dirty feet, she had her way with everyone at home. Her mother and father and nurse had doted on her, her eldest brother had taught her to ride and shoot as well as any boy in the neighboring lands. Until she was nine she thought earth was heaven and the world was made for her...

And then the iron constitution which had carried her through her childhood betrayed her. Her mother and father and older brother had all died. Scarlet fever had swept through out the west country filling the land with burning pits and the stench of rotting flesh. Corwyn had watched it all disbelieving. To see so many cut down, to watch so many die, it had struck her dumb.

It was only when her older brother, now heir to their parent's small estates, had come home, that she had come to life again. She had wept, had told him how her father and mother had died in the same bed, refusing to be parted even in agony. She told him how her elder brother had buried them only to fall ill the same day.

Benjamin Chase, who had sought the sea from his first breath, left it behind for a decade to see his sister grown into a young woman. He had continued to serve in Her Majesty's Navy in administrative functions, traveling to London for half of every year only to return for the winter months to his sister and the bleak marshes and moors of Land's End and Marazion.

In the fall of this year he had told Corwyn she must go to London. Their cousin, the Lady Christina Wakefield, had promised her a home and a coming out. Corwyn would become a woman grown, and Ben would return to the sea. He had been offered his first command of a small ship. He would be patrolling the coast of Virginia for pirates. Their lives must part, he told her, for he had no desire to farm. The estates would be her dowry and he would make his life in the New World.

She had begged him to take him with her and he had declined. The colonies were rough country. She would never be safe amongst the savages and all the rough men of those new lands.

Instead he had taken her to London . . .

Chapter One

Six weeks earlier . . .

Lord Norfolk studied the girl from a safe distance. Her gown of white satin with panniers of indigo blue made her look younger than when they had last met, and the artfully constructed bodice showed her untried bosom to its best advantage. Midnight hair framed a heart-shaped face and sported a strand of pearls. Her emerald eyes sparkled when she laughed.

She leaned forward to whisper something in her companion's ear and he felt a flash of anger. He had made himself quite clear about town in the last few weeks. She was his.

Over a month ago he had agreed to escort Lady Christina Wakefield's newly arrived cousin to the theater. As one of London's wealthiest bachelors, if something of a rakehell, his appearance with the girl assured her acceptance in the highest social circles.

He had been surprised to discover, over the course of the evening, that she was not only a beauty, but also quite the innocent. How long had it been since a virgin had come to London?

During the intermission he led her from the high box seats down to the velvet-muffled stage, promising a glimpse behind the scenes. Once there he yielded to temptation and stole a kiss.

He could still feel those tender lips beneath his, that fragile, coltish body struggling against him. When he finally permitted her to escape, she slapped him with some spirit and delivered a stiff dressing down. The memory still made him laugh.

In the days since, he had pursued her relentlessly. Flowers, jewellery and letters of undying passion arrived at her doorstep each and every day. He appeared at every social engagement she attended, teased her with innuendo and double-entendre until she could not speak at all.

Tonight he planned to press his campaign with Lady Chase to a new level. While humiliating the girl might provide entertainment, it did little to slake his desire for her. Tonight he had made elaborate arrangements that would give them several hours alone. By tomorrow there would be one less innocent abroad.

Corwyn tried to attend to the earnest young man who sat beside her. The sights and sounds of the ball around them made conversation all but impossible, which was probably for the best. Despite Lord Brougham's accomplishment as a dancer, she feared she might not like him so well if she could understand more of his story regarding his success at the recent hunt. He seemed to spend an inordinate amount of time galloping around fields shooting stags square between the eyes.

"Good eve, Lord Brougham." The voice startled Corwyn from her distracted reverie. "I am surprised to find you here with the new crop not yet sold. Since you are doing so well, I am sure you can repay that rather large note you made when last we wagered. Five thousand pounds, was it not?" Lord Norfolk tapped his walking stick against Brougham's leg. "It shall expect it in the morning."

Corwyn closed her eyes and prayed for a miracle. Lord Norfolk, she thought, must fancy himself an actor for he always raised his voice as he played out these scenes.

"Be a good man and your seat," said Lord Norfolk, motioning Thomas to his feet. "My Lady and I have much to discuss."

"No-" Corwyn began.

Thomas stood up as if he did not hear her. His once florid face was pasty now, his movements awkward. He walked away without a word.

Norfolk folded himself onto the lounge beside Corwyn. He was dressed in a suit of gold and silver brocade, and he spent a moment arranging his great coat before he turned toward her. His eyes were the cold blue of a winter sky, his skin the color of new ivory. His blond hair was lightly powdered and caught behind his head in a gold ribbon.

"My dear, I must confess I was quite distressed when you returned my last gift. It was such a small thing." He lay a smooth hand upon her lap. "You must really accept these little presents or you sell yourself too cheap-"

Corwyn swept his hand away as though it were an insect. "I do not sell myself at all, My Lord." she said.

"Then you give yourself away?" and someone laughed.

Corwyn felt the blood rush her face.

Norfolk dismissed the matter with a wave of his hand at a knowing look at those near by who had turned to listen to their conversation.

He continued, "I am looking forward to this evening's supper. Your cousin and a few select friends will make such delightful company-"

"There must be a mistake," Corwyn cut him off. "I have accepted no such engagement."

"It is all arranged," Norfolksaid as if she hadn't spoken.

"I am very sorry," Corwyn allowed her tone to become curt, "It is quite impossible."

Christina had warned her not to offend Norfolk. He was known to be vicious. But under no circumstances would Corwyn spend an evening with him.

Benjamin Chase, heard his sister's raised voice as he passed by and instinctively turned toward it. Having forgotten that he had Lord Black in tow, he pressed through a pair of daringly dressed dowagers and a collection of girls a year or two older than Corwyn.

A blond in jade jostled against him, but he deftly sidestepped the advance. His sister was the one on the block. He would soon leave London behind.

Lord Henry Norfolk, seated beside Corwyn, had turned toward her. "Don't worry, dear Lady, you will be in bed by dawn."

"I'll be in bed by midnight," Corwyn countered, "as I shall be going home after the ball."

"You and I are to ride with your cousin in one carriage," Norfolk explained. "The others will join us as they are able."

"I don't-"

"Corwyn!" Ben spoke before Corwyn could continue. "I have been looking for you everywhere!" He allowed himself a quick look at Lord Norfolk. At first Norfolk's campaign to win Corwyn's heart had been an annoyance. Now it was coming to seem sinister. Christina had assured Ben that all was well, but he was coming to have his doubts. Surely new gifts arriving every day must be considered obsessive.

"You have been looking for me?" Corwyn asked, making no attempt to hide her surprise.

Ben stared at her. Perhaps this was the first time they had spoken for a week. Still, she might have come up with more helpful. He was rescuing her after all.

He felt someone stir behind him, and recalled his original purpose. Well, any port in a storm.

"I wanted to introduce you to Lord Black, the Earl of Kettering."

Then Ben stepped to one side.

Corwyn thought she must be dreaming. The raven-haired man before her was at least a head taller than everyone else in the room. His shoulders were massive, legs well muscled. His hands, square, strong and scarred from hard labor. His face was bronze from long hours in the sun, his eyes such a dark gray they seemed to have no pupil. He looked like some hero out of a fairy tale, a black prince fated to mete justice and steal hearts. He could not have been more out of place here.

He also appeared to have not the least interest in meeting her. In fact, he appeared to be searching the crowd around them for someone else entirely.

"Lord Black," said Ben, "My sister, Corwyn Tyler Chase."

The Earl finally turned to meet her eyes and she felt her heart freeze in her chest. He spoke and she heard the words as if they came from a thousand miles away.

"A pleasure," he said, though the words carried little conviction.

Both men waited for Corwyn to speak, but she could not frame a single sentence.

"My Lord," At long last Ben was speaking again and Corwyn could hear the amusement in his voice. She made a note to kill him the next time they met.

"I see someone I must say something to. Would you do me the honor of attending to my sister for a moment?"

Before Lord Black could answer, Ben had slipped away.

Corwyn, eyes locked in Lord Black's regard, struggled to find something to say.

Instead Lord Black spoke. Unfortunately Corwyn was too over taken to hear what it might have been.

"Pardon me?" Corwyn heard herself speak.

"Would you care to dance, My Lady?" Lord Black offered his hand.

Corwyn stood up without a word. She thought she heard Norfolk make some kind of noise. He must be furious that she had effected yet another escape. One day she would have to set him straight. Never had a man so needed a good clout about the head . . .

Lord Black put a wide hand in the small of Corwyn's back as he led her though the room. The heat of it crawled up her spine and filled her head till it felt ready to fly away. He brought them to rest beneath one of three tremendous chandeliers that illuminated room. As the first few notes of the next piece fell, he turned toward her. A tug brought her into his arms. They began to dance.

Corwyn stared up into her partner's bottomless eyes. However would she explain herself when the dance came to an end, she wondered. Would she say what kept running through her mind?

You are the stuff dreams are made of...

Black found the girl intriguing. He had believed himself immune to the snare of virgins and yet this one gave him pause. He wished she were some farm child, a peasant. He could imagine how he might while away the hours with her, wondered how she would look when she discovered passion for the very first time. There was something mystical in her wild green eyes. That mass of midnight hair reminded him of days long past when desire was something new.

He sighed. It would be so easy to guide her to some forgotten corner and teach her the pleasure of a kiss. And perhaps more, he acknowledged wryly. How could one stop at a kiss when a woman had so much more to offer?

When the music faded away, Corwyn found herself in Lord Black's arms for a moment too long. With a step back, she put a discreet distance between them, and jerked her eyes to the ground. She must not look at him again if she meant to regain her senses. He was a man, she told herself sternly, just a man.

"You are a fine dancer, My Lord," she said in a low voice. There, that did not sound entirely stupid. Perhaps he would not think her a complete fool.

"A pleasure, My Lady."

Corwyn looked up despite herself, meeting his eyes again.

Then he smiled, and the heavens seemed to open over his head. For an instant, she understood him too. He found her desirable, amusing. There was something savage about him, she could sense it. But he would be gentle with her...

She turned away. She had to get hold of herself. What on earth was wrong with her? She searched the room, looking for Ben. Had he meant to embarrass her this way?

To her horror, she saw Norfolk, striding toward her, probably determined to claim her for a supper she had never agreed to. She hadn't the strength to fend him off again.

"I . . . I feel ill," she said. She put her hand out to steady herself on the Earl's arm lest she slip to the floor. The wine, the dance, Henry and now Lord Black, it was all suddenly too much. The room was spinning. "Fresh air-" she said, looking toward the wall of French doors to her right.

"I am afraid it is far too cold to go outdoors."

Corwyn looked up to find Lord Black's smile gone. In fact, he looked quite forbidding now.

"Please," said Corwyn. He had to understand. He must know how she felt.

With an infinitesimal shrug of his shoulders, Lord Black gave his assent. He followed her across the length of the room to the windowed-doors overlooking the garden. In a moment they had emerged onto the long terrace that ran the length of the house. Since the weather was cool, they were alone.

Fifteen minutes later the Earl of Kettering leaned against the wall that ran the length of the terrace and watched the girl before him pace. Why in the world had she brought him out into the chill of an early spring night? He had thought she truly might be ill, but now she walked back and forth along the stone walk ably enough, peering into the ballroom windows as though looking for someone? Could she be afraid of something?

"I assume you did not bring me out here for a stolen embrace," he said. He was too old for these games and it was time she knew it.

"What?" asked the girl. She turned to him as if startled to find him capable of speech. "I beg your pardon," she amended. She approached him then, still casting glances behind her.

Whatever she was afraid of, Devon decided, she was about to find out that he was far more dangerous.

"Why did you bring me out here?" He made his voice harsh.

"I . . . I felt faint." The girl was surprised at his tone. She took a step back. Once again she looked over her shoulder.

"Enough!" Devon grabbed her wrist and jerked her down a short flight of stone steps onto the lawn. He blocked her way back to the lighted walk. Perhaps she would now give him her undivided attention.

"What are you doing?" she cried out.

"Tell me what *you* are doing," he demanded.

"I am trying to avoid someone." She said. "I should think that would be obvious."

"And that would be?" Devon asked.

"Surely you can guess," she said. "And, My Lord, it is none of your business!"

Guess? What was the girl talking about?

"Tell me!" Devon said sharply. Having just murdered his uncle to regain his estates, and after one decade of slavery and another of piracy, he was shocked to find himself caught up in some scandal with this girl-child.

"Lord Norfolk," the girl said, "You sat beside me." Then, as if she thought this might require more explanation, she continued in a lowered voice. "He takes liberties."

Lord Norfolk? That must be the popinjay teasing her in the ballroom. Black's blood suddenly ran cold. What a fool he was! The chit was trying to free herself from an over ardent admirer. She was using him!

"I see," he said. If she had cast him as her new lover, by God he would play the part. In a motion made swift by years of combat he had her by the shoulder.

"Lord Norfolk takes liberties," he said as he pulled her with him into the shadows. In a moment he was half seated along the slanted wall that lined the stairs and she was standing between his legs.

"Let us see," he said, "I am sure he does this."

It was, Corwyn reflected with amazement, everything she had ever imagined a kiss could be. His lips brushed hers, once, twice, then finally lingered. He deepened the kiss, his tongue entering her mouth, exploring her as though he had an eternity to spend.

"And this of course," he whispered. His free hand found the slope of her breast, caressing it through the thin fabric of her bodice. Startled at the surge of heat that coursed through her, she tried to pull away. He held her still, lowered his eyes to watch as he swept the troublesome cloth aside. One full soft globe appeared in the moonlight and his thumb worried its tip into a peak.

"And this too." He bent his leonine head to the untried flesh, tasted her, then suckled gently.

Corwyn gasped, her back arched. Her hand came up, tapered fingers finding purchase in the dark mass of his hair. Then he was kissing her again, standing as he ran his hands the length of her body, pressing her against him.

Then he shoved her away, eyes hard. "No wonder Lord Norfolk takes liberties. You offer them in abundance." He watched as she struggled to right her clothes, enjoying her embarrassment.

"You bastard." Corwyn said the words without thinking.

He cocked his head to one side. "You have no idea what a bastard I can be," he said. "But you will certainly find out if anything comes of this little farce." He brushed past her into the moonlit garden.

Lord Norfolk saw the girl return. She entered the house through one of the side doors away from the ballroom. She was ruffled, tousled looking, tearful from the looks of it. Apparently the slut's lover had declined her bed.

He had watched the pair exit into the garden, and unable to believe his eyes, had moved to follow them. There, from the darkness of the terrace just a few yards away, he had watched Black all but ravish the girl, had been startled by her ardent response. His fury knew no bounds.

He had thought to court the little vixen, but she had played him for a fool! She had a lover, had already taken a man to her bed. How dare she reject him like a schoolboy for but a single kiss? What she could give to another she would certainly yield to him.

And this Black Earl! This man from nowhere! All London knew who owned the girl and yet this cur chose to make her his own?

He would punish them both. By morning everyone would know their little secret. Then he would make an example of them. The Earl of Kettering would die for daring to take what he desired and Lady Chase would find herself debased beyond all reckoning for yielding to another. They would find, as others had, that Lord Henry Norfolk was not a man to ignore an offense.

Chapter Two

Corwyn could not bring herself to get out of bed the following morning. Over and over again she reviewed the events of the past evening in her mind's eye. She was back in that moonlit garden, Lord Black's lips hot upon hers, held immobile in his arms.

Why had she not stopped him? Why had she not wanted to? With Norfolk she felt only revulsion, but she had felt anything but distaste for Lord Black. Had he asked her to do anything for him, go anywhere with him, she would have obliged. She had known him less than thirty minutes, and he had all but undressed her. She had murmured not one word of protest, had wanted nothing more than for him to continue...

Christina interrupted Corwyn's painful reverie with a knock on the door. Despite Corwyn's lack of response, the statuesque blonde let herself in. She swept across the room to seat herself upon the wide bed, draping the ivory and blue silk of her skirts artfully.

"Good Morning." Christina appeared to be in a pleasant mood. "I see you have given up that disgraceful habit of rising early."

"I've given up rising altogether," said Corwyn.

She glared at Christina, so beautiful with her perfect peach complexion and that glorious mane of golden hair. Christina was the belle of every ball, forever composed, never at a loss for words. Christina need not suffer any man's embrace unless she cared to. She was a widow now and answered only to herself. Of course it was a pity that her husband had to die to give her all this freedom, but he was sixty after all.

"So I see." Christina smiled. "I, in a moment of mad energy, rose and went to an early luncheon this afternoon. It was wonderful." She paused to finger the elaborate ruffle of Corwyn's bed. "I heard so many interesting things about you and your new Lord. How excited you must be!" She gave Corwyn a slanted look.

"What new Lord?" Corwyn made herself say the words slowly. Why had she ever bothered to wake up?

"Why Lord Black, of course," said Christina. "How many men did you kiss in the garden last night?"

"One too many, I warrant," replied Corwyn.

"Lord Norfolk himself saw you leave." Christina smiled a little as she continued, "I am afraid he will no longer pay you quite the attention he has in the past."

Corwyn mulled over this unforeseen consequence for a moment. "Well that is something to be thankful for," she said at last. "Nothing else ever drove him away," She took a deep breath to prepare herself for the whole story. "What, precisely, did you hear?"

"Despite your warm response to Lord Norfolk's advances, and your agreement to entertain him privately later in the evening, you exited into the garden to philander with Lord Black. Or so the story goes." Christina sounded as if she were discussing the latest fashion in hats.

"I certainly did not!"

"Which?" Christina asked.

"Either! Both!" Corwyn took a deep breath. Her heart was pounding in her chest and she could hardly think for the fury that washed over her. "I did not do any of those things."

"You did not go into the garden?" Christina asked.

"Well, I did do that," conceded Corwyn.

"Then you did not kiss Lord Black," Christina went on in a more certain voice.

"He kissed me," said Corwyn.

Christina paused, then smiled. "Perhaps you should tell me exactly what you did not do," she said.

"I did not agree to meet that oaf, Henry Norfolk in order to entertain him privately!" Turning away from her cousin's annoying composure, Corwyn scowled at her reflection in the mirror. "In fact, he said you and he had arranged a late supper for me and I was trying to avoid him so I wouldn't have to go. That is why I went into the garden."

"It all sounds a bit complicated," Christina said.

"It is really very simple. I shall never go out in public again," Corwyn said firmly.

"Oh, of course you will." Christina laughed. "If every woman accused of some deceitful flirtation decided to abandon social life, there would not be any of us left!"

"I do not care!" Corwyn slipped further under the heavy covers and waited for Christina to go away.

"But I care," Christina said in a softer voice. "I am afraid Ben will too. Men really have no sense about these things."

"Ben?" asked Corwyn.

"If he supposed you dishonored..." Christina looked worried for a moment. "He would be compelled to defend you."

When Corwyn made no reply, Christina continued. "I know this is some sort of . . . misunderstanding. Every season has a scandal or two and most involve some innocent young girl who never put a foot wrong. Given time these things fade away."

"I don't see -" How could this possibly involve Ben?

"But, if you give weight to this rumor by changing your behavior, some will believe it. If Ben believes it he may call out Henry or perhaps this new Earl." She shook her head. "That would be a high price to pay for a kiss."

Corwyn nodded in silent assent.

"So," said Christina in a somewhat lighter tone, "Arise. Dress. We'll off to Bond where you may forget your sorrows in new gowns."

"I suppose you are right." Corwyn replied. Throwing off the covers when Christina stood, she moved to the wardrobe and selected a pale green gown that was a great deal lighter than her mood. Perhaps it was best to put this all behind her. Why should she punish herself for the crimes of two overgrown brutes?

"You are here at last." The redhead leaned forward to place the glass of wine on the table before her and let the sheet around her slip an extra inch. "I have been waiting for hours."

"What are you doing here?" Devon saw that Barbara had made herself more than welcome with his Madeira. The half-empty bottle stood on the hearth before the fire. He also noted that her clothes lay in a rumpled heap on the floor as though this were not his flat but her own.

"You act as if you are not happy to see me," pouted Barbara.

"I am in the habit of inviting women into my home." Devon wondered how he would he rid himself of the girl. He was not in the mood for diversion this evening.

"You did invite me!" protested Barbara. "Do you not recall?" She stood, leaving the sheet in the chair.

"Yesterday I invited you. You left this morning. Do you not have a husband to attend to?" Devon finally decided to remove his cloak. He would not be driven out into the rain again. He dumped the sodden mass over the back of a chair and he ran his hands through his hair.

"He is at the theatre with his mistress. We have an arrangement, he and I. You needn't concern yourself with him," Barbara smiled.

"I see," Devon responded. He had not been the least bit concerned by her husband. "Nevertheless, I believe my coachman will drive you home." He pulled the bell cord.

Barbara said nothing for a moment, obviously shocked. Then, face flushed and spitting obscenities, she dove for her clothes. She pulled on the corset and crinolines, the underskirt and finally her gown of emerald green.

"You bastard," she spat, lacing the dress up the front with careless fingers. "How dare you dismiss me! I am no tart to be used and cast away."

"Of course not," said Devon. He picked up the correspondence in the silver tray and looked through it while he waited for his servant to appear.

"You have taken up with that black-haired witch from Cornwall," Barbara said as she pulled her hair back. "When I heard the tales, I doubted them. After all, how could you prefer that skinny chit to me?"

Devon let the insult pass.

"She's a trollop that girl. She has lain with half the men in her brother's stables and all of London knows it. She is like her cousin they say, who will spread her legs for any man who so much as looks at her." Barbara hurled insults at him. "She plays the virgin well, but only fools are taken in."

Devon looked up. "I have no connection with that girl, so I have little interest in her reputation." In fact, he had enough about Corwyn Tyler Chase in the last few hours to last a lifetime.

Before Barbara could manage a stinging response, a rap on the door interrupted them. Without another word, she swept past him, then past the butler who stood in the doorway.

When she was gone, Devon rescued his bottle of Madeira from the flagstones and settled into the chair she had so recently vacated.

He remembered that surprised little face, the eyes of a child regarding him with apparent confusion after he had kissed her.

Could Lady Chase be the harlot the rumors claimed she was? He found that very hard to believe. A lifetime spent with pirates, slavers and criminals of every description had given him a sixth sense for deception. He could not credit that his understanding of her could be so flawed.

He could almost believe that Norfolk was her lover, or more aptly that she was his current victim. Black was all too familiar with his type as well. Perhaps she had seen a chance to rid herself of the blackguard, had thought that he might protect her, and had led him into the garden. Maybe she had hoped that Norfolk would discard her if he saw her with someone else. But that kind never let go. Her attempts to escape would only inflame him further.

He swallowed another mouthful of wine. Under other circumstances he might have taken up her cause, would have delivered the beating Lord Norfolk so richly deserved. He had rescued a woman or two in his time, and thrashing heavy-handed brutes was always a pleasure.

But, he simply could not involve himself in this struggle. He could not make a habit of killing aristocrats even if quite a number truly needed killing. Norfolk was first cousin to the Queen, or was it second cousin? Nephew? His wealth and status made him a formidable enemy for a man whose past could not withstand a moment's scrutiny.

So the black-haired vixen, innocent or well used, would have to find another knight in shining armor. Which was all for the best, because she was turning into something of an obsession. He wanted her, wanted to drag her into a bed and take her in every way possible. He did not care if she had slept with one man or a hundred, were a virgin or a whore. He wanted to see her face again, wanted to hear her gasp as he entered her. He wished that he had finished what he had started on those steps under a cold sky. For all the trouble she had been and was going to be, he should have demanded what little honor she had left.

Chapter Three

Henry Norfolk, irritated at the pace with which the matter proceeded, sat in his uncle's study. It had been almost four weeks, and still Black was a free man. He had even seen the rogue at the gaming tables the night just past, obviously untroubled by his precarious position in society. What audacity!

Norfolk had hired spies to watch him, was paying men to solve the riddle of his mysterious reappearance, and had offered bribes to two of the peers who were all that stood between Black and a prison cell. And all for naught! The man still remained at liberty.

Feet resting upon his uncle's desk, Henry waited for the frail old man to finish the missive he was penning for the Spanish emissary. How could a man of means devote himself so completely to the Queen's business? What satisfaction could he find in a practice that resulted in no personal gain?

Lord Pembroke, looked up from his correspondence long enough to respond to his nephew's demands. "The matter is being investigated most carefully, my boy. We have little doubt that Lord Black is guilty of his uncle's murder. We are simply waiting for one of his conspirators to recant."

"Recant!" Norfolk could not believe his ears, "What do confessions have to do with arresting the man? Arrest him first and press him for the truth." Henry dropped his feet to the floor and stood up. "While you delay, a young girl is being despoiled by that . . . murderer."

Lord Pembroke looked up again. "Surely you have no interest in the girl. I will not have you disgrace your mother-"

"No, no," Henry shook his head. "Nothing like that. But she is such a pretty thing. I just cannot let him continue to . . . use her." God's truth, the idea of Black touching Corwyn drove him mad with jealousy.

"You aren't thinking of calling Black out, are you? The girl has got a brother. If she is being interfered with, let him settle the matter." Lord Pembroke set aside his work to give Henry his full attention. "Your mother would die if anything happened to you..."

"Yes, I know. She faints if I lose a farthing on a horse race. I will not offer myself as the Lady's champion. Still, I cannot stand by while he has his way with her. He should be arrested immediately. His story will fall apart once he is in jail. I am sure of it."

"In time the matter will be resolved to your satisfaction," responded Pembroke. "We will draw up a formal charge soon enough and then your little girl will be safe."

"A week?" Norfolk sat up.

"A month at best, my boy. He is a peer of the realm and he picked his cohorts carefully." Lord Pembroke shook his head, was silent for a moment. "How curious. In recent years I had worried over your character and yet here you are defending some country maid as though your life depended upon it. It is good to see you acquire a conscience my boy."

Norfolk made no response. How could man in his uncle's position be so blind?

"But Henry," Lord Pembroke tapped the table to get his attention. "Do not get carried away in this endeavor. You are your mother's only child and my heir. Do not take matters into your own hands. We have indulged you far too much, and you have had your way in many things, but Lord Black is not a man to be trifled with."

"I have no intention-"

"Listen to me, my boy. Those Ketterings are a vicious, vindictive lot." Lord Pembroke leaned forward. "You will note that no one mourns the murdered uncle. No one doubts that the late Earl killed his own brother to take the title. Murder runs in that family the way madness does in others." He pointed a gnarled finger at Henry, "So promise me you will stay well away from Devon Black."

"I will, Uncle." Henry lied without compunction. It was obvious that using the King's courts to destroy Lord Black would take far too long. He would have to take a more direct approach.

Lord Norfolk watched Devon Black emerge from his coach and step into the rain that poured from the midnight sky like water through a sieve. As Norfolk's spy had predicted, the man was right on time. He was dressed in rough, dark clothes, like a common tradesman and appeared all but unarmed. Black said something to his driver and then waved the coach on its away.

The Earl boarded one of the dark ships that huddled in the swirling river and spoke to one of the crewmen standing watch on the vessel. A moment later the man went below, returning a short time later with a taller fellow. Together Black and the tall man left the ship, heading into one of the inns nearby from which light and music poured.

Henry and his pair of burly associates left the relative comfort of the hired carriage and walked down the cobbled street into the inn. They moved through the crowd of lecherous drunks and dirty serving women to sit at a rough-hewn bench in the back corner of the taproom. Norfolk turned so he could watch Black talk to the tall man. He wondered what on earth such an unequal pair had to discuss.

"That's the one then?" said one of the thugs beside him. "Course its 'im" said the other.

Norfolk spoke to the oversized pair without turning his head. "Do you think you can take him?"

"An' 'im bein' nought but a slummin' lordling?" said the bald one. Then, as it suddenly aware that Norfolk, dressed in old clothes and a battered hat might be considered in the same light, he added, "Beggin' yer pardon, sir."

The other, though somewhat younger and built like a prize bull, was more cautious. "A fighter I'll warrant. Look at 'is arms."

"But no match for mean' Jake," said the older man to Norfolk. "We c'n put 'im down."

A barmaid came by to offer them drinks. She gave Norfolk a long slow look as she took their order. He obliged her by examining her breasts as she bent over.

"'as the 'ots fer you, she does," said the older man as she moved away. He gave Norfolk a snaggle-toothed smile.

"Shut yer yap, Merrick." Jake gave his partner in crime a glare.

"I want you to kill him." Norfolk gave them both a hard look. "Just follow him from this pub, and kill him when he is alone."

Jake nodded. "Ay sir. 'E's no match for me an' Merrick. Big as 'e is, we can do 'im."

Norfolk nodded and rose from the table. He dropped a pair of gold coins before them. "Thank you, gentlemen. I look forward to hearing of our friend's untimely demise."

"Wot?" Merrick asked. "Wot did you say?"

"Shut yer 'ole I said," Jake reached out to clout his brother on the side of his head.

Norfolk left without waiting to see the end of the argument. He walked back to his carriage and sat inside.

Black knew he was being followed from the moment he left the taproom. The pair behind him were big, probably farm boys come to make a life for themselves in the city. Seamen were usually smaller, quicker on their feet than these two.

He felt his blood sing as he led them away from the wharves into the silent streets between the warehouses. London seemed full of enemies these days, but these were the first two who had presented themselves to him in such a forthright fashion. He found himself wanting to thank them for giving him such a pleasant way to express his frustration.

They called to him as he entered a dead-end alley. He knew the area because it was near one of his own warehouses. Having a title made dealing with revenuers easier, so his crew had taken up smuggling. In a few weeks he expected to be able to send them home, free to take ownership of everything he had left behind. He just wanted things here firmly settled first.

Once he had the boys thirty feet from the main road, he turned to face them. It was dark, but he could still make them out.

"Did you want something, gentlemen?"

"Me ‘n Jake were wonderin' if ye ‘ad some gilt ye'd like to give up, yer Lordship."

Black smiled, turned to the smaller of the men, "Is that what you were wondering Jake?"

"Shut yer trap Merrick!" The man called Jake was coming around on Black's right. He held something in his hands, a club of some kind.

"You two wouldn't be brothers, would you?" Black slid his hand down his thigh, found the haft of his knife. "The last time I killed a pair like you, they were brothers."

"Listen to ‘im talk!" Merrick stepped forward. He must have a blade because he was taking the lead.

Black heard the man's arm sweep toward his chest and he took a step back. He dropped down to one knee and drove his knife through the man's side. With years of long practice he curled the blade up into the man's heart. Merrick dropped like a stone.

"Let us see," said Black as he turned. "We have Jake left, do we not?"

"Merrick? Merrick?" Jake had the club extended, was breathing hard. His night vision was weak, it appeared, because he did not seem to understand that his brother was bleeding to death at his feet.

Black grabbed the club and jerked on it hard, as if trying to wrench it out of his hands. Jake struggled to maintain his grip and was dragged forward. Black ran his blade up into the man's throat. Jake's fell atop his brother.

Barely winded, Black looked around to insure that he had not missed any other assailants. At the end of the alley he saw that a carriage was stopped. Its windows were dark, the driver a statue. He started toward it just as it pulled away.

Norfolk evaluated the results of his last attack on Lord Black dispassionately. The man was obviously competent at defending himself. Of course, garden-variety thugs were hardly a match for a well-trained man, but it was rather surprising that Black had dispatched them so easily. His uncle was right, Black was a killer.

Norfolk had no doubt that he could best Black in a duel. He had years of training under his belt, and had put more than a dozen in the ground. Lord Black was obviously a street fighter. He probably preferred to settle his affairs in dark alleys with a short blade. Make him fight with a rapier in a cold dawn and he would fall easily.

Of course a duel was out of the question. While his uncle lived, Norfolk could not go against him in the important things. Lord Pembroke could easily select another heir, and then Norfolk would only inherit his mother's estates. He had already inherited his father's title and properties, and his mother's death would return her dower, so he was quite well off already. But his uncle, miser that he was, had more money than God. There was no use jeopardizing those funds over a cur like Black.

On the other hand, it would be nice to kill the man himself, preferably with the girl watching. That would be ideal. Black would bleed to death; she would hold his head as he gasped his last. And later Norfolk would take her brutally, would describe all he had done to have her. But how could such a thing be arranged? He would have to give the matter some thought.

Chapter Four

"You have been working for the man for almost a month. She has not come even once?" Henry scowled at the servant over the breadth of his desk. How irritating it was to be thwarted when one had developed the perfect plan.

"No, yer Lordship," said the man, running a hand through his bright red hair. "I swear she hasn't. I should have come to you immediately if I had seen her."

"I dare say they have decided to slack off a bit," said Norfolk. Early on his ire had driven him to spread wild rumors about the couple a

cross London. Perhaps neither wished to be seen in the company of the other just at the moment.

The servant's pale face began to take on some color as he realized that he would not be punished.

"But what will you do when she does come?" Norfolk sat back in his chair.

"I will summon you immediately," said the man.

"And what will happen if you delay so much as an instant?"

The man swallowed. "You will kill me, My Lord."

"Indeed. I will cut out your heart and cook it in front of you, as they did to your grandfather."

The man swallowed again.

"It was a common punishment for Irish treachery in days past, and I think it a good one to carry forward into the future."

"I swear I will summon you." The man ran a hand through his red hair, wiped at the sweat beaded on his upper lip. "I swear I will."

"You should see her within the week," said Norfolk. "So, be vigilant." Norfolk waved a hand to dismiss the man and watched him skitter from the room like a frightened deer.

Norfolk shook his head. He had destroyed so many in his time, and he wondered why Lord Black should present such a challenge. In order for his plan to work, the Black Earl and his little tart simply had to meet. Now, since they would not come together of their own accord, he would have to flush the girl toward her lover, the way that servants flushed game into a blind for him to shoot. He sighed. Perhaps it was for the best. It would be a pleasure to see her again, and a joy to make her play such an active role in his plan.

Six weeks after the disastrous ball, Corwyn found herself at a private club wishing she could be almost anywhere else. Fires blazed in two enormous hearths and the small windows along one wall were closed to prevent even a breath of air from entering the room. Why had she decided to wear this heavy gown of cream velvet? In fact, why had she consented to take part in this wretched outing at all?

Rising, Corwyn approached Christina. When an opportunity presented itself, she pulled her away from the gaming table.

"I feel truly unwell," she whispered into her cousin's ear. "My head is pounding. Would you be quite upset if I went home?"

Christina laughed as if she had said something amusing. Leaning close to her cousin, she whispered. "If you try to leave early you will only make them believe you are scurrying off to yet another assignation with one of your lovers." Christina's quick smile softened her words. "Really, I think it might be best if you just left with the rest of us. Do you think you can wait an hour or so?"

"I can wait," Corwyn replied. How cool Christina looked in her pale blue gown, powdered hair curling softly upon her head like a cloud. "I am sure I will feel better in a moment."

"You know, my dear," said Christina as she took her arm, "You should be quite pleased. It has been days since I heard anything truly scandalous about you." By then they were standing at the table, and she handed Corwyn a handful of coins. "Maybe your luck is changing."

Corwyn managed a smile and laid a wager. She threw the dice, and lost all her money on the first pass. She shrugged her shoulders, and Christina gave her a little hug as she drifted away.

Moments later she stood to one side watching Christina preside over the dozen or more people in their party. Her cousin's ability to banter with the company filled Corwyn with envy. Where had she acquired such skill? Was it something a person could learn?

A steward interrupted Corwyn's contemplation of the social graces.

"Milady," he leaned forward to whisper in her ear, "Your brother is waiting for you in one of the small sitting rooms. He says he must speak with you immediately."

Corwyn turned to confront the young man who had spoken to her. Could this be true? Why had Ben come to her here? Her heart skipped a beat. Could he have heard one of the stories circulating about her? Had he come to demand an explanation? What would she tell him?

Ben ventured every day to his ship anchored in the Pool of London, between the Tower and London Bridges. She had hoped he was too caught up with making plans to leave for the colonies to listen to London gossip.

"Take me to him," she whispered. She stood and followed the man from the room, her heart pounding.

Moving into the private areas of the club, the meeting rooms set aside for card games and more delicate assignations, terrible images filled Corwyn's mind. Ben would surely do something foolish if she told him the truth. Yet the lies circulating about her were even worse.

What would she do if he chose to call Norfolk out, or worse yet the Earl of Kettering. She could just imagine him upon the cold ground, blood pouring from his chest. What in the world would she tell him?

Corwyn stopped to look back down the way they had come. Christina would know how to handle this. She did not have to face Ben alone.

"He is this way My Lady," the steward said. He opened a door just to her left.

It was too late to turn back. Corwyn took a deep breath and stepped into the room. Somehow she would make Ben understand that it would all blow over sooner or later.

Where was he? Corwyn looked around the room. She saw the red leather chairs, oriental carpets, a card table and a bevy of candles that filled the wall sconces. A fire burned in the hearth and a decanter of gin sat open on the mantle.

A sharp click made her spin about.

"My dear, how kind of you to come," Lord Norfolk placed the key he had used to lock the door in his waistcoat. Today, dressed all in black and silver, he looked particularly predatory. "This is the first of my invitations you have ever accepted."

"Open the door!" demanded Corwyn. She was at once relieved and enraged. So Ben had not come to demand an explanation. Henry was just toying with her again.

"I wanted to see you." Norfolk did not seem to hear her. "This was the only way to speak with you in private. You seem to be constantly in the company of your cousin these days." He took a sip of his drink, and gave her a smile. "I am sure you understand."

"I do not understand!" Corwyn took a step toward him. This time she would set him straight. In her fury she could imagine nothing more pleasant than slapping that smug expression off his face. "Henry Norfolk, I never, ever, ever want to see you again!"

"Oh, I would never agree to that, My Lady," said Norfolk shaking his head. "You see, I am quite determined to have you. You cannot imagine the plans I have-"

"I would sooner die." Corwyn spat.

"Well, that would be quite contrary to my purpose." Norfolk said. "But I do agree that someone should die." He paused, as if contemplating their previous encounters. "Someone who has kept you from me."

"Kept me from you?" Corwyn asked.

"Another man," said Norfolk. "And once he is out of the way you will give me the attention I am due." He moved toward the fire. "You really should feel terrible, forcing kill a man to win you." He refilled his glass from the decanter.

"Black?" Corwyn queried after a moment's mystification. "You are going to kill the Earl of Kettering?" Shaking her head, she laughed. "He means nothing to me," she said, "nothing at all."

"Will you say that when you see him hang?" Norfolk seemed startled by her declaration. "If you have a mind for a last tryst with your lover, you should make haste. He will see Newgate day after tomorrow."

"I could not care less," Corwyn did not permit herself to wonder if that was true. "Well, if that is what you have brought me here to say, I have heard it. Unlock the door." She wondered if Christina had begun to miss her. It certainly would not do to be found cloistered, alone, with Lord Norfolk.

Norfolk was silent for a moment. "Perhaps I should pick a new target," he said thoughtfully.

"What?" asked Corwyn. Her blood ran cold as she realized her mistake.

"Your brother? Your cousin? Who would suit you best?"

"You cannot be serious."

"In two days, Lord Black will be arrested," Norfolk put his empty glass on a gaming table. "I think you will credit my sincerity then."

He must be insane, Corwyn thought, utterly, terribly mad.

"Let us see," said Norfolk as he came to stand just inches away from her. "I believe your brother is due to sail soon. That must be stopped." His pale blue eyes followed the curve of her face, explored the soft mounds that rose from her bodice. "How shall I treat him? Shall I call him out and carve him up like a Sunday roast? Or shall I take away his commission?" An ivory hand rose to caress her lower lip. "I believe my cousin serves on the board and there are always ways to get a man in trouble."

Corwyn was too frightened to move, to say anything.

Norfolk leaned down to whisper in her ear. "Now will you have me?"

The citrus smell of his cologne wafted over her, his breath stirred her hair. "Come, it is not as bad as all that. What can a man do to you that has not been done?"

"I need . . . time." Corwyn had to stop him from talking. She put a hand on his chest, tried to push him away. "I just need time." She slipped away and turned to face him.

Norfolk searched her eyes. Then he smiled. "Three days. After Black, I will move on to your brother unless you present yourself at my door. Together we will derive the price of your ... virtue?"

Corwyn nodded. She had no choice but to agree to whatever he said.

"And now we will have a kiss to seal our bargain." He reached for her, pulled her in front of him, pushed her back against the door. He pressed his lips to hers, hands moving to her breasts as he forced his tongue between her lips. He seemed pleased by her struggle, pressed her back into the hard wood. He was laughing in her mouth. Did he mean to rape her?

Loud pounding startled them both, "Lord Norfolk, are you there? Are you there, sir?"

Cursing, Norfolk moved away. Corwyn, faster than he, turned and pounded upon the door until it opened. She pressed past the worried steward, and flew down the hall in search of Christina.

Once she was gone, Norfolk's good temper returned. Things had gone very well indeed. Retrieving the gin, he threw himself into one of the comfortable leather chairs. He really could not wait to have the girl to himself.

Chapter Five

The next morning, Corwyn rose early. Unable to sleep, she walked in the rose garden that framed Christina's town house. She noticed the cold damp air and the gray clouds shrouding the sky only after she sat down in the long green grass.

She had no doubt that Norfolk would carry out his threats. He could arrange an arrest, a court martial, even a murder with little difficulty. He possessed enough money and influence to ruin anyone if he so desired. Though Ben could claim a title and a certain income from their estates, they could offer no defense against someone with Norfolk's resources. If she did not find a way to stop Norfolk, he would do all he had promised.

If she told Ben anything like the truth, he would call Norfolk out and then Lord Black. Now, there was a man more than capable of killing if she where any judge of scoundrels. She would rather die than lose Ben.

Corwyn had run through her few options over and over again, always returning to the same solution. Lord Black was her only hope. He would hang unless he found a way to stop Norfolk. Perhaps, if he knew of his imminent arrest, he would murder Norfolk as some said he had his uncle. Perhaps he would call Norfolk out as a gentleman should. Maybe he could just manufacture a convenient accident. Anything, Corwyn thought unhappily, that would stop Norfolk from carrying out his threats against Ben.

Time was of the essence. Norfolk had promised to have Black arrested in only three days time. If Black were in prison, then he could not defend himself, defend her, defend Ben from this madman.

Coming in from the garden, Corwyn climbed the stairs to her room. She changed into an old gown, hoping that during her trip across London the drab outfit might help her avoid notice. She had to remind herself repeatedly that she was fighting for her life, for Ben's life. She wanted Norfolk to die and she wanted Black to kill him. She would do anything, sacrifice everything to achieve her aim.

Even if she acquiesced to Norfolk's ridiculous demands, who knew when he would tire of her? Then his promises would mean nothing. And suppose she displeased him? He would want to punish her. No, he must be stopped at all costs.

Christina could not have been more surprised by Corwyn's demand to go shopping. The ominous gray of the morning did not bode well for the condition of the roads. By all appearances the rain would be falling hard and heavy by mid-afternoon.

"All the more reason to go now," Corwyn argued.

"All the more reason not to go at all," Christina replied eyeing her cousin curiously. Having decided to spend the day with a wealth of long overdue correspondence, she was disinclined to rise from her escritoire and begin bundling for the rain.

"But I simply must have gown for the Lantry affair. Marie says she has no cloth that will suit the pattern and I must buy some today if I want a gown to be ready in time! "Corwyn looked panicked, as though the lack of a good gown were a matter of life and death.

"You are being ridiculous," Christina said. For the first time she was truly annoyed by her young cousin. Finally, after demanding a firm promise that they might turn back at the first sign of rain, Christina agreed to the outing. After all, she could remember a dozen times in her life when a new dress or a hat had lifted her spirits. Maybe Corwyn had decided to try something new.

Corwyn found it was no mean accomplishment to pretend to look at fabric while Christina watched.

In the first shop, which carried lawn and linen, Christina stood near the door peering out the window as though she would leap into the carriage at the first sign of precipitation. Corwyn's questions about color and thread count were met with cold, clipped responses.

In the second store, Corwyn tried to entice her cousin into examining the fashion dolls. Often Christina would spend hours looking at the dolls in a shop, seeking elements she could use in her own gowns. This time, however, she gave them only a passing glance, then turned back to her stoic contemplation of the sky.

In the third establishment, owned by an Italian importer, Corwyn decided drastic action was necessary.

"I am sorry to have made you come out," she said as she fingered a pale silk. "Usually we have such fun-"

"You know it is only the weather," said Christina, softening a little. She left the doorway and ran her fingers over the fabric displayed on the table.

"Is it?" Corwyn asked. "Perhaps you are tired of me. Maybe you wish I had never come to London." She made a great show of turning to a new bolt of cloth.

"You know that I love having you here! You are like a sister to me-" Christina's voice betrayed her concern. "Something has come over you-"

Corwyn interrupted her, afraid that her cousin's kindness might start tears that would never stop. "I overheard someone say that my gowns make me look like a harlot," she said softly. Actually, the words were true. Lady Barbara Ryan had said it just loud enough for her to hear at a recent party. It was just one of a hundred barbs she had suffered in the weeks past. "Can you help me?" She felt terrible praying upon Christina's emotions, but she had to get away, and she could not do it while Christina stood in the door of every shop.

"All your gowns are beautiful, of course," said Christina after a pause. "But we shall make you something wonderful to wear." She had tears on her face. "These silks are just the thing, of course, but these pale colors will not suit you. I will ask the shopkeeper to bring us everything he has in blue. That color always serves you best . . ." With that she slipped behind a curtain ostensibly in search of the bearded owner.

Corwyn suspected it would take Christina several minutes to regain her composure, to find the merchant, and to dredge up more than a few lengths of blue fabric. Now was her chance. She felt guilt-ridden and cruel as she slipped from the shop, knowing how much Christina would be hurt by her trick.

Once onto the street, Corwyn put aside her misgivings and darted into an alley. She ran down the narrow streets until she found a broad avenue lined with drooping oaks. There she forced herself to walk, looking about to insure that no one had witnessed her strange behavior. Reassured to see the lane all but deserted, she began to scan the avenue looking for a carriage to take her to Black's address.

It proved more difficult than Corwyn had imagined to hail a cab. Most had left the streets in deference to the heavy clouds. The remainder responded to her request for assistance with lewd smiles, and rude words. Watching them rush past, she ignored their insults. She had no time to feel embarrassed or afraid.

Finally she approached an old coachman, bent with age and labor, who sat atop his carriage outside one of London's numerous clubs. Sheets of rain began to fall as they bartered over the fare. Finally she paid the man an exorbitant fee and climbed into the musty interior of the ancient rig. Cold, damp, Corwyn let her head fall back against the cracked leather of the seats.

The rain rattled across the carriage roof and the day was so dark it seemed as if night had already fallen. No doubt this storm would last days. The last thing Corwyn wanted was to spend more than a moment with Black, so she would have to leave almost as soon as she arrived. She doubted that he would risk one of his horses to drive her home and she had no more money to hail a cab. It looked like she would have to fight her way back on foot.

When the carriage finally clattered to a stop, Corwyn drew a deep breath and put a hand to her chest to still the pounding of her heart. Lord! What would she say to him? What would he do?

The old man gave her a fierce look, a rheumy cough punctuating his snap of the reins as he rattled off into the rain leaving his passenger across the lane from her destination. The street, a river of muddy water, clutched at Corwyn's skirts as she picked her way across it, drenching her shoes and matting her dress to her legs. Finally in the relative shelter of Black's doorway, Corwyn rapped on the door.

Black's servant seemed startled to see her when he answered the door. Recovering his good manners, he informed her that Black was not at home. He stepped aside and invited her in from the rain.

Gaunt, tall, with shocking red hair, Corwyn was sure she had never seen the servant before, and yet he called her by name when he led her up the long flight of dark stairs to the small parlor of an upper flat. Peculiar though this behavior was, he extended her every courtesy and proved proficient at attending to her comfort. He sat her before a warm fire and gave her a draft of wine as well as a light meal. Obviously he was used to entertaining lone women in his master's house.

Corwyn found Lord Black's absence disheartening. What if he decided to remain away all night rather than return here though the storm? Sooner or later someone would think to look for her here. What would she do then?

Curled in the deep chair, Corwyn was only dimly aware of how the time passed. The small glass of wine she had taken from the servant had affected her strangely, making her re-live days long past as though she were in a waking dream.

The licking flames of the fire reminded her of afternoons spent in her father's study where the pulse of the rain and the occasional crack of thunder had filled her with fantasies of magic and fairy folk. It had been years, she realized, since she had felt so young and so completely out of control, not since those horror filled days immediately after her parents' death.

Darkness was at hand when Corwyn realized that she was alone in the flat. Where the servant had gone she could not imagine, but it had been fairly two hours since she had last seen him. Perhaps he lived elsewhere and had departed to let her wait for his master alone. Leaving her chair, Corwyn took the long steps required to look out the window into the flooded streets. Now, truly a mire, they seemed impassable.

She would have to leave soon if she wanted to reach home before midnight. Ben and Christina were probably frantic with worry.

The sound of a door slamming brought Corwyn's head up as she stood near the fire retrieving her cloak and slippers. A clatter of boots on the stairs and the sudden opening of the door to the parlor where she had waited for so long revealed a fierce

Lord Black, obviously irritated at the disappearance of his servant.

How she had haunted him! The little waif with coal black hair and sooty eyelashes. He felt the familiar tension across his back, coiling down his arms, his hands flexed looking for the weight of his blade. Blood lust? For a girl? Or did he simply feel power curling about him.

"You are a fool," he said as he removed his cloak and dropped it into a chair. He had just spent several hours on the turbulent Thames making preparations for his immediate departure, and now the girl had appeared. He had almost decided to let her wait for his return. His revenge would be all the sweeter for the delay he had decided. Yet, here she stood.

"Norfolk is going to have you arrested," said Corwyn. Her voice sounded distant to her own ears. Why did not he seem real? Midnight eyes, ebony hair catching the light of the fire, broad shoulders encased in a thin, damp shirt, he took her breath away. He was like the men in those silly stories from her childhood, a black prince wrapped in dark armor dispensing death to his enemies. She had forgotten how words caught in her throat when she saw him, how aware she was of his every move.

Black nodded, moving to the sideboard. He poured himself a drink and waited for her to speak again.

"I wanted to warn you," she whispered.

"You want me to kill him for you," Black replied, his eyes cold.

"I -" Corwyn broke off, wishing for all the world that she might have imagined some other way to end this nightmare. She could feel the hate behind that stern facade. She shook her head to clear away her lethargy. It was a mistake to come here. She started to pull on her cloak. She had been mad to consider such a plan. "I should never have come. I will find another way-," she said, making for the door.

"I think not," said Black, taking her arm as she moved past. He pulled her to him, ignoring her resistance. Without preamble, he brought his lips to hers, his hand biting into the flesh of her upper arm.

Corwyn did not fight him. Some part of her wondered if this had been her intention all along. As he filled her senses, she recalled her words to Norfolk yesterday. Had she lied? Did she care for Lord Black? Did she love him? Was this heady desire to surrender to him called passion? She never wanted him to stop touching her.

Black slowed his assault. He drew away to search her eyes. His next kiss was more gentle, searching.

Corwyn wondered at the perfection of his touch. He compelled her response, making her grow more hungry for him with every measured caress. His hand moved over her body till it found her breast, was tender when it discovered the rosebud nipple through the fabric. He drew it to a tingling point. With deft fingers he untied the chord that held her bodice closed. In a moment his head came down, lips and tongue exploring the soft flesh.

Corwyn gasped. Caught in his arms, his willing captive, he encompassed the entire world. She could believe that he called the rain and the darkness like a shroud around them, filling every sense with this dark mystery, this all consuming need for him.

"I want you." His voice was rough. He buried his head in her hair and held her for a moment.

"Please," Corwyn whispered against his chest. She did not know what she was begging for, whether she wanted him to stop, or to continue. She knew the answer when he tilted her head back and his lips found the pulse of her throat.

The sound of voices in the stairway came to Corwyn's ears as Black thrust her away from him. Before she understood what was happening, a dozen men pushed through the door, their voices stilling suddenly when they confronted the couple that waited in the near darkness.

The servant had reappeared, Corwyn noted dully. He stood just behind Lord Norfolk, his eyes averted for some reason. Only when Ben also averted his eyes, did Corwyn realize that she was all but naked before them all. Reflex drove her hands to cover her breasts, passion and curiosity melting into fear. They had come to find her.

Christina appeared and helped to draw her dress and cloak over her body. Corwyn buried her head in her cousin's shoulder to blot out the shouting.

"You Bastard!" Norfolk's voice betrayed his satisfaction at finding them together. "How dare you dishonor a lady so!"

Corwyn pulled her head away to regard her self appointed savior. He was triumphant. She saw that he held a heavy dueling pistol, and she watched as he brought the weapon to bear on Black.

"I will teach you," said Norfolk, "not to take what does not belong to you." He let the ball fly almost before the words left his lips.

Corwyn screamed, watching Black recoil as the bullet took him in the chest. She saw him drop to his knees and an instant later he had a blade. It flew from his hand to bury itself Norfolk's throat.

Norfolk sank to the floor as if he too had been shot, blood pulsing from his throat with every heartbeat.

There was a stunned silence, as though no one could quite fathom what had just occurred. Then Ben and the servant fell upon Black. The other men stumbled into action a moment later, two trying desperately to staunch the flow of blood from Norfolk's throat while the remainder joined the fray with Lord Black. Even with a ball in his chest, he was a formidable foe.

When they finally pulled the Earl to his feet, blood cascading from his wound, Corwyn came face to face with him. His twisted features stole her breath away, banished all thought. For a moment there was no one else in the room, just this great, raging beast, and herself. She could feel his hate for her as if it were a physical attack. She was grateful for the darkness that finally claimed her.

"He's going to die?" Corywn could not believe her good fortune. What wonderful news!

"Try not to sound so hopeful my dear." Christina shook her head. "He is probably dead already. He lost so much blood his flesh was the color of bone."

"Did you see him?" Corwyn sat up in her bed.

Christina shook her head. With nary a bow and no lace to enliven the dark gray gown, she might have been in mourning. "Lady Norfolk would not let me past the parlor. She seems to hold you responsible for the entire affair."

"Me?" How could any one be so blind? "I did not hound Lord Norfolk hither and thither across London, or spread vicious rumors about his character. I did not invite him to Lord Black's apartments and certainly did not tell him to shoot the Earl on my behalf."

"She says Henry truly loved you. Apparently he went to his uncle, the Earl of Pembroke, and all but confessed his intention to marry you. She's sworn to see you publicly humiliated, and I think Lord Pembroke may actually see you as Black's accomplice. He seemed to think you were lovers-"

Corwyn put her hands over her ears. She could not bear to hear any more. When Christina left the room, she fell back against her pillows and started to cry.

"Absolutely not!" Ben pulled the gown out of her hands. "What can you be thinking of?"

"Why should not I go?" Corwyn asked. "After all, I am hardly a young lady in danger of ruining her reputation." Standing in her bedroom, surrounded by open trunks and clothing, she waited for Ben to see reason.

"Virginia is no place for a girl. There is no suitable society for you there," Ben paced the floor.

"Suitable society will not have me." Corwyn dropped another gown in a nearby trunk. "It is the only way," she told him, her eyes meeting his when he turned to face her. "You asked why I should go? Should I wait here for Lord Black to kill me? A man who can escape Newgate can certainly manage my window. I can guarantee he will hunt me down if I stay here. With you, I will be safe."

"Do you not see," he said in a softer voice "You will not be with me. I cannot bring you onto the Verity. Even if it were allowed, we are filled to the gills already. There is simply not room for one more person, let alone a woman."

"There are other ships traveling under your escort," said Corwyn, "I could sail on one of those." No matter what Ben might think, she would not, could not remain here. Sooner or later Black would seek her out, and she refused to imagine what might happen then.

"I do not know any of the ship's masters well enough to trust you to them and we do not have time to find you a suitable companion," said Ben uncertainly. "It would not be safe. I insist that you remain here."

Corwyn drew a shaky breath. She had never disobeyed Ben in all the years since her parents' death. "I am afraid I have no alternative," she said, refusing to meet his brown eyes. "If you do not take me with you, I will book my own passage."

"Surely not!"

"Norfolk is dead, Black has escaped, and someone must pay. I am the only one left." Corwyn shook her head. "I will not stay here, I cannot remain in England. When we return from the colonies, if we ever return, this wretched business will have been long forgotten. I will make a quiet life in the country and no one will be the wiser."

"You cannot do this," said Ben. "Its ridiculous even to consider the idea."

"Ben, please help me," Corwyn sat down on a trunk and put her head in her hands. "I do not want to die."

Ben put an arm around Corwyn's shoulder and drew her to him. For a moment he was silent, considering the alternatives. He knew of at least one ship, the Albatross, sailing the same day as his vessel. Though not a large ship, he assumed it would be well armed due to the cargo of gold plate it carried, and he knew the owner by name. Perhaps something might be arranged in the few days remaining.

"Will not you help me?" asked Corwyn turning her emerald eyes, bright with tears, upon him.

Ben gave in to the inevitable, "I will see what I can do."

Chapter Six

Her first evening on the Albatross, Corwyn dined with the captain and his mates. The five men squeezed into the small, disorganized room did not deign to offer her any conversation so dinner was an uncomfortable affair. Prior to beginning the meal, those gathered were subjected to a heartfelt, seemingly endless prayer to an unforgiving God. Corwyn found the Captain's reference to heartless sea wolves and beasts of the deep rather frightening. When the meal was finally presented, she found that even more distressing. The food, though they had just left port, was comprised mostly of salted meat and aged bread. Had not anyone thought to purchase fresh supplies? In a quarter hour, after eating some hardtack dipped in water, she excused herself. Would the entire journey be this pleasant?

As the days passed Corwyn began to notice things about the ship that did not seem to reflect an iron hand at the helm. For example, though the vessel was heavily manned, the rigging and sails were in bad repair and the deck was warped. Her one expedition to the hold was terminated abruptly when she saw hundreds of rats scurrying along the beams and heard water rolling across a deck somewhere far below. She hoped this ship's cargo was immune to damage by water or rodent.

The only comforts of the voyage were the ships she could see arrayed across the horizon when she ventured on deck and Margaret who provided her with distracting conversation. The slightly older girl did not seem concerned by the ill-mannered crew or the poor repair of the ship.

"My brother James once sailed on a ship with so many holes that the captain himself had to bail for half a shift each day. We will make port, you wait and see." Margaret took Corwyn's cloak and hung it on a hook on the back of the door.

"I suppose the crew will hardly let the ship sink merely to spite me," said Corwyn.

"You can be sure that every man aboard will work to keep us afloat." Margaret dimpled. "After all, they cannot swim."

"How can that be?" asked Corwyn. She and her brother had both learned to swim as children.

"James used to say sailors took to ships because they would do anything to stay out of the water."

Corwyn found herself smiling again. Margaret's words were always comforting. She seemed incapable of feeling anything but contentment. Corwyn shook off her momentary foreboding and reminded herself that while she could still see ships on the horizon she was completely safe. Ben would surely rescue her if she were in any danger.

For a short time the weather could not have been better. The wind blew cold and strong, filling the sails and driving the ship onward at an immense rate. The sun, bright despite the occasional cloud that appeared along the edge of the sea, danced on the deep green water. It was so beautiful that Corwyn wanted to spend every moment on deck.

This good fortune held for five days into the ship's second week. On the morning of the sixth day, Corwyn went above to find the skies filled with ominous clouds, and the wind so hard upon the ship that the sails were being trimmed lest the masts snap from the pressure. She watched the crewmen scurry from one end of the ship to the other with fascination. Why did they not fall as the ship leapt beneath them? What kept them from freezing in the biting wind?

By noon, both watches had been called to man the ship, all hands serving to keep two sails high and maintain some speed despite the wind and rain.

With the storm and the accompanying turmoil, Corwyn decided to remain in her cabin. She did not like the way the ship twisted and turned beneath her feet. It was hard to stay upright.

Margaret, on the other hand, was quite at home. "They will keep sails up as long as they can, trying to outrun the worst of the storm. If it gets bad enough they will bring the big ones down and just use one or two small ones to keep the ship turned into the waves."

"Into the waves?" Corwyn thought of the water that would break over the bow, pounding the deck with untold force.

"The ship would capsize if it got struck broadside by a big wave," Margaret said without apparent concern. "My brother said he saw that once. Its very unusual."

"I certainly hope so," said Corwyn shivering.

"Do not be afraid," said Margaret. "I am sure the crew has weathered more than one storm in years past. They will have the good sense required to keep us afloat."

Corwyn wished that she could share Margaret's confidence.

Having finished stowing most of the loose gear about the cabin in sea chests, Margaret stood up. "I think I will take a last turn around the deck before we tuck in for the duration."

Corwyn nodded. "Be careful," she said as the girl left the cabin. "It is quite slippery."

"One hand for myself, and one for the ship," said Margaret. "I have heard that so many times that I plan to embroider it on a pillow one day."

Corwyn laughed and curled up under a blanket.

Margaret never came back. Several hours after her departure the first mate rapped on Corwyn's door. Without preamble he told her that Margaret had been swept overboard and instructed her to stay below until someone told her otherwise. When Corwyn started to cry, he turned away, his disgust evident.

Chapter Seven

His crew was probably right, Black reflected as he peered through the slim spy-glass at the ship just visible on the horizon, he had lost his mind. He could just make out seventeen men on deck, scrambling to make repairs in this unexpected lull in the storm. Heavy clouds and a sullen sky promised renewed fury by nightfall.

As he had for several days, Black contemplated a paradox. Could a man be mad and know it? Black's crew certainly thought him mad, that was obvious enough. They scuttled away from him when he drew near, and obeyed his orders as if they were afraid he would cast them overboard for the slightest delay. Of course, they had seen him kill before and knew he was in a killing rage now. That, in and of itself, did not make him mad. But they knew his target was a woman and that he would drive his ship into the sea to have her. That was passing strange.

Of course the master of the other ship was also quite insane. Aware that the Albatross was being shadowed, its captain drove his vessel mercilessly forward into the endless storm. Where, Black had wondered several times, did the man think he was going? Did he really believe he could escape by tearing apart his rigging and ripping the masts from his ship? Why else put every sheet to the wind? A sudden thought made

Black laugh out loud. Who was more ridiculous, the lunatic who led, or the one who followed?

Enough, Black decided. He turned to regard his own ship tossing in the swollen seas. He would take the girl tonight, reward his crew with the contents of hold, and be done with the matter. He had wasted enough time playing cat and mouse. Far off course, sails so ripped they could not hold the wind, the ship ahead presented no challenge for him. This evening, when the storm rose again, she would be his.

Corwyn awoke to deafening thunder. Startled awake by the loud crash and alone in the tossing darkness of the cabin, she was frightened. It was so cold, so dark.

The horror of Margaret's loss was overwhelming. How horrible it must have been to tumble into the churning seas, falling forever into the infinite night.

Casting about in her damp bedding, Corwyn sought the candle and flint that she always kept near at hand. She could not bear to be blind any longer. When the sputtering wick finally took flame it exposed the violent shifts her luggage had undertaken while she slept and threw dark shadows around the room.

The thunder came again, and Corwyn covered her ears to hide from its echo. The lightning must be just overhead! Perhaps the ship would be struck, would catch fire and sink. Then she and Margaret would share a watery grave.

The sound of pounding footsteps on deck brought Corwyn's head up. Another loud crack of thunder punctuated the distantly heard shouts. The ship suddenly listed to port, throwing Corwyn to the floor of the cabin. She landed in several inches of water. There were more voices, frantic now. Corwyn heard men descend into the companion way and pass by her door.

It was strange how unfamiliar the voices sounded. She could not hear the captain's voice, or even the mate's. They must be on deck fighting the storm.

She climbed back into her bed and pulled the covers over her shivering body. If the vessel were truly sinking she would be called for the boats. Until then she should stay out from under foot.

Heavy strides walked past her door, heading for the hold. Other voices climbed the stairs to join those shouting above deck. So much activity! What could they all be doing?

When the voices quieted, replaced with the ominous sound of wind and rain, Corwyn's fear returned. Where had everyone gone? Was the ship sinking? Surely they would not abandon her.

A sudden tilt of the deck made her cry out, certain that the movement to one side would never end as the boat capsized.

When the ship righted itself, she began to struggle from the tangle of blankets. At last she found her feet on the ever-shifting deck. She had to know what was happening.

Opening the door to her cabin set loose a tide of seawaterthat flooded the floor immediately. As the ship rocked, the water ran from one side of the cabin to the other. Each shift drenched Corwyn to the knees. When the ship once again listed to port, Corwyn followed the motion into the hall.

She found the companion way completely dark except for the light from the candle in her cabin, and the dim light pouring through the door at the top of the short flight of stairs just ahead. She still could not hear anyone. The ship felt empty, desolate.

Corwyn found it difficult to keep her balance as she crept down the narrow corridor. The boat seemed to tip in all directions at once, making progress possible only when she managed to find purchase along the wall. With each step forward, icy sea water washed up her thighs. It was as though the entire Atlantic were intent upon coming down the crude wooden stairs to fill the hold.

A sudden pitch of the vessel cracked her head soundly against a wall. She pressed her hand to the pain over her eye, felt the slick blood between her fingers. She stumbled on, feet finally finding the short flight of ladder-like stairs that led to the deck. She heaved herself forward, climbing out of the ship like a condemned man escaping hell.

Corwyn could not believe her eyes. Pounding rain fell through the yards and yards of sailcloth that filled the deck like a white sea. Only shreds of sail remained aloft, hanging from the spars of the fallen mizzenmast that had all but crushed the door.

Panicked, she made her way to the edge of the ship, pressing through canvas, rope and water to find the railing where boats should be waiting. What she found instead made her wish she were already dead.

Another ship was rolling in the water alongside the Albatross and was tied to her with long thick ropes. On its decks she saw men carrying blades. There were sea chests scattered about them on the deck. While she watched they pitched the pale body of one of the Albatross mates overboard, his throat slit from ear to ear.

She turned away, pressing back into the sails. Better to die in a cold sea than in the brutal hands of a pirate crew. She fought her way back to the companionway door, prepared to enter a darkness she might never leave again.

She saw something shift in the shadows and fell back. There before her, a man emerged. He was tall, as tall as the tallest man Corwyn had ever seen, and black, cloaked all in darkness but for the skeletal gleam of a white shirt that clung to his chest. Devon Black.

He caught her hand before she could take a step. She tried to jerk away from his iron grasp, brought her nails across his face, pounded his chest with all her might. This nightmare could not continue.

Lord Black's hold remained firm. He dragged her across the deck, through the sail to the railing. He seemed completely unaware that she battled to free herself. Once at the side of the ship, he turned to crush her against him. He held her still while he pulled at a length of rope tied to the rail of the Albatross. When it was free, he wrapped the length about her, pinning her arms to her side. It burned her skin as she struggled against it.

He was going to tie her up and throw her into the sea! Please God, Corwyn prayed as he dragged her to a gap in the railing, do not let him kill me. In another moment she was over the side, the black mouth of the sea gaping below her.

A jarring thump signalled their arrival on board Black's ship. Dizzy, frightened, Corwyn could not move. Black thrust her into the arms of wiry seaman without a word, and she started to struggle. Over the wind she heard the fierce crack of Black's voice. A moment later, the crewman dragged her below.

Chapter Eight

Corwyn paced the cabin like a caged animal. Feet numb, salt encrusted nightdress plastered to every curve of her body, she was chilled to the bone.

She had to escape. Turning again toward the crewman at the door, she wondered if she could kill him. She could kill him if she had to. She could do anything she had to do to get away.

But what if she failed? What then?

How long had she been waiting? She crossed the room again. How many times had she traveled the distance between the only two weapons she could see, the beveled glass of the bookcase and the locked gun chest?

Once again at the gun case, she stared at the lock. If only she might be left alone for a moment, just an instant. She could pick the lock or break it, then load a gun and kill Black when he came for her. Then she would escape, perhaps take one of the boats she had seen on deck. She would have little chance on the open sea, but anything was better than remaining here.

Turning, Corwyn tried to judge the time by the darkness outside the windows. If this ship was like most others, the captain's cabin was located aft. She wondered what direction she faced. Did it matter? It looked like midnight outside the window.

The captain's bed, built into the wall of cabinets surrounding the window, caught her attention. Panic rolled over her in a long wave.

It took an immense effort of will to calm herself. She had to find a weapon. She had to defend herself. She looked around the room again.

She saw a polished table bolted to the floor with six chairs surrounding it. Black's minion sat in one of those chairs. Tilted back against the wall, his hard eyes followed her every move. He had red hair, a thin, muscular build, and he had already proved himself to be a formidable opponent. It gave Corwyn a moment's satisfaction to see the four long red streaks running the length of his face. She had not exactly lost their last engagement, and by God she certainly would not lose the next one.

Corwyn's eyes skipped to the door just to his right. Was it locked? She glanced back to find him still watching her.

If she had a weapon she could kill her jailer. With the guard dead she could break open the gun case, load guns and kill Black when he entered. Then what? She would get out, take a dinghy and throw herself upon the mercy of the storm. Even to herself it sounded ridiculous.

She buried her face in her hands and tried to think. This was all so insane.

Both Corwyn and the crewman were startled by a sound at the door. Its broad width swung open and Lord Black strode into the room. Blood flowered in streaks across his shirt. Water beaded in his dark hair, soaked his clothes so they fit his body like a second skin.

The crewman settled his chair to the floor with a thump.

"Get out," Black said to the guard. He stepped aside to let the man pass. Black shut the door and shot the bolt home.

Lord Black did not seem to be aware of Corwyn at all, did not even look at her, as he dropped his saber onto the table. A moment later the knife he kept strapped to his thigh joined it.

Weapons at last! Corwyn looked up to find Black's eyes heavy upon her.

"No." His voice was cold.

Corwyn drew away from the table with her hands behind her back. She had seen him three times. Each time he seemed stronger, larger, more menacing. Was he human at all? Did she stand before the devil himself? Oh Lord, she did not want to die!

He pulled off the blood stained shirt. Dozens of welts and scrapes etched his sun dark skin, and low on his midriff Corwyn could see a deep scratch caked with blood. Had a knife done that? If only his attacker had finished the job! When her eyes moved up, she saw a well-scabbed wound high on his chest, a healing wound. Norfolk's ball had almost done its work.

Her eyes leapt to his at this realization. By mischance or by intention, it made little difference. He had almost died because of her.

His face was an expressionless mask. They might never have met before. "Come here."

Corwyn shook her head. Her heart pounded in her chest, blood rushed in her ears. Was it to start so soon?

He moved toward her so quickly that she recoiled without a thought, pulling a chair down between them in her panic. He was every inch the predator, unstoppable, relentless. The weapons on the table rattled as she bumped against it.

And then, as if by magic, she had his saber in her hand. He was reaching for it. She stepped back and to the right, brought the blade down across his path. It sliced across his body from shoulder to hip as he jumped back. An instant later she stood in the corner between the bolted door and the bookcase, the blade held high in two shaking hands before her.

Black looked at the ribbon of blood welling from his chest and shook his head.

He studied her for a moment, then he stepped back. He pulled the smaller blade from its sheath and moved to sit on the edge of the table before her.

He waited.

To her dismay, Corwyn found the tip of her blade slipping lower in just a few minutes. Every time she dragged it up to point it at his heart again, her hands shook with the effort. She could feel him watching her, waiting for an opportunity to take the weapon back. They both knew who would be the victor in this contest.

She wondered, as she waited, if he was going to kill her. Pirates often killed women right after they raped them, did they not? She was so cold, and her wet clothes made it impossible to get warm. Her head ached from where she had bumped it on the Albatross. She could not think for the pain, the fear and the cold. Perhaps death would be better.

"So, do you plan to stand there across the whole Atlantic?" he asked. His voice startled her, so low and calm. It sparked a memory. He had asked her to dance once.

"And what do you suppose will happen to you if you actually manage to kill me?" He was using the small blade to clean his fingernails, apparently no longer interested in watching her. "There are thirty-nine men on this ship."

"Please," said Corwyn. "Let me go."

He looked up, shook his head slowly. "Put it down."

"Please," said Corwyn.

He shifted his weight, moving to rise. He would open the door, summon his men. She could see it in his eyes.

The blade slipped from her hands and clattered to the floor.

He moved to scoop it up. She watched him put it back on the table. He returned to his seat and to watching her. It was an eternity before he spoke again.

"Come here!" His voice filled the chamber like a gun shot.

She was startled into a step forward, found herself nearer to him, trembling with cold and fear. She did not let herself think as she took another step, and another until she stood just within his reach. She could not bring herself to move any closer.

He hooked a finger over the neck of her gown and brought her forward. Lifting one hand, he turned it palm up to expose a row of pearl buttons. He slipped the tip of his knife between the folds of fabric and drew it toward him. The buttons fell to the floor like rain. He took up her other hand, releasing a similar cascade. He pulled her forward, then moved his hands behind her back.

Corwyn took a final step so she could lay her head against his chest. He was the only warm thing in the world, the only familiar thing for hundreds of miles. She felt the kiss of the blade as it found the buttons that ran up the back of her gown, heard them drop to the floor and roll everywhere. She closed her eyes.

Black pushed her back and pulled at the fabric at her wrists, dragging the dressing gown forward and down until it puddled around her feet. Time stood still.

Her breasts were perfect ivory mounds tipped with coral peaks made hard by the cold. Her stomach was flat, hips swelling into gentle curves that begged for a man's caress. A black thatch nestled between perfect thighs that tapered to slender legs and tiny feet. She stood before him still as a statue, eyes closed.

He could feel her heart pounding in his own chest, feel the fear sliding along her veins like lightening. Predator and prey, they were one being.

He used his fingertips to trace her shoulders, to follow the curve of her arms to her hands. He lifted them finding the calluses he had seen just a moment ago. She had spent time in the saddle, this one. Her hands were rough from gripping the reins.

He continued to hold one hand as the other slipped forward to touch a hip. Her skin was smooth, soft. She moved under his hand, unconsciously shifting her weight toward him.

His mind struggled against a wave of emotion so strong that it swept away reason. What did he feel? The words that came to him made no sense. Power? Possession? Despair? She's just a woman, he thought. Just a woman.

He swept her up and carried her to the bed.

Corwyn opened her eyes, watched Lord Black sit on the edge of the bed to tug off his boots. She looked away as he undid the drawstring to his britches, staring into the darkness outside the window, watching the swell of the sea that she could just detect in the broken moonlight.

She was afraid, afraid to disturb this fragile moment. He had been ready to kill her when he entered the cabin, she had felt it in her bones. Now he was . . . She stopped. There were no words.

He turned out the lamp and she felt him lie upon the bed. The little light that came through the window showed her his face. Broad forehead, full lips, sculpted features, square jaw, was there ever a man this handsome? A dark Apollo, she found herself thinking, dragging misery in his wake as Apollo pulled the sun across the sky.

His head was resting on one hand, the other traced spirals across her belly, trailed lower to follow the curve inside her thigh.

His hand found the entrance to her body and she gasped as it opened her. His lips found hers then, his tongue exploring her mouth as his fingers entered her. She found her legs parting for him, felt her heart start to pound like a hammer in her chest. She felt him press into her, felt something tighten, pulse.

"Christ!" he said.

She raised her head to look at him. Had she done something wrong? Was he angry with her?

In the silver light that illuminated them both, she saw him shake his head as if in disbelief. With a sudden movement he put himself above her, between her legs. He cradled her head in his hands, began to kiss her. Then she felt him enter her, fill her, felt him press through the tightness to bury himself in her body. Without pause he began to move, sliding into and out of her with long strokes.

In an instant her hands were on his broad shoulders. She had to keep him inside her some how. Her fingers sought the curve of his back, slipped lower onto his buttocks. She couldn't get enough of him, wanted him to stay inside her forever. She cried out as the unexpected convulsions hit her, writhing beneath him.

Her orgasm pushed him over the edge and he drove into her mercilessly. He felt his seed spill into her, felt her legs wrap around his.

She was asleep before he left her body, curled up like a kitten in his bed. He dressed in fresh clothes, even going so far as to put on a coat against the cold.

Later he stood on the foredeck watching the wind pull the waves into white peaks.

One minute he wanted to kill the girl, the next he wanted to make love to her with every fiber of his being. The little virgin had cost him everything. He was sure of that. Whether that had been her intention or not, he didn't know, but she had condemned him to a living hell he had spent twenty years trying to escape.

One thing was absolutely certain. He would never give her up. He was going to take her every night of this crossing, and perhaps a thousand more nights besides, until he could look at her without feeling anything at all.

Chapter Nine

Corwyn awoke the next morning feeling battered. Her head ached as a result of multiple contusions, her body felt rigid and abused. Worst of all, what she could remember of the night past could only be described as a nightmare. She had been so cold and frightened and then ... then she had wanted him more than life itself. In the wan light pouring through the cabin window, she could hardly believe that it had not all been a dream.

Black lay behind her, molding her body to his even in sleep. His leg, thrown over hers, curled reflexively when she shifted to look out the window.

She hated him. She hated herself. She wished she had never gone to London, had never met Henry Norfolk, and most important that she had never met Lord Black.

She should have died before she permitted him to take her. Isn't that what the stories said. Weren't young girls supposed to die before surrendering their virtue?

He was awake. Though at first he made no move, she could hear the change in his breathing, feel the tension suddenly alive in his body. Closing her eyes, Corwyn willed him to leave. Had not he done enough to her?

Propping his head up on one elbow, Black swept the tossed coverings aside, baring her to the waist. Bruises marred the features of her face, dried blood, his blood he supposed, etched the ivory of her arms. Like some roman skirmisher she wore the evidence of her many battles.

With a return of all too familiar feelings of anger and loss, he brought his hand to the smooth plane of her stomach. Perhaps he should make love to her, hear her crying out for him once again. Perhaps then he would feel a moment's peace.

Corwyn did not try to stop him. He was strong enough to force her if he chose to. She endured his slow caress of her breasts, the hand that moved to part her thighs. It was only when he leaned forward to kiss her that she turned away. She was rewarded with a low laugh.

It was, she reflected the very first time she had ever heard him laugh. Could the blackguard really find her misery amusing? Then he was gone, slipping away to leave her alone in the cold bed.

"So, we have a few battles left," he told her as he splashed water on his face and pulled clean clothes from a press built into the cabinets around the bed, "I cannot say I am surprised. Shall we wager on who will win them?" He pulled on his boots and left the cabin.

Corwyn thew off the blankets, eased off the bed and onto the deck. Looking about she saw her nightgown on the floor. He had taken it off her and left it there when he had made love to her. She and Christina had purchased that gown together, and when she had put it on just yesterday, it had smelled of French perfume. But, all that was long in the past. She would never wear it again.

Moving to the ewer of water on the table, she washed herself, careful to insure that nothing of his scent remained on her. She would never allow him to touch her again. Never.

Once clean, Corwyn turned to the cabinet she had seen Black open to retrieve his clothes. Looking through the garments, she found a red shirt, very heavy and very warm. When she put it on she found that it fell almost to her knees and the cuffs dropped off her hands. She rolled the sleeves up enough to free them and then took a moment to examine the rest of the small closet.

There were a dozen or more neatly folded shirts, pairs of britches, even stockings. Though all the clothes were simple, sturdy fare, they were well crafted. It would seem that Black demanded quality. Staring at the closet full of tidy clothes, Corwyn wanted to scream. How could he take her away from everything she had ever known, rape her as he had, and yet still have well made clothes hanging in a tidy press?

She closed the closet door and looked out the window. The sea was calmer today, but the clouds promised more rain and the white tipped water bespoke violent winds. She just could not bear to remain his prisoner, could not bear to have him touch her ever again. But what alternative did she have? As long as she was on his ship, he owned her. If she killed him, his crew would rape her. There had to be a way out.

If only the storm had not come up the flotilla would still have been together. Corwyn stopped for a moment. Had she not seen a sail on the horizon just yesterday? Perhaps she might take her chances in a dinghy. If she were fortunate, one of the boats in the flotilla might stumble across her. It was a dangerous wager, but it was better to die alone at sea than let him take her again and again until he tired of her.

But, in order to commandeer a dinghy, she would need to get by Black, and in order to do that she needed a weapon. Corwyn turned toward the iron banded gun chest. Moving to kneel before it on the hardwood floor, she examined the crude lock. She could make out the three large tumblers just by peering through the keyhole.

If she managed to pick the lock and get one of Black's guns from the cabinet, she could force him to give her food, water and a boat. Surely he would not want to die simply to stop her from leaving his ship. She would force him to let her take her chances on the open sea.

But, in order to accomplish her goal, she would have to find something long and sharp with which to pick the lock. Looking about the tidy room, Corwyn saw nothing that would fill her purpose. When her eyes lighted on the cabinets and drawers surrounding Black's bed, she felt a surge of hope. Surely she would find what she needed there.

The first drawer surrendered only linen bandages to her gaze, long strips of clean, white cloth obviously meant to bind wounds. Two cupboards under the bed rattled hopefully, but refused to be prized open. Corwyn had no doubt that Black kept a wide variety of blades in these cases, and only the fear that he might return before she was ready forced her to continue her search elsewhere.

One of the drawers presented Corwyn with a number of personal possessions. The first that came to eye was a well- worn bible. That he should own such a pious effect galled Corwyn. She wondered that it did not burst into flame in his hands. Below the bible she found a bundle of scented letters, each on lavender paper and written in an obviously feminine hand. Feeling no compunction, Corwyn pulled the ribbon apart and began to read.

Dear Devon.

I cannot tell you how much I enjoy the gowns you sent, and how much I miss you. You really are far too good to me --

Corwyn dropped the letter back in the drawer. How could anyone have been so deceived by this monster? If the milk of human kindness flowed in Black's veins, it had never been apparent to Corwyn. Fine gowns? Corwyn could not imagine that Black's hands had ever caressed a garment with an eye for beauty or been kind enough to a woman to earn her love.

She continued her search. When her hands felt the sharp prick of a needle, she smiled with satisfaction. She pulled a scrap of sailcloth from the drawer and found three needles poked through the rough cloth.

The lock proved stiff, but after several minutes of prying Corwyn finally yanked it open. There before her were a dozen guns. Three were muskets, designed to deliver a very heavy shot, and almost too big to hold. Reluctantly, Corwyn replaced these weapons. There were some dragoons, hammers too stiff to cock, and she had to abandon those as well. In the end, Corwyn selected a pair matched dueling pistols. Light, well oiled, they showed the burns of repeated use. How many men had died, Corwyn wondered, as a result of these weapons?

Corwyn was careful to keep her mind blank as she loaded the guns. As much as she loathed Black, it was hard to imagine killing him. But, if he refused to allow her to escape, she would have to do exactly that. She had to be willing kill or be. He had made that abundantly clear.

He found the girl sitting on his bed, dressed in one of his shirts, a book in her hand. She did not look up as he entered the room, perhaps in an attempt to ignore him. Well, they would see how long that would last.

His things had been disturbed he realized as he opened the drawer where he kept his log. Finding some clothing was one thing, rifling his possessions was another. He had only been back in his cabin for a moment and already she had managed to irritate him. As shoved the drawer closed, he heard a hammer click.

Slowly, very slowly, he turned to find himself confronting his own dueling pistols.

"Again?" he shook his head, "I thought we had this discussion already."

"Do not make me kill you." Her voice shook with fear and he relaxed a little.

"I might ask you the same favor." In two days she had offered to kill him twice. He wasn't going to put up with this kind of behavior for very long.

"I want you to order your men to prepare a boat for me," the girl said carefully. "Food, water, enough to last for a few days," and she paused. "A lamp, and clothes."

"Where are you planning to go?" Black relaxed against the wall of the cabin, watching her.

"I want off your ship." Her lower lip trembled a little.

Black was silent for a moment, looking out the window at the darkness and the rain. She would not last twenty-four hours.

"You will die," he said at last. Surely she could see that the storm was rising again, the waves were growing rough. He could just picture her bobbing about in the water like a kitten in a pail. "Is that what you want?"

"I'd rather take my chances with the sea than with you." Again her composure wobbled.

Shrugging, Black stood up straight. "Let's go," he said, feigning disinterest. "If you would rather die than stay with me, I will not stop you." He shook his head to emphasize his point, "In fact, I will let you keep the guns. I do not think you know how unpleasant waiting to die can be whereas I have had some previous experience in the matter."

In a perverse way, he admired her for her ingenuity in acquiring a gun. He wondered if she would be able to use it.

Back on deck, they stood in the drizzling mist. He ordered his men to bring food, water and a lamp to the dinghy. The cabin boy surrendered half his meager wardrobe when she asked for clothes. When everything was prepared, he turned back to her. "There you are. Everything you asked for is in the boat."

She motioned them all away with one of the pistols, eyes wary, even frightened. Dressed in one of his shirts she showed his crew a fair amount of thigh as she scrambled into the dinghy.

Once she was in, pistol now leveled at his chest, he shrugged his shoulders and motioned for his crew to lower the boat into the water.

Putting the weapons down, Corwyn looked around. In the darkness, the horizon was just a narrow line along the water's edge. The sea was black, choppy, and the only illumination came from the single lamp the sailors had placed in the dinghy and those still on the ship. It was like being lowered into an abyss. Had she made a grave mistake? Were there really other ships near by? Was she really choosing to die? Corwyn looked up to find Black leaning on the rail watching her.

Just after the boat touched the water, something fell from the ship, dropping onto Corwyn and knocking her to the bottom. It was a net, a heavy net like those used for deep sea fishing, and she struggled to throw it off while looking for the pistols she had dropped. While she scrambled about, the dinghy climbed back up the ship until it could be pulled over and dropped onto the deck.

The net lifted up and away from her and Corwyn finally found one of the pistols. She stumbled to her feet and leveled it at Black. He stood with his arms folded across his chest as though he were watching the antics of a misbehaving child. He lifted an eyebrow and she looked about to find herself facing a sea of men, each one poised to take her when the opportunity presented itself. In despair she found the gun sliding round to point at her own temple. She could not bear anymore.

In one swift move Black slapped the gun out of her hand and then brought his hand back across her face. The gun discharged as it struck the deck, the shot splintering the wood and making the men jump back. Corwyn dropped back into the boat, stunned by the force of his blow.

"Get her out of there," Black ordered. While his crew obeyed him, he picked up the gun that had fallen to the deck, and a moment later retrieved the other pistol from the boat. Without a word he threw the pair overboard.

"Well, I think we have had quite enough entertainment for the evening," he said as he turned toward her. Moments later he was carrying her past his gawking men down the stairs and through the companionway. Once back in the cabin he deposited her upon the bed and she buried her face in her hands.

Black watched her weep. Had she meant to kill herself? When he had seen that white face peering up at him in the darkness, he had known that she had come to her senses. She did not want to die alone in the middle of the sea. He had rescued her, pulled her back aboard his ship and she had turned the gun upon herself. That sight would stay with him for the rest of his life.

He found it hard to believe that she would surrender her life so easily. This was the woman who had tried to disembowel him the night just previous. Where was her courage now?

He shook his head to clear it, found words "I have killed, by my last reckoning, more than a score of men." He paused, as if in thought, "No, I am mistaken, it is a score and one with that last bastard in London."

She stopped weeping to look up.

"And then there is the crew from that ship you were on. The Albatross wasn't it?" He pulled out a chair and sat down. "Since the fools abandoned ship in approximately the middle of the Atlantic during a gale, and their ship sank, I think we can safely assume they are dead."

He leaned forward. "By any reckoning I have killed quite a number of men and if you insist I will kill one more." He knew he had her attention. "That brother of yours should be easy to find at his new post and bluff as he is he is no match for me."

He saw her face turn white.

"The next time you try to kill me, I suggest you succeed. Failing that, you survive this voyage or I will send Captain Benjamin Chase to his grave as soon as I can find him. Do you understand me?"

"I will see you hang one day!" She spat.

Black smiled, success was bitter-sweet. "Only if you live, My Lady." Her hair was tangled; her cheek flowering with the effects of his blow; her eyes were red. But her expression was resolute. Hate flourished where hope foundered. Wasn't that always the way?

He stood, watching her draw back. "Well, it seems we understand each other." He left the cabin, locking the door behind him.

His crew were all on deck despite the fact that half had not slept for a week and the watch wasn't due to change for two hours. Their heads swiveled as he made his way to the bow and looked toward the approaching storm. From their stunned silence he assumed this particular episode would insure that he was painted the blackest pirate in all of Christendom.

He felt the wind come up and the saw the waves stir and rise. "All hands!" he heard Heal call. "All hands on deck!"

Now that was an unnecessary order if ever he had heard one. He smiled as the ship began to toss. There was nothing like a fight for your life to clear the mind.

Chapter Ten

Black did not return to the cabin that night and yielding to the bitter cold, the temptation of dry clothes, and a bone deep weariness, Corwyn finally raided his wardrobe for another long shirt and climbed into bed. When she woke the next morning she was surprised to find herself alone. Perhaps he had managed to get himself washed overboard.

She could only hope.

For lack of better occupation, she searched the rest of the cabin. She found the things she expected to find, stockings, boots, britches, liquor, all the things a man would need to live months at sea. She found other, more curious objects. A leather whip coiled in the bottom of one drawer, cracked and burnished brown with old blood. A stack of law books, passages marked and old letters pressed between the pages.

She spent several hours reading the correspondence and before she was done she had decided that Devon Black knew more law than most of the barrister's appearing in the king's courts.

And finally four long log books surfaced, each bearing the name of a vessel. She found what appeared to be the oldest one and opened it at random.

7 April '15 readings, lat & long

Brisk wind from the SE. Crew at half rations. 40 lashes to first mate for insubordination. Stock holding.

8 April '15 readings,lat & long

Light wind from the SE. Crew at half rations. First mate in brig until Sunday service. Stock holding but for one whelp taken ill.

Whelp? Who would transport wolves? Dogs? Corwyn shook her head and pushed on. It struck her as strange that Black had such unsteady hand. He was a strong man.

9 April '15 readings, lat & long

Trade wind. Crew at half rations. Whelp poorly. Physic administered. Stock holding but for one whelp taken ill.

10 April '15 readings, lat & long

Sunday service. Restoration of full rations. First mate broken to second. Crew subdued. Stock holding but for one whelp taken ill.

Corwyn broke off and flipped a few pages looking for more than a mere recitation of dates, crew rations and stock measurements. After a dozen pages or more she came to a long passage.

11 June '15 readings, lat & long

For the good of the ship I shall hang Second Mate Devon Black for mutiny on the morrow. He has made clear his intention to commandeer this vessel and its cargo, and has enlisted the aid of some of the crew. Since his arrival on this ship he has proven to be a miserable officer and a poor Christian. I shall be glad to put an end to him. Stock failing, three lost during the night.

The next entry was harder to read, and since it did not have a date she assumed it was written the same day.

Second Mate Devon Black has compelled the rest of my crew to mutiny. Even now they make preparations to hang me. In my 57 years I have always endeavored to serve my God and my country. I have endeavored to run my ship with good Christian discipline and in the service of its owners. I go now to a better world. May the Lord have mercy on my soul.

The following entry, written in a firm, determined hand proved the captain right.

12 June '15   readings, lat & long

We have this day hanged Elijah Riles. From this day forward, this ship has a new master, Devon Black, Earl of Kettering.

"Are you going to look through my possessions every day?"

Corwyn looked up to find Black in the doorway. He actually managed to look patient, tolerant even, as he stood there. He shook his head and closed the door. He moved to the table, picked up the log she was reading, scanned the open page and snapped it shut. "Leave my things alone." He gathered up the rest of the books and put them back in the drawer.

"You mean to keep me here naked?" Corywn heard herself ask.

"Primarily," said Black, "Although you may borrow clothes as it suits you. You may even read my books if your thoughts turn to idle fancy. You may not read every letter and log in my possession."

"Are you afraid I will learn your secrets? Should I think less of you because you are a mutineer as well as a murderer and a pirate?"

"In a long career of villainy, the execution of Elijah Riles stands out as one of the better things I have done." Black shrugged. "Be that as it may, if I find you have disturbed my papers without my permission again, I will quarter you in the hold. The accommodations will be less hospitable, and I assure you, overall, I am better company than the rats."

"I would rather sleep with the rats." said Corwyn. "You are deluded beyond all redemption if you think mutiny is laudable."

His expression wavered for a moment, registering something very like surprise. "Well, you do have a voice. I recommend that you keep a civil tongue in your head because I do have something of a temper."

A rap on the door prevented Corwyn from replying. While she watched, a young dark-skinned man carried in deep bowls full of stew, bread, ale and cheese. He left without looking at her.

"If I am not mistaken, you may be hungry by now. When was the last time you ate?" Black pulled out a chair and seated himself at the table.

Corwyn could not remember. Two days ago? Could that be right? Reluctantly she sat across from him, picked up her spoon and took her first bite. The beef stew tasted better than anything she had eaten since she had left London, and the bread was fresh baked. It seemed that Black was unwilling to suffer the normal privations of men at sea.

It was a long time before she noticed that he was watching her, his arms folded across his chest, feet resting on a chair.

He was huge, she realized again, a giant of a man who managed to make her feel he was too close though he sat six feet away.

"At least I do not have to force you to eat."

"Pity," Corwyn replied, mocking his dispassionate tone. "You would enjoy that."

"How much farther do you plan to push me?"

Corwyn put her spoon down. "Well, let us see. So far you have taken me captive, raped me, beaten me and starved me as you have so kindly noted. As I make it out, there isn't much more you can do, is there?" She could hardly hear herself speak for the pounding in her chest, but she would not cower before him.

"Raped you?" Black raised an eyebrow. After a moment he inclined his head in agreement. "You are quite correct. I am afraid my heart is so black with sin I had not noticed the addition of a new variety."

"What is going to happen to me?" the words were out before Corwyn could stop them.

"I haven't decided yet." Black might have been discussing the fate of a horse he had just purchased, or an investment he had made.

"Will you kill me?" She had to know, now, what he had in mind for her.

"I do not know," Black said, "Probably not. That seems . . . wasteful."

Corwyn wondered how to phrase the next question. When she finally found the words, they took a long time to say. "Will I ever see home again."

Black shook his head slowly.

Corwyn buried her face in her hands and started to cry. She could hardly believe what she was hearing. How long could she live without knowing what would happen to her? Was life worth living if she never saw Chase Manor again? Never saw her brother or Christina?

Black stood up to answer a knock on the door, and Corwyn watched through bleary eyes as two men rolled a deep wooden tub into the room and filled it with six huge buckets of hot water. In a moment they had disappeared. After they left, Black collected soap and linen from one of the cabinets and placed them on a chair near the tub. Then he pulled off his clothes. He stepped into the steaming water and scrubbed his skin until it was red. Then he washed his hair, working up a rich lather with the bar of soap.

"Will it be necessary for me to force you to take a bath?" Black asked after he had rinsed his hair with a bucket his men had left behind. In the blue light that poured into the cabin from the last minutes of the day, his eyes were the color of pitch.

"I want a bath," said Corwyn, finding she could just remember how to speak. "But I will not take one in front of you."

Black turned away and rubbed his face with his hands as though he were weary. "I find myself in the awkward position of wanting to give you advice." He stopped, as if wondering whether or not he should continue. "I do not know why I bother since I doubt that you will take it, but I shall endeavor to help you come to a conclusion you will arrive at in your own good time."

"And what is this pearl of wisdom?" Corwyn inquired. He took her captive and now he meant to give her advice on being a model prisoner. That was rich.

"Pick your battles."

"Do what you tell me to do, whenever you tell me to do it, until I cannot stand it any more." Corwyn translated. "I see."

Black pulled himself up. He stepped out of the water and came toward her, skin glistening blue in the half light.

He took her hands and pulled her to her feet. When she would have jerked away, he turned her around and drew her back. His arm was like an iron band around her chest as he unbuttoned her shirt, tugged it away from her body. He let her go.

"Is it worth the battle?" he asked her. "After all, you want a bath and I want you to have one."

Corwyn could not reply. He had managed her so easily, using just enough force to accomplish his objective.

Black stepped aside and gestured at the tub.

After a moment, Corwyn walked past him to the back. The water was still warm, fragrant from the soap. She sat down and picked up the discarded linen square he had used as a washcloth. Black, behind her now, took it away from her and began to wash her back. When he moved to caress her breasts with the warm, sudsy water, she tried to push him away. He captured her hands and brought the cloth back and forth across her nipples, making her gasp with surprise. He spiraled lower, finding the secret place between her legs and she fell back against him, eyes closed as he explored her.

He pulled her from the bath and took her to the bed, laid her so her legs fell over the side. He lifted her hips, drew her forward, onto him. She gasped as he filled her. He held her legs over his arms and began to move.

Corwyn arched her body to bring him deeper, she wanted to feel him everywhere, to replace all his rough words with this silent power. When the climax finally came, she cried out, reaching for him, dragging him down to kiss her. She could feel him spend inside her, heard his release.

After a long moment, he pulled up and away. Corwyn rolled to her feet and walked unsteadily to the tub. She descended into the still warm water and washed herself again while he dressed.

When she reached for the bucket to pour water over her head, Black picked it up instead. Without a word he helped her wash her hair, even handed her a towel when she left the bath.

"I want to comb your hair," said Black.

Corwyn shook her head. That seemed too intimate somehow, something a lover or a husband would do.

He retrieved a comb from him wardrobe and sat behind her on the bed. An hour later her hair spilled across her back, clean and drying into gentle waves.

"Do not hope," said Black.

"What?" Corwyn asked, looking over her shoulder to find him toying with a strand of her hair.

"Do not hope. It isn't fear that destroys you and it isn't pain. It's hope. Hope brings expectation and expectation brings disappointment."

Corwyn felt the blood rush to her face. She pulled away from the bed and whirled to face him. "How dare you offer me advice on how to survive your abuse!" she spat. "I would not be here if it weren't for you. You want to offer me help? You want to be kind to me? Take me home! We are enemies, you and I, and we will be enemies until I see you swing from a gibbet."

Black made no reply, face growing harder with her every word. When she stopped, he stood up and tossed the comb onto the table. He started to speak slowly, deliberately as he dressed. "Well said. We are enemies. We were enemies the day you forced me to kill Norfolk."

He collected instruments and paper from the drawer that contained the log, then walked to the door. "You cost me everything, everything, that day. As you have just so eloquently pointed out, that is enough to make one want to kill. I suppose it is fortunate for you that you have another coin to pay in." He walked to the door.

"I hate you!" Corwyn wished she had killed him when she had had the chance. How dare he compare their situations!

"You are going to hate me a great deal more," Black promised as he left the room.

Black returned to his cabin two hours later. For the first time in weeks he had been able to take readings, and as he expected the ship had run far to the north. In seven or eight weeks, if the winds were good, the ship would make Port Royal.

She had not turned down the lamp before she had fallen asleep. In fact, she lay like a broken toy on his bed, obviously having cried herself to sleep. Clean, hair spilling about her like a satin cloud, she had new bruises on her temple and cheek. Her arms and legs had new scratches, as well, probably from all the fighting she had done in that dingy.

In summary, the whole picture was obscene.

On the other hand, he would see her in hell before he would let her go. That was the truth of the matter. Yes, he was quite insane where she was concerned. He could run his ship, command his men, chart his course across the wide sea just as though he were the man who had sailed into London a little less than a year ago. But that man had been purposeful, logical, reasonable. The man who watched this woman sleep had no purpose except to return to an island fortress where he could force this girl to give herself to him over and over again until surrender became a habit. This man had wanted to kill her once, wanted to ravish her now. Who knew? In two days might well have decided to sell her into the slave trade. And, by God, if he were a mad man, she had made him one.

Chapter Eleven

Two days later Black returned to his cabin at mid morning. He spared Corwyn, seated on the bunk and silhouetted by the window, barely a glance. Without a word he moved to the gun case and unlocked it with one of the keys on a ring he carried with him. He pulled out several weapons, dragoons as well as muskets, and placed them upon the table. Pulling powder and shot from the case as well, he turned to replace the lock. Then he moved to sit at the table, brown hands loading the weapons deftly.

"What are you doing?" Corwyn leaned forward to watch him.

"Loading guns," Black poured powder into a musket.

"Why?" Her heart started to beat faster. She swung her legs off the bed and came to stand behind him.

"Why do you suppose?" Black spared her a look. "If you move to touch one of these weapons, I shall probably shoot you. I haven't time for your foolishness now."

"You cannot mean to say you are going to take a ship?" Corwyn came around the table so she could stand in front of him. "With me on board?"

"We are, after all, pirates," said Black, "I am sure you do not expect us to give up our livelihood simply to spare your sensibilities." Through with the third weapon, he picked up the fourth, using the back of his hand to brush a lock of dark hair from his eyes. "I suppose we could throw you over board."

"You have no right to drag me into this... danger with you."

"What danger? It is a British ship and we are flying the Union Jack. Before they know we are anything other than a brother at sea, we will be close enough to sink them," With his guns loaded, he moved to the door. "In any case, I do not suppose you have any alternative."

"They will hang you," said Corwyn, "Someday you will die for what you are doing now."

"If you really want to see me swing someday, stay in the cabin. There might well be bloodshed on both sides. I do not want you to be a casualty." Then he disappeared into the dark hallway, locking the door behind him.

When Black finally returned, long after night had fallen on the sea outside the window. Corwyn found herself torn between relief and revulsion. So, the attack had been successful. Black had survived and he stood before her with even more blood on his hands. She watched him return his weapons to their cabinet, their charges spent. He stripped then, pulling his shirt over his broad shoulders and dropping it onto the floor. He moved to sit on the bed and Corwyn could not control a gasp.

"Rediscovered your virtue?" Black asked her over his shoulder as he began to remove his boots.

"I have never met anyone so contemptible," said Corwyn. "How many men did you murder today?" she demanded, "Was the gold worth those lives?"

"Since you ask, yes the take was fairly good. Not that I had much of it. You are an expensive little baggage and I am paying for you in hard cash."

"You are buying me?" Did he have a right to buy her? What kind of a world did he live in? "You cannot buy me!"

Black looked at her and laughed. "Do not be ridiculous. What is surprising is that I have to buy you when you belong to me already." He looked down and pulled off one of his stockings. "And since you ask, the captain was the only casualty. His crew had him strung up before we boarded."

"I should have known." Corwyn's blood ran hot.

"Elijah Riles." Black said. "We are talking about Elijah Riles, now."

"He was an old man and you killed him."

"You are defending Elijah Riles?" Black laughed again, "Now that is rich!"

"Why should I not? You stole his ship and his cargo, convinced his crew to mutiny, murdered him-"

Black's eyes narrowed. "What, exactly, was his cargo?"

Corwyn remained silent. Wolves? Dogs? What else had whelps?

"Slaves." Black laughed again. "Elijah Riles, you will be surprised to hear, had no difficulty in trafficking in human flesh. When his cargo would sicken, due to bad food and poor ventilation, he would administer one of his physics, an emetic that usually forced his patients to vomit blood before they died." Black stopped as if gauging the effect his words had on her. "He is dead. I killed him. I would do it to him and to all of his kind if I had the chance."

"And you are better than Captain Riles?" Corwyn fought back. "Should I thank God lam wearing your chains and not his?"

Black said nothing for a moment, blood draining from his face. When he spoke again, his voice was low, dangerous. "First, by all rights, you should be dead. You aren't. That is more mercy than I planned to show you. Second, I do not care what you think about me and I do not care what you have to say about what I do. Keep your mouth shut or I will stop trying to pretend that I am human at all."

Corwyn put her hands over her mouth. One moment he was laughing, the next brutal. What was wrong with this man?

He reached for her and she did not try to draw away. She let him drag her toward him, under him, felt his hand slip between her thighs. "You want this," he whispered. "You want to belong to me. You want me to master you over and over again. You wanted it in London and you want it now."

"No," Corwyn felt him hard against her, felt the wetness between her legs, the familiar tension coil in her belly. "Please-

"I've lain with a dozen women, a hundred women, even more. Do you think you can hide from me? You want this." He loosened his britches and, without preamble, entered her. "You want me." He began to move and she felt him watching her, waiting for her response. Her back arched. She did want him, wanted him to possess her, to fill her. Because he was human then, human and sometimes kind. He increased the tempo, driving them both onward. Corwyn reached up to pull his mouth down on hers. She wanted him to share this madness, not punish her. She felt him spend inside her, and then the shudder of her own release.

He held her until she fell asleep.

In the weeks that followed, there were times when Corwyn wanted to cry out that he was destroying her. There was no point, during their lovemaking, that she could claim was painful, but nevertheless she knew he was tearing her apart.

He returned to the cabin each evening, and they ate, sharing a full meal together in silence or occasionally in terse argument. Then he would lay out a sea chart and plot the day's progress, using measurements from the sextant. The ship's journal would be duly marked with the information, and notes would be made regarding any events above deck. He would read for a short time, taking a volume from the shelf and turning the pages laconically.

Corwyn avoided the bunk as much as she could. Once he entered the room she tried to put as much distance between herself and the object of her dread as was humanly possible. She would sit across from him at the table, reading, perhaps modifying one of the shirts she had appropriated, her hands plying the needle nervously.

When he stood, at last, and began to undress, her heart would stop for a moment. She would pretend that she did not see him, that she was unaware of his movements. The ruse would not last long. When he finally turned to her, gesturing in an offhand manner at the bed they would share, she would be forced to put her modesty aside and approach him.

She would allow him to undress her, would feel the familiar breath of air as her garment fell away to reveal her flesh. Though his expression would not change, she could feel the full force of his intelligence focused upon her, feel him listening to all the words she did not say.

His lovemaking was skillful, tender sometimes, passionate at others. Worst of all, he never had to force her to share their mutual fulfilment. She wanted him to take her, just as he had said.

After the passion had slipped away leaving her remote from herself, from her loss and anger, she would turn to him, nestling into his arms like a child. Sometimes she would try to breach the silence, seeking some common ground between them, but his gentle laugh and tender caresses always drove the words away.

Later, in the dead of night, waking from a sound sleep, she would hate herself for her weakness. She wanted to deny that she could surrender so easily, to forget his touch and her response. Her pain and self-imposed distance would slide into the next day where she would castigate herself over and over again for her lapse. Never again, she would declare, would she let him arouse her. She would lie like marble beneath him, cold and unyielding. Every night her body would answer his demand with one of its own despite her wishes.

"I do not understand why you keep me here," she declared one day, as he dressed to leave the cabin. Her voice, to her own ears sounded childish. She wanted to appear strong and defiant, but when she spoke to him her control always slipped away. How could he steal her courage so easily?

"We are at sea," pointed out Black, "What else should I do with you?" Pulling on an indigo shirt, he regarded her.

"But, surely you have had your revenge," Corwyn pointed out. She was on the bunk, curled into a corner near the window. Her green eyes sought him guiltily. She hated the smooth planes of his body, the coal black intensity of his eyes, his voice. "Why not confine me in the hold? Put me somewhere else on board. Anywhere but here."

"I do not want to," Black said, watching her.

"But I want you to!" said Corwyn, frustrated. "I cannot stand this any longer. Do you not know what you are doing to me?" She tried to communicate something of her pain, her self-loathing.

"Do I hurt you?" Black asked. "That is not my intention."

"Please," Corwyn began. "I do not want-" she stopped, seeking words. "I cannot stop myself," she tried to explain. "Please, I will do anything if you will just leave me alone."

"No," said Black, his head cocked to one side as if he found her curious. "I do not want to leave you alone." Moving to sit beside her on the bed, he pulled her unwilling frame toward his. "There are too few pleasures left to me in this world to deny one more," he told her. "You might consider adopting a similar attitude."

Corwyn, crying, was unable to reply. When he left the cabin, she sought refuge beneath the blankets, hiding from the sun and from herself in Black's bed.

Chapter Twelve

The days, with the passage of the ship into southern climes, grew longer and warmer. In a few short weeks Corwyn could almost believe it was summer, not early spring. At home the trees would just now be acquiring their leaves, and new buds would be making their first appearance on the dark branches.

At first Corwyn had welcomed the heat. It was such a relief from the dampness and chill she had experienced since England. Then, day by day, the heat became more oppressive. In the late afternoon, the cabin was filled with motionless air that seemed like the breath from the bellows of a blacksmith's forge. Her head ached, sweat beaded her brow, and her anger over being held prisoner grew minute by minute. She had never enjoyed confinement, and suffered greatly under it now. How she longed for the freedom of the upper deck!

"I would like to go above," announced Corwyn, more than a month after she had been captured. Each evening she had wrestled with the idea of making this request. Each time, she had lost her voice when confronted by her captor. This time she forced herself to speak to him despite her fear, the words stumbling over one another in her hurry to have them said.

"Do not be ridiculous," Black replied without looking up from his work.

"I could wear some of your britches, cut them to fit me." Of course he would reject the idea out of hand. He did not care what she felt about anything.

"No," Black shook his head.

"You do not understand. Its too hot in here," said Corwyn. She stopped, willing herself to keep the strain from her voice. Speaking more slowly, more calmly, she continued. "Its inhuman to keep me confined so."

"You, My Lady," said Black, "are not a guest. I do not care if you are comfortable."

Corwyn turned to stare out the window at the placid, moonlit sea, she tried to control the tears that coursed down her cheeks. His every word to her was unkind, his look betrayed contempt, he owned her, and he hated her, and day after day her frustration increased.

Even the way he touched her, she decided, was like a surgeon practicing his trade. He felt nothing, simply probing for a specific response, seeking a particular end. It seemed that even this might be part of his revenge. He laughed, sometimes, when she bit her lip to stifle her cries.

Almost a week after Corwyn had made her request she decided that any punishment was too little to confine her to the cabin. She simply could not stand it anymore.

Opening the clothes press, she pulled a pair of britches from the lowest shelf. Gray, and frayed at the cuffs, they were obviously well worn. Pulling them on, she tugged at the laces. Even at their tightest, they rode low, barely managing to stay on her hips. The legs were far too long, folding under her feet when she tried to walk. With a sigh Corwyn found Black's razor and cut the legs to a ragged end at her shin. Reaching into the clothes press again, she pulled out a faded white shirt. Reviewing the considerable excess length she sighed. With the razor she cut off a ragged hem so that the shirt would fall just below her buttocks instead of to her knees. She used the length of fabric salvaged from the shirt to fashion a makeshift belt for the britches. Reflecting that she might as well die for a sheep as a lamb she trimmed the arms of the shirt so they would end at her hands instead of flopping about.

Finally dressed in the ridiculous garb, she braided her hair. Dropping the long tail down her back she hoped she might pass, at first sight, for a boy, rather than the captain's personal strumpet. Doubtless Black knew every man aboard his vessel, but she hoped to cross the deck unobserved. Perhaps she could tuck herself away in some unnoticed corner for a few hours before he discovered her.

She went to the door, struggled to pull back the bolt, and stepped into the long dark corridor she had not seen for so many weeks.

Her heart pounded in her chest as she approached the door at the top of the flight of stairs. Creeping toward the light, she prayed that no one would find her here, least of all Black.

At the top of the stairs, she hesitated, looking out across the too bright deck at the endless expanse of turquoise sea. A crewman's shout startled her and her eyes dropped back to the deck. Where could she hide? Two boats rested just across from the companionway. Perfect! High enough to obscure her from view, close enough to minimize her exposure. She could not have asked for better luck. Before her courage faltered she dashed into the open and across the deck.

Sandwiched between a boat and the rail, Corwyn held her breath. Had she been seen? Her heart pounded so hard she was afraid she would not be able to hear Black shout at her when he followed her to her hiding place.

Minutes passed and her heart stopped racing. Perhaps she would have her day on deck after all. Thank heaven for small mercies. With a sigh of relief to stuck her feet through the railing and over the side of the ship, wriggling her toes in the warm breeze that caressed them. How long since she had last felt the sun on her legs? Months? Perhaps her last day at home, before Ben appeared to tell her the carriage was ready to depart. Why had she ever left the west country?

Since she was seated near the end of the ship, she could examine the rush of water as the ship cut its wake. Above her sails snapped with the sudden changes in the wind. No land marred the horizon, though Corwyn knew the ship was running close the southern colonies now. Georgia? Further south? It was hard to study the charts as Black plotted their course. She gave up watching the horizon and lent herself to the serenity of sea and sky, the steady power of the vessel as it plowed the water. Who knew when she would see daylight again?

Corwyn almost cried out when she felt something brush her hair. She turned, looking up and back, sure she would see Black towering over her and ready to punish her for disobeying him. But no one seemed near. How curious! She felt about her and discovered an apple core at her side. Then she looked up into the sails to discover a sun-bronzed sailor hanging some twenty feet above her head. He had a wide smile on his face.

At first, uncertain of his intentions, Corwyn feared he would alert Black. When that horrible fate failed to materialize after a little time, she wondered if he intended to do her some greater harm. She watched him climb up and down the rigging, navigating the ship like a spider in its web. When he saw her watching he tossed her a carefree salute and returned to his work. Corwyn relaxed again. For the moment it appeared she was safe.

As the evening approached Corwyn found her contentment turning to anxiety. She had never expected to go this long without being apprehended. Should she stay the night on deck, taking in as much fresh air and freedom as she would be allowed this trip? Should she return the cabin and try again tomorrow? One day out of the cabin hardly seemed enough now that it was almost over.

At last she decided she wasn't going to leave the deck until she saw the sun set. After all, she might never see it again.

Cat calls and whistles finally broke through her contemplation of the sinking sun and Corwyn looked up to find a half dozen sailors hovering above her head. Dressed in all manner of brightly colored clothes, most bare-chested and some with earrings, they looked like a flock of parrots. With one accord they pointed to the foredeck. Just an instant after Corwyn had divined their intention, she was jerked to her feet by her collar.

Without a word Black dragged her out from behind the boat and through the companionway door. Just before he thrust her through it, Corwyn glanced up to find nearly the entire crew watching her. Did she see pity in their eyes?

"I should have known!" said Black fiercely as he pushed her into the cabin. "I spent the whole day waiting for my orders to be carried out, looking for my crew, only to find them hanging over your head like monkeys!"

Corwyn made no reply. Jerking her arm from his grasp, she went to stare out the window.

"I told you not to go on deck!" Black continued.

Corwyn spun around to face him. "I do not belong to you! I never will!" The fury and fear she had felt for so long were coming to a head. She did not care if he killed her. She would rather die than live like this.

"Actually, you can own people. Black, white, male, female, it is commonplace. In fact, to be specific, I have paid several hundred pounds for you since the day you set foot on this ship, and a thousand times more than that before we left England." Black took a step closer. "Furthermore, I can prove I own you in every way a man can own a woman. Shall I prove I own you once again?"

Corwyn felt the blood rush to her face. "Lay one hand on me and I swear I will kill you." How dare he talk to her as though she were his property!

"Is that what you will do to me?" He asked, moving closer.

Corwyn drew back. "You are an animal!" she shouted at him, "A huge, cruel, vicious animal!"

Black's face grew white with rage and she saw his hands clench into fists.

"You are devoid of every feature, every characteristic that sets a man above a beast! I would rather lay with a rutting bull or a mangy dog than share your bed again!" Corwyn heard the words pour out of her mouth.

"Shut up!" he grabbed her by the arm, jerked her toward him.

"What more can you do to me? What sin have you omitted? Shall you give me to your crew? Please do. I'd rather have all of them than you-"

He threw her on the bed and her head struck the frame.

She could not see for a minute, could not breathe, but she rolled forward, onto her feet. She stumbled along the cabinets, cutting a wide berth around him on her way to the door. She bumped against his shelves and she heard glass rattle. She saw him reach for her and she grabbed the brandy decanter and threw it at him. It smashed against the cabinets, spilling like blood down the wood.

She reached blindly for something else to throw. Then he had her by the arms, was speaking to her. Pushed past all endurance she attacked him, she felt nothing, heard nothing, wanted only the pleasure of hurting him as much as he hurt her.

Black left the room hours later. He did not know if the girl was sleeping or unconscious. He had wanted to stop it all after he had thrown her onto the bed, but she had not let him. She had fought him when he had tried to hold her, twisting in his arms so hard he expected to her bones break. And when he made a move to release her, she clawed him across the eyes, across the chest. He had held her until she exhausted herself.

Once on deck Devon made no attempt to wipe away the blood that ran across his face or down his arms. He walked aft, ignoring his men, wondering how the girl would fare if he simply jumped overboard. He had never struck a woman in his life before he met her, never forced a woman to do anything she did not want to do, never held a woman captive, rarely even argued with a girl under even the most trying of circumstances. What had happened to him? He buried his head in his hands and tried to think.

When he was with her he felt so many things. Rage one minute, pain the next, grief, sorrow, wonder, passion, a symphony of emotions. He could not ever remember feeling anything except hate before, hate for his uncle and the determination to take back what belonged to him.

Now, for the first time in almost twenty years he thought he might weep. The girl had to go home. He had made a horrible mistake in taking her captive in the first place. In fact, he was quite sure he had lost his mind. She had to go back where she belonged, where he would never have to see her again. That is what he wanted. He wanted her off his ship, out of his life.

But what if she were pregnant? Another wave of despair broke over him. If she bore him a child ... He reached for the rail. A child? He could never part with one of his children. He knew what happened to unwanted children. They were alone in the world. What had he done?

He shook himself. If she was pregnant, he would care for her until the child was born then send her back to her family. He would keep the child, and no one would ever know she had born one. If she was not pregnant, he would have her sent back by the fastest ship he could lay hand to.

And no, he told himself sternly, he would not take her home personally. He would hang if he got caught within a hundred miles of England. He had no right to drag his crew half way around the world again, toward Newgate and a hangman's dock, simply to put right a mistake he had made. And, by God, if she was not pregnant by now, the return voyage should certainly remedy the situation. He was disgusted to find that he wanted her yet again.

She had to get off his ship and away from him at the earliest opportunity. The sooner they parted company, the better.

And once she was gone ... Despair again. What would he do? Where would he go? Back to his island to lick his wounds? Would he kill a few more men? Sink a few more ships? Was that all he had to look forward to? A life of murder until one day he could surrender his own life to a blade? He had always thought himself superior to those who surrounded him. They killed because it pleased them or because they had no choice. He had always had a loftier goal to guide him, to revenge himself upon his uncle and regain his estates. Now he was like the others, a man with no hope and no future.

She was still sleeping when he returned to the cabin. Unwilling to have his men see her thus, he picked up the glass from the shattered decanter himself. He cut his fingers and watched the blood well, perversely satisfied to see he was human after all.

Later he cradled her head in his lap, staring out the window at a midnight sea. His hands absently brushed the hair from her brow as he waited for her to wake. When he looked down, he was mesmerized by the shadowy lashes that trailed across her face, the cupid's bow of her mouth. He traced the line of her jaw, marveling that it could hold such determination even in sleep. He did not think her nose was broken, but a bruise was forming on her left cheek bone, he could see bruises forming on her arms from where he had tried to hold her. Christ, what a bastard he was!

She stirred, and a moment later her eyes fluttered open. She started to sit up, move away from him.

"I am sorry." He said the words before she could say anything that would stop him.

"For what?" the girl made her escape, sitting as far away as the bed would allow. "Beating me? Holding me captive for weeks on end? Taking me prisoner? Or turning me into a whore?"

The words bit into him. "You are not a whore. A whore is paid for her services. I forced myself upon you. I thought that was clear from the outset."

She cocked her head. "So, what else do you want to do to me?"

"Do you want to go for a walk around the deck? It is a pleasant night, and I am sure the crew would be relieved to see you alive."

Her eyes narrowed, obviously anticipating a trick. "No," she said, "I think I have done enough for today."

Black slipped off the bed and stood up. "Let's go."

A warm breeze filled the sails that stretched like ghostly columns toward a starry sky. Standing on the shifting deck, Corwyn could not believe the beauty that surrounded her.

"It is beautiful," she offered, moving to the rail, "Like being in a cloud." It was something from a fantasy, a child's dream. So clear and bright were the stars that she felt she could almost touch them.

"It is beautiful," Black replied. He stood a few feet behind her, outside the dim glow of the lamp hanging from the jib. "The northern skies seem so remote. Southern stars always welcome me home."

"Home," said Corwyn, "I thought England was home. Isn't that why I am here?" She wondered why she wanted to turn the knife in the wound. Was she punishing him? Testing his new found demeanor?

"I do not care if I ever see England again," Black replied. "Now that my uncle is dead, it means nothing to me." As he said the words, he realized they were true.

"Curious," said Corwyn. She moved away from the rail, and turned toward the bow of the ship. "It seems to me you used to care quite a great deal."

"My uncle killed my father, I killed him. Its finished."

"What a lovely family." Corwyn responded dryly.

"Indeed," Black said.

Corwyn walked the length of the deck, wondering in which direction home might lie, and marveling at the magnificent sky. She found Black's presence almost comforting, a shadow master of a ghostly ship.

"It is time to go below," Black said after a time. He had walked beside her e for more than an hour as an unobtrusive guard. "Though you might have little enough to do during the day, my daylight hours are quite busy."

"I do not ever want to go below again," said Corwyn. Looking into the distance, where the dark sea met a sparkling sky, she waited for Black to tell her he had been lenient enough already.

"Is it so terrible?" Black asked. He turned toward the companionway door.

"It is unbearable" said Corwyn. "Its very hot. Too hot to read, to sleep, and there is nowhere to hide from the heat." How could she admit that she spent every hour waiting for him to return to the cabin? She was so bored even fear was entertainment.

"Would you like to come up again tomorrow evening," asked Black. He made no sign that he had heard her words.

"It is hot during the day," Corwyn replied. "Would that I could spend every minute on deck, but the days are the worst."

Black led her down the corridor to his cabin. Once inside he closed the door behind them and poured two glasses of wine. He presented one to Corwyn, who sat at the table. He moved to sit on the bed.

"I paid a bride's price for you, Milady," he offered. "My share is several times a crew member's, and your ship was a fine take."

"Why should this matter to me?" Corwyn stared into the dregs of her wine. Was he planning to tell her he owned her again?

"If I let you on deck during the day, some of the men may forget what you cost," Black went on as though he had not heard her speak. "If that happens, I will have to kill someone. That breeds bad blood that might make trouble for both of us."

"So now you keep me prisoner to protect me?" Why did he bother to lie to her? Her head was beginning to ache and her struggles earlier in the day had tired her. She just wanted to sleep now, to forget she ever knew him. "Do what you like."

"If I let you up on deck, you had better not decide to incite some sort of riot," Black did not appear to have heard her words. "Like as not, you'd be getting an innocent man killed."

"If lever go on deck again, I will try not to incite mutiny," said Corwyn. She pushed her chair away from the table, stood and walked to the wide bunk. She climbed over Black's legs to lie down. In a moment she was fast asleep, facing the midnight sea.

Chapter Thirteen

The next morning Corwyn wondered if it had all been a dream. The cabin was stifling, and she was locked within. Only the pain in her head offered any reassurance that she had not imagined the events of the day past. At noon she sat with her eyes closed and her head against the cool glass of the window, praying for the heat to subside.

"Let's go," said Black, leaning against the doorframe, watching her.

"Go where?" Corwyn asked. This was too good to be true.

Black jerked his thumb up, his look sardonic. While Corwyn stood, coming reluctantly toward him, he spoke, "I've just spent the better part of the morning threatening my crew with the most dire consequences for looking at you."

"Is that what took so long?" asked Corwyn. "Your communication with me seems somewhat abbreviated in retrospect." It was probably a mistake to goad him, but the pain in her head made her less than cautious. She stood up and walked toward the door.

"It hard to box the ears of twenty grown men," Black replied. He allowed her to exit the cabin. "You are not so much as to look at one of my crew. You will stay on the foredeck, move as little as possible, and speak to no one at all. To a man they think you lovely, and most of them would be willing to serve as your champion because I am undeniably a brute. I do not want to have to kill anyone."

"Aye Aye, Captain," agreed Corwyn. She followed Black down the companion way toward the sunlight. Whatever the terms of her freedom, she would be glad to pay.

True to his word, Black escorted her topside each and every morning, allowing her to sit on the foredeck. Content to simply be in the open air, she whiled away the hours by staring at the sea or watching him work.

At first Corwyn had tried to ignore him. After all, he had shown her no special courtesy. She continued to be his prisoner, only the terms of confinement had slackened somewhat. But after a week passed she found herself able to believe that the days of her captivity were over. Then her eyes began to search him out as he paced the long ship.

A fair master, Corwyn had to admit, stern, uncompromising, but fair. Stripped to the waist, bronzed skin bright in the sun, feet bare, he moved about the ship like a solider. No idle hands found mischief while he commanded. He insured that every man was fully occupied from dawn until dusk. Corwyn could see that his crew respected him, not from fear but from something more akin to pride. They tended to their tasks adroitly, sparing her not a glance as they moved by.

Black worked alongside his men until late in the evening, till the stars filled the heavens and the moon danced on the waves. Then he escorted her to his cabin and they shared an evening meal. Sometimes, despite her intention to remain sullen and silent, she found herself speaking to him, seeking to know more of him and his past.

Black would answer her questions, for the most part, his eyes sardonic as though he saw something more than mere curiosity in her words. Some questions he left unanswered, those about his parents most obviously. Upon the one occasion he had allowed himself to discuss his childhood, relating what he could recall of his mother, his dark eyes had watched Corwyn, their expression unreadable.

"She had midnight hair, and a cat's green eyes," Black said candidly, "I suppose that accounts for my attraction to you."

"So you attribute your mistreatment of me to your mother?" said Corwyn. "Even I would not add that to your long list of crimes." Why did she goad him? Why not leave well enough alone?

"With a heart as black as mine?" he queried, "I would not be so sure."

Uncertain what reply to make, Corwyn looked into the glass of wine she cradled. When she looked up he was at the door, watching her. "I am taking a turn on the night watch this evening. I will be back at dawn," he told her. Then he disappeared into the hall.

From the night he had struck her, Corwyn had been spared his advances. Though they shared the same bed, he made no move to do more than hold her at night. At first this respite had been more than welcome, and yet, as time passed, Corwyn found herself wondering how he had come to be disinterested in her. After all, she assured herself, she did not believe that he had simply stopped molesting her due to a belated remorse. Like as not he had found something repulsive about her, something unattractive.

This, she was ashamed to admit, had piqued not only her curiosity, but her vanity as well. How dare he despoil her only to cast her aside without explanation! And yet, she could not demand that he interpret his behavior. He would think she wanted him to touch her.

She sat on deck one day, watching the sun shade him the color of an Olympic god, golden and bright, she wondered that he could seem so foreign now. Just weeks past she would have sworn she could recite every defect of his character, every blemish of his form, and yet now she found him to be like some brutal Galahad, rough and beautiful, with no imperfection at all.

Black gave her no attention when she sat on the foredeck, not a word or a look. She did not exist for him while the ship plowed through the waves at the mercy of the wind. She watched him consult his first mate, the man who had carried her to her cabin so long ago. Neither man ever turned her direction. This lack of attention troubled her more than she would have cared to admit.

Corwyn scanned the horizon, looking for the narrow line that would indicate land was near. She knew Black had them skimming along the coast, perhaps past the tip of Las Floridas, into the West Indies. But instead of a dark still ridge of black, she saw something flicker on the horizon. She found her sighting confirmed when a voice shouted "Sail Ho!" from the crow's nest.

The ship was startled into action, every man running to some appointed task. Corwyn moved to the mast that shadowed the foredeck. In one lithe move she had stepped into the rigging and was climbing to the first level of the mast. Then, bare feet on rough wood, she followed the mast higher, watching the sails billow below, her eyes scanning the horizon over and over again for the other ship. Perhaps this was an English ship, one that could rescue her.

"Steer Clear!" Corwyn heard Black's order from far below. Almost three quarters of the way to the topsail, Corwyn glanced down. There, far below her on the seething ship, he stood. He pointed at her and then at the deck. His expression was unreadable from so far away.

A wave of dizziness washed over her and Corwyn sat down on the crossbeam, steadying herself against the mast. In a moment, she knew, the giddiness would pass. She had experienced this sudden fear before when she had climbed too high. She closed her eyes and listed to the wind caress sails.

She was quite aware when Black joined her, seating himself on the other side of the mast, one hand upon hers.

"Have you decided to kill yourself again," he asked, his voice loud in the silence all around them.

"No," Corwyn replied. "I would have come down in a moment or two," she tried not to be aware of the warmth that emanated from his skin, or the heat of his hand as it covered hers. She forced herself to open her eyes and look at him.

"One way or another," said Black said with a rare smile.

After so many weeks, how could his smile make her heart skip a beat? How many times had he smiled at her? Once? Twice? What if he could smile at her every day? Corwyn look down. "I've climbed many a tree My Lord," she said firmly, "I have never needed aid in the past."

"My ship is not a tree," Black pointed out. He still smiled, eyes dancing as if he knew that he disturbed her sitting there.

"You are such a savage," said Corwyn unguardedly. He looked at home here high in the sails, sun beating down on him as if it shared the amusement of its favorite son. If he could be this man before her every day, how lovely it would be! She closed her eyes again, wanting to blot out her vision of him.

"If," said Black softly, "I were a savage, I would probably do this," and he swung himself around to sit beside her on the long spar. He leaned forward and brushed his lips across hers, and his hand caressed her hair for just a moment.

Corwyn's eyes fluttered open.

"Let us get down," he said, staring forward into the tremendous curve of sail before them, "Before we fall." There was no indication that he had touched her.

"You first," said Corwyn, her voice unsteady. Suddenly she felt she truly might topple the long distance to the deck. Surely anything was possible.

When they both stood firmly on deck, once again in the presence of his crew and lost in the sound of water rushing past the ship, he gave her a nod and returned to his command. Feeling lost and slighted somehow, Corwyn moved to sit as far as she was able from him.

That evening Corwyn felt inexplicably unnerved. When Black led her below decks, she found it all but impossible to hide her agitation. She wanted, desperately, to reach through this dark silent creature to the man she had met this afternoon. And yet she could find no words to say. Her every thought seemed vacuous, empty headed and unimportant. She sat silent and uncomfortable through their meal.

"How long before we reach port?" the words were out before she realized she was going to say them. Of course, she reflected, this was quite an appropriate question. A prisoner might be expected to inquire this after weeks aboard a pirate vessel.

Black looked up. His eyes narrowed for a moment as though he sought some dark intention, then he shrugged. "Soon."

"Where are we bound?" She hated the high, childish pitch of her voice. Why was she only now asking these questions? What had she been thinking all this time?

"Port Royal," he replied. He watched her as if waiting to see where this line of questioning would end.

"When will we set sail again?" Corwyn asked curiously.

"The Wraith will leave a few days later," Black replied.

"The Wraith," Corwyn mused out loud, suddenly caught up in the curiosity of the word. "What a curious name ... It sounds lonely," she offered. "Why ever did you name it that?"

"It is a name," Black replied. "A good name for a pirate ship."

"I suppose," Corwyn went on. "But why did you name it that?"

"Why are you asking so many questions?" he asked in response. He seemed intent upon her reply. In fact he leaned forward to await it.

"Well," Corwyn could feel the amusement lurking behind his impassive demeanor and it unsettled her. "I just wanted to know ..." She turned to look out the long window.

Black stood up, and the sudden tension in her body made her a statue, holding her motionless as he knelt before her. She thought she saw a smile tug at his lips when he began to speak. "No, this is what you want," he said, a rough hand coming to her chin. Then he kissed her, his lips brushing across hers in a whisper.

Corwyn shook her head, unwilling to take responsibility for initiating this moment. Massive before her, Black once again stole her words away.

"Quiet now," noted Black, leaning back to regard her face, his head cocked to one side. "No questions for me?" he asked, raising a gentle, work roughened hand to caress her jaw, to raise her eyes to his. He leaned forward to kiss her eyes, "Why do you not ask me to kiss you?" he whispered. Touching her cheek with careful lips, he said "Ask me to make love to you." His hands slipped to caress her thigh. "Do you want me?"

"Please," she whispered, "make love to me." She placed her hands upon his broad shoulders and relinquished all thoughts of pride to the passion that stirred her blood. Why should she pretend that he did not give her pleasure? Why could she not be as much as a savage as he was? What did it matter anymore?

Black swept her into his arms and moved to the bed. In a moment he had removed the peculiar assortment of clothes she wore for her excursions on deck. Then, when she was naked before him, he turned to remove his own clothing.

Corwyn watched him undress. Such physical perfection, she found herself thinking, was something that should exist only in dreams. When he moved back to her, she shifted close to the window and raised her head to watch him.

Black lay upon the bed and moved to take her in his arms. Corwyn stopped him with a gesture. Then, as he lay immobile under her scrutiny, she placed a small, cool hand on his chest.

His skin still held the heat of the day, radiant with the light of the long afternoon at sea. As she moved her hand lower, she caressed the curve of his ribs, felt the taut muscles of his stomach ripple. He was indeed perfection, she thought as her hands circled lower.

Finding his passion, she touched it tentatively at first, taking in its size. Could it be that her body accepted such a shape each time he made love to her? Exploring him, she was aware that he watched her, eyes growing dark with desire.

To Black's surprise, Corwyn moved to kneel astride him. Her small body felt cool against him, cool and feather light. Then, she was holding him at the entrance to her body, eyes closed as she slipped down upon him. The sensation made them both gasp.

She set a slow, steady rhythm, moving inexorably toward fulfillment.

Black endured her slow assault for as long as he was able, then tumbled her over upon her back. Then he was driving into her, slaking his own thirst even as he catered to hers.

When the moment came, Corwyn was shocked by its power. The pleasure rippled through her body over and over again, making her cry out with each thrust. She thought she would faint when she heard Black gasp his release and she called his name as she followed him.

When Corwyn had drifted into slumber, Black kissed her upon the forehead and slipped from the bed. He dressed in darkness and left the room. Once on deck he sat in her place on the foredeck watching the ship drive toward the sliver of land on the horizon. They would make Port Royal before two. It would be a hard thing to surrender the girl to Andre, but he had survived worse. In a day or a week his memory of her would have dimmed and he would be himself again.

When he returned to her bed just before dawn touched the sky, he found her waiting. Without a word she lifted her arms to him and they made love again.

Chapter Fourteen

Corwyn regarded Port Royal, Jamaica, with a mixture of fear and elation. As the Wraith entered the deep, bowl-shaped harbor, her eyes scanned the verdant hills that towered on either side of the narrow entry. When she examined the ancient Spanish battery that had guarded this bay for a hundred years, she could just make out cannon. Two long rows of artillery were focused on the narrow passage, ready to destroy unwelcome vessels.

The city flowed away from the water and up onto the hillside. Narrow winding streets ran from the busy wharves through the one and two story plastered buildings, to the less dense, more varied houses scattered on the perimeter of the town in all directions. On the rim of the enclosure Corwyn saw a fortress, its walls crumbling into the jungle surrounding it.

It was easy to understand, she decided, why this bastion of villainy had survived so long. The harbor could not be breached by even the largest warships. Cannons would blow them apart as they filed into the bay and foliage, so dense that it appeared to occupy every free inch of space, would deter any attempt at a march across the island. Corwyn felt a moment's respect for the Spanish officer who had first seen this tiny harbor as a strategic installation.

From the ship, Corwyn could see nearly fifty vessels, some bobbing near the dock while others were scattered throughout the cove. Many of the ships flew colors, some from Holland, a few from France and there were other flags Corwyn could not guess at. After a careful examination of the vessels filling the harbor, she admitted that her hopes of discovering an English ship had been naive.

Though Black anchored the Wraith some distance from land, Corwyn could make out men scurrying along shore like brightly colored ants. Each ship had cargo to be discharged, new cargo and supplies to be loaded, and while the vessel was in port crews could make repairs.

Corwyn made her decision and turned to leave the deck. She had to escape and Port Royal might prove her only opportunity. Once free of Black she would be able to find a way home. She knew she was taking a great risk, but she could not remain Black's prisoner forever.

In the overheated cabin, she explored the cupboards surrounding the bunk she shared with Black. The linen bandages she had discovered on an earlier search soon came to light and she moved to sit upon the bunk. She pulled off her shirt, she began to bind her breasts. If she could pass for a boy for just a few days she would certainly be able to find a vessel with a captain willing to help her. They could not all be blackguards and rogues.

Black entered the room without warning. He had known when she left the deck what he would find here. Her body had grown used to his, but her spirit was not broken. She still hated him and in her place he would have felt as she did. "It is useless," he said, "I do not know that you ever did pass for a boy, but you certainly will not in the future."

The girl made no reply, discarding the bandage after a moment's thought.

"But you are leaving the ship. You'll be staying with a friend of mine while I tend to business elsewhere." Black steeled himself for the battle.

She was silent for a moment, frame suddenly rigid. When she finally raised her eyes to his, the hate was apparent. "I see." she said after a time.

"I guarantee that you will be safe and well taken care of, until I return." Black found the lies more difficult to deliver than he expected. What should he say? Stay here until I know if you are pregnant or not? Wait here until I know for sure whether or not I can send you home? Hope was the enemy.

"You are finished with me." she said. "You do not want me anymore."

"That is not true. It is just best for you to stay here for a time." Why did he bother talking to her at all? It would not change how she felt about him, what he had to do or where she had to go.

"I hate you."

"Yes." Taking up one of the bandages she had discarded, he gave her an order, "Give me your hands."

"What are you going to do?" Her face went white and she put her hands behind her back. "You are not going to tie me up."

"Do not make me force you to do this." Black shook his head. How many times would she fight the same battle?

"How can you do this to me?" She looked up at him. "How can you discard me here?" Her face flushed red as the emotions she sought to control got the better of her.

"A minute ago you were preparing to jump ship rather than stay on board with me." The irony of the situation was far from amusing.

"I was going home."

Black shook his head. Should he try to explain that she might be carrying his child? Should he try to tell her than he could not keep her aboard because he found it torture to keep his hands off her, that if she was not pregnant now another month or two on his ship and she surely would be? Should he try to explain all the reasons why he could not take her home right away? What would be the point? "Just give me your hands and let us get this over with, shall we?"

She stood up and stuck out her hands.

"Turn around," he said. When she complied he tied her hands behind her back with the length of linen.

"Thank you," said Black, when the operation was complete. He stepped back and she turned to face him. Her look was filled with contempt. Placing one hand on her shoulder he guided her from the cabin.

Once on deck, Black handed Corwyn over the crew. He pretended to be unaware of their morose faces and pitying looks. She had a ship full of champions here now. This episode should just about insure he was painted blacker than any pirate since Blackbeard. While he watched, they lowered her over the side of the ship into a small dingy waiting to be rowed ashore. Black joined her at the stern of the small boat, sitting beside her on the narrow bench. The sooner this was over and he was sailing away from this god-forsaken port, the better.

On the long way to shore, Corwyn rubbed the bandages entwining her wrists against a short iron bar that thrust against her spine. Though the metal was anything but sharp, the cloth was loosely woven. Her diligence finally won out and the material separated to leave her hands free. She kept them behind her back and held the cloth about her wrists as though she were still bound. She waited until the boat had bumped against the long wharf, and Black had already climbed the rope ladder to the wooden planking.

The crewmen lifted her to the deck and she moved to stand just behind Black. Let them think she had come to accept her fate. She waited until Black leaned over the side of the wharf to call an order to the oarsman and then she shoved him hard in an attempt to push him over the side. To her chagrin, he did not drop into the water as she had hoped. He did however miss his footing and he had to scrabble for the rope ladder in order to prevent a drenching. Corwyn darted down the long wharf toward the narrow buildings that lined the shore, dodging ropes, nets and crewmen from other vessels as she ran.

She felt free as the footsteps behind her seemed to fall farther back, but a sudden tackle from behind brought her crashing headlong into the rough planks. For a moment all was dark, and when she recovered her wits she found she had been dragged to her feet.

"A commendable effort," Black offered when she stood before him. "It was, however, as unsuccessful as every other plan you have ever attempted. Let us see if we can travel the next half mile without any excitement, shall we?" By this time her hands were once again tied behind her back. When she refused to walk, he threw her over his shoulder and made for the long alleys leading into town. Breathless and bruised, Corwyn had never felt so humiliated.

Black carried her through the twisted streets, past whorehouses and taverns, mounting narrow winding avenues that climbed to the summit of the hill. Corwyn railed at him as they climbed, each jostle, each step flamed her fury. She hated him, she swore viciously, and nothing would prevent her revenge.

In all too short a time he had dropped her to the polished floor of a Spanish villa's front hall.

Corwyn struggled fiercely in the arms of a slave that had been brought in to control her. She cursed her innocence over and over again as she watched Black finally decide her fate. She could not hear their words across the great distance of carpeted floor, but she knew Black had sold her to the dark skinned aristocratic man who even now gestured her way. For nearly an hour she had watched them, impatient and angry while Black reclined in a delicately-made cherry wood chair across from the tall, immaculately dressed man. The stranger's voice, all but inaudible over such a distance, revealed a French accent that belied the almond color of his skin, the deep brown of his eyes.

She should never have trusted Black, she realized. She should have fought him every minute of every day. She should have forced him to kill her aboard his wretched ship. He had turned her into his slave, his whore, and finally his lover. She had been a fool to believe that he felt anything for her. How stupid she had been to let down her guard. Next time they met, by God, he would be begging the hangman for his life.

"She is obstinate, conniving, and vicious," Black said. He toyed with the cigar Andre had provided him with and tried to ignore the struggles of slave and young woman that broke out periodically behind him. "The most difficult thing you will do is hold on to her until you can send her home."

"What a task you bring me, ami," responded Andre, his eyes gesturing to the girl with a wealth of amusement. "You seem to have expended a great deal of effort to capture this creature, and now you set it free. That's a curious thing for a good business man to do."

"Perhaps she is a curious woman," replied Black. He wished the intelligent, over curious half-breed would turn his mind to the matter at hand. "If she is not carrying my child, I want her sent home on an honest ship."

"She seems a beautiful girl, beneath the grime," Andre pointed out. "Why not sell her?"

Black felt the blood rush to his face. If Andre said another word he would be a dead man.

"Perhaps not," Andre amended. "I know you have no taste for human trade."

"Home," repeated Black, "Unmolested. On the next ship."

"Why does a young girl fight so when she is to be returned to her home and family?" Andre queried suddenly, watching the girl's struggle continue. "She is quite determined," he noted.

"I have not told her I am sending her home. If she is pregnant, she will have to stay with me until the baby is born. Maybe longer." Maybe forever, Black thought. "I've told her she is to wait her for me. You can tell her you are sending her home once you are sure she is not pregnant." Black examined the cheroot burning in his hand. After a moment, he went on, "I want her treated like a lady. New clothes, a maid, everything a woman of her class is accustomed to, until she is on board an honest ship or until I return for her."

"Perhaps you are unwise," Andre began cautiously. "She is English, no?" At Black's nod he continued. "It may be that if she returns to her homeland, you cannot. She may live to see you hang one day."

"Perhaps that would be a pleasant reunion for both of us," Black returned emotionlessly.

For a moment neither man spoke.

"Why not just keep her?" Andre asked. "She is pretty enough for a wife, I think."

Black, coming to his senses, regarded Andre with annoyance. After a decade of profit and what passed for friendship in this part of the world, he might have expected something more than unbridled curiosity and intrusion. He stood up. "I apologize for the inconvenience that she will surely cause you. Please see that my instructions are carried out." Black looked out the window. He would be happy when he was free of the girl and his head was his own. "A hundred pounds to cover her cost," he finished abruptly. "I will bring you the money in a month or so."

"No, please," said Andre. He pulled out a purse heavy with coin from his desk. "I owe you money from our last transaction as it is." He stood and tossed Black the bag. "As for the girl, no payment is necessary." He moved around the broad escritoire quickly, and was just in time to escort his guest out of the room. "This is a trifling matter, too little to require payment between friends." Neither man looked at the girl as they left the room.

"You will do as I bid?" Black asked. "I do not want her sold, seduced, or beaten. Just kept here until you are sure you can send her home."

"Exactly as you have asked. And if she is enciente, she will be waiting for you when you return." Andre reached to open the heavy front door. As he opened it, he moved to block Black's path for a moment. "I apologize for my curiosity. I should have understood that this is a private matter."

"Take care of her," said Black as he pushed past him. "Thank the Lord she is your problem now."

"Maisoui," replied Andre with a slight bow.

Corwyn listened to the door close. She would not have believed it unless she had seen it with her own eyes. He really had sold her!

The dark skinned man returned a moment later. He walked across the room to his desk and sat against it, watching her.

At his nod the slave dragged her forward, her arm twisted behind her back. When she struggled, he tightened his grip and she cried out with the pain. When she stood before the stranger, he shook his head in apparent distaste.

"You have some manners to learn, ma petite," he said, his accent making him difficult to understand. He moved slave's hand away from her Corwyn's mouth.

Corwyn spat epithets at him, in French to be sure he understood her slurs, until he placed his scented hand over her mouth and nose, stopping her breath. When she struggled, tried to scream, he shook his head.

"Non. Be silent. I have not the patience for this game."

When she stilled, eyes frantic, he spoke again, "Do you like to breathe, little one?" At her hysterical nod, he went on, "When I let you breathe, you will remain quiet?"

Corwyn nodded her acquiescence and his hand fell away. There was no point in angering him. Let him do whatever he pleased, she would escape at the first opportunity. She waited impatiently as his cinnamon eyes examined the scratches on her cheek which had come when she had tried to escape on the wharf. His touch was impersonal, almost professional, when he pushed the hair away from her eyes. Then moments later his hands took the measure of her hip and waist, while Corwyn stared at the floor, blood rushing to her face. Was there no indignity she might be spared?

"Very good," he said, tilting Corwyn's head back to look at him. "You need a bath, some fresh clothing, perhaps some food."

Corwyn, met his warm brown eyes. The very instant she was alone she would escape. She was on dry land now, not lost in the middle of the sea. If Black meant to maroon her in this terrible place, he would soon learn a most important lesson. She would be his victim no longer.

Her new owner sighed. "I can see you hate me and we have only met. One day I think you will like me very much." When Corwyn shook her head, he laughed. "For the time being, perhaps you will allow the maid to help you bathe."

Corwyn nodded, let her body relax. "I would like a bath," she said.

With a nod he made the slave release her. "If you will follow Dimitrius he will take you to your room. Your maid will be along shortly to help you."

"Thank you," said Corwyn, but he had dismissed her already. She followed the slave out of the room and up the carpeted stairs to a room at the far end of a hall. The slave opened the door for her, eyes narrowed as if he did not believe her sudden change in manner. He closed the door and locked it behind her.

Corwyn barely had time to examine the elegant room, done in pale blue and lemon before she stood at one of its windows. To her satisfaction it overlooked the long roof overhanging a garden veranda and a small portion of the street outside the manor wall. Trying the window, she found it opened easily, obviously a credit to the carpenter who had crafted it. In a moment she was through, feet unsteady upon the rocking red tiles as she crept toward the two story drop over the narrow, muddy street. When she found herself hanging feet dangling at least ten feet above the lane, Corwyn's courage failed her. What if she broke her leg, or even her neck in the fall. One of the red tiles she knelt on slipped. She fell off the roof and to her freedom.

Her landing was as painful as she might have expected, and for a moment Corwyn could not move. She was sure she would never breathe again. When she recovered her senses the knowledge of her regained liberty helped her stagger to her feet. She had to move, had to start running. Before she could decide which way to turn, she heard voices at the window above her. In a moment the sound of tiles slipping against one another came from the rooftop.

Corwyn darted away. She heard the impact of a man dropping to the ground behind her, and desperation coursed through her veins. She turned at the first corner she came to and found herself in a wider street. Two women, only half dressed in the filthy clothes they wore, pointed at her as she sprinted past them. Down another avenue, longer than the last, with even more people to navigate. She passed by stalls, carts, they were multiplying, crowding the streets. Now Corwyn could barely hear the steps of the man chasing her, she was gaining ground. More turns followed and Corwyn emerged into a crowded market square.

Simple canopies of dyed canvas and a hundred carts and stalls divided the area into long allies. People of all races jostled one another, buying fruit, fish, meat, bread, and more exotic food. Some rummaged through bins of clothing, dishes, and more personal possessions, apparently unconcerned by the origin of such property. Unwashed bodies, horse dung, strange foods filled the squared with a miasma of noxious fumes. Corwyn shoved her way through the crowd, sometimes ducking down to dart through a stall rather than going around. Some of the sellers cursed her when jostled their goods or their customers, but she kept her head and ignored them.

A corner of the market had been set aside as an auction block, and she knelt on the ground at the back of the crowd, wondering where she could hide. She saw a cow auctioned off in a matter of moments, then a child. The next time she glanced at the block she saw a woman, white skinned with black hair, struggling with the auctioneer. She was dressed in rags that might once have been fine clothes. Her face was bruised. When the auctioneer lifted her skirts. Corwyn turned away.

Along the far edge of the square, past the auction crowd, she saw carriages waiting. She darted between the ring of stalls and the auction block crowd and made for the most attractive one. It was a red carriage with gold piping, and the largest of the few stationed here. She slipped inside. She sat on the floor, her back against the door, and prayed that her pursuers would give up before the owner of this conveyance wanted to go home.

As she caught her breath and her heart stopped pounding, she let herself think of Devon Black. How angry he would be when the dark man wanted his money back. He had tried to cage her over and over again, but she had finally escaped. She was free now and one day she would see him in chains. She closed her eyes and began to pray that her nightmare was finally over.

Chapter Fifteen

The carriage door was jerked open and Corwyn rolled out of the carriage onto the ground. Had she fallen asleep? The square was almost empty now, the sky dark.

"Merde!" A man, probably not much taller than herself and obviously very angry, gestured at her. In response to his order, a huge black slave appeared and pulled her to her feet.

"Who are you!" the man demanded in terse French. "What are you doing here?" Sharp gray eyes flicked across her. They lingered on her ripped shirt and the bruises on her face. He was dressed in immaculate blue britches, black boots and a blue great coat fitted with gold buttons and matching epaulets. He reminded Corwyn absurdly of a toy soldier.

"Please you must help me," Corwyn replied without thought. Her French, though unpracticed was at least understandable. "I have been abducted and you are my only hope."

"Qu'est-ce que c'est?" the marionette demanded. "Why should I help you?" he asked coldly. "Why should I not have you whipped for your trespass?"

"My name is Corwyn Tyler Chase. I have just escaped from pirates. Please, you must help me. My family will reward you."

"You are a Lady?" the man inquired. His suspicion was obvious. He switched to English, "An English Lady?"

"Please, help me," Corwyn followed him back into her native tongue. "I can explain everything. It is not safe to talk here." She tried to look over her shoulder, in the direction from which she had come so many hours ago but the man holding her blocked her view. "I will tell you everything," she promised, "If you will only help me."

With the master's nod, the black giant released her, and Corwyn darted back into the carriage. Her diminutive escort followed, seating himself as far away from her as the small space allowed.

"Why were you in my carriage?" He spoke in French again. Guarded, suspicious, he looked inclined to disbelieve anything she said. "Did your... abductors follow you here?"

"There was nowhere else to hide," Corwyn told him, trying to keep her voice level. "I saw your carriage and prayed that the man who owned it might help me." Well, that was almost true. She had hidden in his carriage and she had hoped to find someone who could help her. She just had not assumed they would be one and the same man. "I truly had no choice, Monsieur."

"How did you come to be here, alone. You were taken captive? Alone? No family? No servants? What became of them when you were abducted?" His sharp eyes darting to the dirt caked on her feet to her tangled hair.

"My maid died before my abduction," Corwyn replied uncomfortably. "My brother is a Captain in the English Navy, stationed in Virginia. I was coming to stay with him, but my ship was taken at sea." She moved away from the uncomfortable topic. "I am know my brother will pay handsomely for my return," she added.

When her unwilling savior made no reply but to peer at her speculatively, Corwyn turned to stare at the night that had fallen outside the carriage window. Please, she prayed silently, let him help me.

The man spoke again. "I am sorry, Mademoiselle, for my previous manner. You can have no idea of the kind of people that frequent this island."

Corwyn nodded her assent. The change in his manner was startling to say the least. "I only arrived this morning."

"I am Francois Du Joles, Marquis du Lyon," here he reached forward to tap her hand. "I will certainly do everything in my power to aid you." Shifting position to regard her more directly, he continued, "I cannot tell you how fortunate you were to find me .. ." and he trailed off as though he could not sully her ears with the alternative.

Corwyn evaluated him with as much composure as she was able. He was going to help her, that much was clear. "I am very grateful to have found man of honor here. I know my brother will be overjoyed at my return and will want to thank you generously."

"Certainly, Mademoiselle," Du Joles replied. "Rest assured, I will attend you until we can find others better suited." Moving to open a small cabinet built into the side of the carriage, he offered her a cordial to help her recover from her shock.

Corwyn shook her head. His last words troubled her, a double entendre if ever she heard one. She shrugged. Even if her savior turned out to have villainous plans, he could not be as terrible as Black had been and now that she was on dry land she could always run away again.

"Can I offer you no comfort?" Du Joles asked.

"Perhaps a bath could be arranged? Some fresh clothes?" Corwyn responded. While she looked like this he would never believe her story. Clean, decently dressed, she was sure they could come to some arrangement.

"Of course," he replied, "We shall provide you with every comfort as soon as we arrive at my residence."

Corwyn whispered a word of thanks when they rumbled through a wrought iron gate on to a half circle of pebbled drive. The carriage had clattered up the narrow streets for twenty minutes or more since they last spoke, winding this way and that toward the top of the hill. All the while Du Joles had watched her, eyes moving from face, to hands, to legs and breasts.

Du Joles resided in a brick town house that would have been at home on any fine street in Paris. Isolated from neighboring houses by a high outer wall, the inner enclosure featured a wide lawn and flowering plants of every variety. The house itself was red brick, obviously imported since it was entirely unlike any of the structures she had seen so far. The windows on the first floor were relatively small, and were protected from weather and worse intrusions by heavy white shutters. A second floor with more generous apertures overlooked the white pebbled drive, reminding Corwyn of Christina's home in London. A high brick wall extended from the side of the house, and she could just make out the tops of some small trees inside it. Obviously the house featured a private garden.

A number of servants in white and green livery came to attention as the carriage approached. Some were black, others Indian. When the carriage came to a complete stop, one of the servants moved to pull the coach door open. Du Joles disembarked first, assisted from the carriage by his massive body guard. One servant moved to take his cloak from him while another collected his gloves. There was something ominous in the military precision Du Joles commanded in his staff. Were free men ever so flawless in the performance of their duties?

"Adam, take our guest in." Du Joles said in French. "Put her in the spare room."

The giant servant leaned forward, and despite Corwyn's reflexive movement to avoid him, he scooped her into his broad arms. He removed her from the coach as though she were as light as a feather and he carried her past the impassive attendants into the house.

They passed through the marbled foyer and then turned right to climb a flight of stairs to an upper hall. From her peculiar perspective, Corwyn saw elegantly dressed women watch her from gold picture frames along the walls. Vases, chandeliers, polished cabinets, her host apparently made every effort to appoint his home with the finest furnishings.

The massive slave shouldered his way through the door and set Corwyn upon her feet in the cream and gold bedroom. For a moment their eyes locked. Corwyn waited for him to say something, but he made no attempt to do so.

"Thankyou," she said.

For a moment she thought she saw some something like pain or pity move in his eyes. Then, with a curt nod, he was gone, disappearing into the hall.

Corwyn took a few moments to explore the room. The late afternoon sunlight filtered through lace curtains, making patterns upon the pale carpet and light wood floor. The bed, walnut with an ornate headboard, sported a blue satin counterpane and a canopy of matching silk. The mattress, Corwyn discovered when she pressed her hand into it, was down. Across from the bed was a magnificent armoire featuring a spectacular silvered mirror. The mirror was darker than she had ever seen before, like a pool of silver black water.

The strange object filled almost an entire wall of the bedroom, the dark wood glowing with care and cleaning. Small copulas and tiny drawers marked it as a relic from a previous age. She was startled by the detail represented in each carved ribbon, every carefully sculpted flower. It intimidated her somehow, overshadowing everything else in the room with its vacant eye. Corwyn shuddered and moved to the window.

Looking out the window, Corwyn knew that this time there would be no daring escape across a rooftop. Both her windows overlooked thirty-foot drops, and she doubted she could survive that without breaking some bones. One of her windows, however, did overlook the garden. As she had expected, it was filled with small trees and hundreds of flowering plants. A lush lawn, fountain and several benches completed this private yard. It was hard to believe such an island of civilization actually existed in this wilderness.

Before Corwyn could complete her review of the garden, a young maid with skin the color of pale cream appeared at her door. As Corwyn admitted the woman, she discovered two dark skinned attendants trailing behind her, a deep porcelain tub swinging between them. They disappeared a moment later. The young maid motioned for Corwyn to seat herself before the armoire's long silver mirror. She took up a brush and pulled the tangles from Corwyn's ebony mane while bucket after bucket of hot water was poured into the great tub.

Hours later Corwyn contemplated herself in the full length mirror, clean and appropriately dressed for the first time in weeks. Having been bathed and perfumed by the young maid, she found felt almost human again. Though the low cut gown of bright yellow gauze she had been given might not have been her first selection, Corwyn decided that it fit her well enough. After all it was the first dress she had worn in almost two months. She could only count herself lucky that it fit her at all.

Shortly after dressing, Corwyn joined her host in a dining room off the main hall. Seated across the long lace covered table from Francois Du Joles, she marveled yet again at his diminutive size. Surely he stood not one inch taller than herself.

He too had dressed. A gray silk shirt, an embroidered vest of silver satin, and gray britches had replaced the somewhat martial apparel he had sported earlier in the day. Corwyn noted that his clothes were perfectly tailored for his compact frame. He could have been a gentleman from any of the finest houses on the continent. How in the world had such a man come to live in a place like this?

"It would appear that you are most perfectly recovered, Mademoiselle," said Du Joles. "You have survived a most difficult time, from what you say, and I am very glad that you have come to me safely." As he spoke his eyes wandered across her form, moving from hands, to face, to the bodice she wished were a fraction less snug.

"Merci," said Corwyn, demurely. Uncomfortable under his gaze, she seated herself. "I am glad to be in safe hands at last."

"Indeed," said Du Joles. "It is quite remarkable that you were not hurt." He rose and moved to stand behind her chair. "Few women survive capture by pirates," he promised as he touched her hair.

Corwyn stood, turned away from him, and took a few steps to put a comfortable distance between them. Obviously it was time to discuss the nature of his reward for rescuing her, lest he decide that her hair was not the only thing he would like to handle.

"My brother," she began, "is Lord Benjamin Chase, currently serving as master aboard Her Majesty's Ship the Verity." She turned to face her rescuer. "He believes me dead I am sure, and will pay a great deal when you return me to him alive and well."

"Despite the animosity that always seems to exist between our countries, your safe conduct can be assured," De Joles promised. "After all, there are," and here he paused, searching for a word, "matters of class that transcend le monde des politque." He put a hand to her elbow and guided her back to the dining chair. With a nod, he admitted two servants bearing an elaborate meal of cold beef, cheese, bread and fruit. While the meal was laid upon the table, he continued, "Now, you must tell me of your misfortunes. Who took you captive? What is the blackguard's name that I might see him punished?"

"I do not know his name," said Corwyn. The last thing she needed was for Du Joles to decide that returning her to Lord Black was more profitable than waiting for a long lost brother to appear. "I was thrown in the hold for the entire voyage, I never saw him."

"How terrible for you to be treated so! A lady's virtue is her most prized possession..." clucked De Joles. He sat at the table, apparently disinterested in the food that Corwyn had already begun to heap onto her plate.

"My virtue," said Corwyn, "remains intact. Perhaps the captain feared reprisal, or hoped to ransom me, or perhaps he just did not like women. In any case, I arrived here, and he sold me." She could not let Du Joles sense her discomfort about this topic so she regarded him with a level gaze.

"To whom?" queried De Joles, "I will see that man punished at the very least." It was obvious, by the tone of his voice, that he would brook no evasion on this matter.

"I know not," said Corwyn. "A crewman told me I had been sold, and bundled me from the ship. I escaped once we were on shore, and here I am, with your grace." She made her voice grow colder as she spoke.

"But surely," De Joles pursued her, "You know the name of the ship, or at least the name of the crewman. You must tell me everything. Justice must be done," he stood and began to pace.

"I do not want justice," said Corwyn, "I want to go home. My brother will decide how to avenge me once I have returned to him." Before he could ask another question, she spoke again, "I find this topic particularly unpleasant. That experience is behind me now. I am sure you will agree that punishment of the transgressors is less important than returning me to my family at the first opportunity."

For a moment, there was silence, as though her host contemplated further interrogation. Then, with a short nod, he let the matter rest. "I am sure you are right," he replied. Leaning back in his chair, he folded his hands and regarded her a patient smile, "How shall we begin?"

"If you would, My Lord," began Corwyn, "please send a missive to my brother in Virginia. I am sure he will seek me out immediately." At last, he had turned his attention to the task she most wanted him to undertake!

"Indeed we shall. Of course, correspondence sent from such a barbarous location as this may take several weeks to arrive, even with my safe passage. But, as you say, I am sure he will come to you as soon as he can. If you will draft the communication, I will forward it in the morning."

"I shall attend to the matter immediately," said Corwyn. She prayed this strange little man meant what he said. Perhaps she would soon be safe in Ben's arms, away from Black and his minions forever.

"And," Du Joles continued, "while we wait for the letter to perform its task, I shall pursue an investigation into your abduction. We shall not let the criminals languish for attention. Even in this terrible place there are laws and those who dare to enforce them." Turning his head to one side, he met her eyes, "I am sure you will aid me in this task."

Corwyn nodded, unable to make any reply. He had given her what she wanted, and therefore she must oblige him. She rose and left the room. His investigation would certainly wait until she could be more certain of his intentions.

Corwyn penned the letter that evening, as she had promised. Sure that Du Joles would read the missive, she carefully considered each word. She knew it contained precious little information, but after all, what more need she say? She was alive and waiting for rescue. Sealing the note with a short, fierce prayer, she addressed it to Ben at his station in Virginia.

Dora, the young quadroon assigned as Corwyn's maid appeared shortly after Corwyn finished the letter. The young woman refused to meet Corwyn's eyes as she moved to the wardrobe. Pulling out a silk nightgown, she presented the garment to Corwyn for her approval.

Corwyn found the assortment of women's clothes that had appeared so suddenly in the clothes press of the dressing table rather oppressive. Where had Du Joles managed to acquire them? Of course, it had come to her immediately, such a man would surely have lovers and those lovers would have clothing. It would appear that his last *petite femme* was of a similar size to herself. The idea alarmed her.

Glancing up, Corwyn found the young quadroon watching her. "Thank you," Corwyn said with a smile. "In just a moment I shall try it on."

At this Dora looked uncertain. While Corwyn regarded the envelope she had just sealed, she tried to ignore the presence of the young slave. Why did she not depart? A natural desire for personal privacy made Corwyn unwilling to undress again before her. She had never really enjoyed the attentions of a personal maid, and she did not plan to accept them now. After several moments Corwyn turned to regard the girl again.

"You may go to bed if you like," she offered, "I am sure you must be very tired."

The girl shook her head slowly. Fear sparkled in her dark eyes as she regarded her mistress.

"Must you see me in bed before you sleep?" Corwyn asked, wondering if Du Joles had given the girl explicit instructions about the matter.

The young slave, appeared uncertain for a moment then nodded, as if she had just come to comprehend the question. She placed the nightgown on the bureau before the mirror, then moved behind Corwyn and began to undo the long line of buttons down the back of the yellow dress. When she was naked, Dora dropped the nightgown over her head and buttoned the collar and cuffs.

Corwyn slipped into the deep feather bed and beneath the weight of a down comforter. The sheer bliss of the soft mattress made her sigh with pleasure and weariness. Dora left her with the light of a single lamp to keep her company until she slept.

Where, Corwyn wondered as weariness overcame to her, was Black? Did he know she had run away? Was he looking for her? He had probably forgotten all about her once she was no longer his property. He was probably glad that he no longer had to suffer her presence aboard his clockwork ship. That other man, the man Black had sold her to, would be searching for her. But Black, Corwyn found herself thinking forlornly, had probably already discovered a new woman to pleasure him.

Burying her head in the down pillow, Corwyn forced herself not to cry. She would never allow herself to mourn the loss of Devon Black. She was glad to be free. She hated him with all her heart and would be overjoyed if she were never to see him again.

The girl was bruised, neck and breasts marked with black and blue blooms. Her lips were swollen, and her eyes, when she looked up, were vacant with pain. She sat with her thin arms wrapped around her legs and from where Black stood he could see that bruises flowed along her thighs. She shivered uncontrollably, as though the tropical night chilled her. She wore only her long black hair.

Black stepped out of the room, and shut the door. Leaning his head against it, he drew a deep breath. It wasn't Corwyn, and for just a moment he was glad he had not found her. Yet, wherever she was, she might well be in worse shape.

He had returned to Andre as soon as he had received the message regarding Corwyn's escape. The stoic trader, obviously well prepared for the abuse Black had heaped upon him, only shook his head.

"I had no idea she would try to escape so soon," he said. "You said she was difficult, mon ami, not suicidal."

"I told you she would try to run away," Black said, voice cold. He was standing, hands clenching and unclenching as he spoke. How hard it was not to kill him for losing Corwyn.

"She climbed out a window on the second floor and dropped to the street," Andre said, shaking his head. "My men chased her into the market where she disappeared." Cocking his head to one side, he went on, "A woman of admirable ... courage."

"A fool," Black amended crossly. He should have realized that Corwyn would not be confined. She had been willing to die on his ship in order to escape him, to buy a moment's freedom. What had made him believe that she would simply sit idly by waiting for him to return?

He shook his head in disbelief. He had wanted to return her to England, to her family, to a normal life. Suddenly she was lost in his world, the world he had fought so hard to leave behind. The girl had probably already discovered that he was a tender lover compared to the men that frequented Port Royal.

A wave of despair passed over him. Once he had wanted her to suffer, but now he could think only of saving her from those who would do her harm. "Where the hell can she be?" he asked, "How in the world will I find her?"

"There are over two dozen brothels," Andre offered, "not counting the taverns that occasionally keep women. I have already had my servants investigate those closest to the market." When Black made no reply, he went on, "Of course, a man who found her might sell her to a ship, or to a slaver." Finding one girl in Port Royal was likely to prove quite difficult. More difficult perhaps because anyone smart enough to find her was likely to want to keep her to himself.

She could also be dead, Black forced himself to admit. One man, or a ship full, could drop her into the water with no one ever the wiser. She would be just another dead body in a bay of the dead.

Devon stood. There was no point in remaining here, doing nothing. If Corwyn was to be found, the search had to start immediately. "I will have my men start looking for her. We will start near the water and work our way up."

Andrew followed him to the door. "I have men still searching near the market. We will not rest until we find her." When Devon did not respond, he added, "I am sorry I did not treat her as you told me to -"

Before he could finish, Black was gone, disappearing into the darkness of the street.

Shaking his head, Andre closed the door behind the obviously distraught man. An affaire du coeur, he thought, what a tragedy it would be if the girl were already dead.

Black mustered his men swiftly, calling them out of brothels and taverns where they had gone to spend their share of the profits from the ships taken on the last voyage. Gathered in a circle, illuminated by a ship's lantern set on the rough wood of the wharf, he ordered them to look for the girl. He divided the city into sections and made terse assignments for each pair of men. He noted their grim faces as they turned back to face the city that climbed out of the bowl shaped bay. They knew the odds.

For himself, Black reserved the darkest portions of the benighted city. At fifteen stone he had every reason to expect cooperation in his search from the people he met. If she was here, he meant to find her as soon as possible.

It was a walk through hell, thought Black, as he left one brothel behind. One scarred, battered, abused woman after another. Due to his loathing of such establishments, Black had made little use of them in the past, preferring the company of an established mistress whom he shared with no one. In fact, he had left one behind to go to England. She currently lived in the house he had kept for her in Port Royal, the one he had given her on his departure. He could imagine how happy she would be to see him again. That was yet another matter he would have to straighten out.

His first ray of hope had been after an inquiry yielded word of a girl, supposedly stolen from an English ship, newly arrived in port that day. Though a number of men seemed to know of the girl, no one knew where she was being kept. He had hunted for her then, his irritation growing until he stumbled across one drunk who claimed to have been with her. Shoving the man's back into a wall, Devon managed to wake enough of his wits to find out where the girl was being held. Heart pounding, he had followed the man's garbled instructions to a tiny tavern, closed now due to the lateness of the hour. Rousing the owner of the dilapidated establishment, Black insisted on seeing the girl.

The small frame and long black hair had given him a start. It was only as she looked up at him, shaking her head in mute rejection of another assault, that he saw her face.

Standing in the hall with head against the door, Black swore. He had seen enough battered women this day to imagine Corwyn's body broken a hundred different ways. Images flicked through his mind. Her face lost in passion, reaching with him toward fulfillment. He could easily imagine the same face, bloody, bruised, body struggling beneath someone who wanted to hurt her. Christ! Why had he ever taken her from that leaky tub in the first place?

Black arrived at Andre's door, girl heavy in his arms. He had paid a tidy sum for the wench, who the owner admitted easily, was well used and not a little addled. Rapping on the door with little consideration for the early hour, Black was finally rewarded as the door opened to reveal a young slave, a girl with wide brown eyes, who regarded him as though he were the devil himself.

When Andre appeared, garbed in a dressing gown and obviously resigned to losing the rest of the night's sleep, Black ordered the damaged woman bathed and put to bed. When the she was gone, he lay down on a love seat, his muddy feet hanging over the edge as he placed his arm over his eyes.

"That girl," said Black, making a half-hearted gesture at the girl upstairs, "get her cleaned up and ask her if she wants to go home. If she does not, find out what she does want and arrange it."

Andre nodded, pouring himself a drink.

"As for Corwyn," Black continued, pausing as though he could not bring himself to finish, "you <u>will</u> find her. I do not care how much it costs, I do not care if all you end up with is a dead body. Follow every rumor, every hint, every wild hunch until you know where she is or what happened to her." And Black sat up, eyes narrowing. "Then you will contact me. If I am not in port, and the girl is alive, you will make arrangements to buy her. You will pay any price, no matter how high, with the assurance that I shall return the sum."

Andre nodded again. He had never expected to see a man such as Devon Black brought to his knees by the loss of a woman. Love was a terrible thing. Nevertheless, he was a good client, one of the most honest privateers in the area, if such a thing could be contemplated. He was well worth the effort of some inquiries. Doubtless the girl would turn up one way or another.

Chapter Sixteen

Corwyn presented her letter to Du Joles the next morning, as he sat in his white and gold study reviewing his correspondence. She watched him scan the note briefly, and then saw him enclose a card along with the short missive in an envelope. He summoned a servant who departed without a word, message in hand. "There," he said turning to her across the expanse of his desk, "you see. It is finished. We should hear from him in a few weeks."

"Thank you, My Lord," said Corwyn quietly. "You are very kind." And with that she left the room, unwilling to let him see the tears filled her eyes. She was going home at last!

For a time Corwyn's fears were allayed by this very simple act. Du Joles had promised her that the letter would be delivered and she had wanted to believe him. Before long she had discerned that he sold slaves, and much as she disliked the idea of trading in human flesh, she knew that he had unlimited opportunity to send correspondence to the colonies because so many of his customers resided there. Surely, with the promise of great reward, he would make sure that her note got through.

In the course of her days in his house, she saw him meet with several well-dressed men, obviously interested in purchasing consignments of slaves for sugar, tobacco, indigo or cane plantations. Some, she noted were Spanish, while others were obviously European. She avoided them all assiduously, fearing that someone might recognize her and report her whereabouts to Devon Black or the man who had purchased her.

In all honesty, Du Joles seemed a most considerate and attentive host. His concern for her comfort and entertainment grew every day. He provided her with recent copies of several newspapers, including those most popular in the English colonies. He offered her the consolation of his library, and his completely enclosed garden. When he could not be by her side, he left his personal body servant, Adam, to watch over her and attend to her smallest wishes.

Du Joles even insisted on purchasing her fine gowns, equal to her station, as he was wont to say. He summoned a seamstress to have her fitted. In most matters, he seemed a perfect gentleman.

Corwyn tried hard to ignore any doubts she had about the good will and concern he constantly professed for her. After all, he spared no cost in caring for her comfort. She had but to mention a need and he moved to fulfill it. Even when his behavior seemed somewhat strange or unreasonable she forced herself to see things from his perspective.

Her confidence in his good intentions remained constant for several weeks, until late one tropical afternoon when he summoned her to his study. Without preamble, he asked her to sit in an overstuffed red velvet armchair. With growing insistence he began to question her regarding her abduction, forcing her to describe something of the months she had spent upon the Wraith, her escape, even how she had come to find his carriage. The onslaught was difficult to bear. His questions, probing, incisive, betrayed his irritation at her silence. She denied that there was more to her story than he knew. At long last he let her go with a curt dismissal.

When the dresses Corwyn had been fitted for began to arrive, she found herself forced to confront him with a problem. Despite her preferences in color and style, her new gowns featured low bodices and stiff whalebone corsets. Cut in the modern French fashion, they were suited more for a young woman making her debut than a castaway waiting to be returned to her home and family. When she told him this, Du Joles frowned. With ill grace he offered to have her measurements taken again, and new dresses made up.

Corwyn eventually declined his proposal. She would have to make do with the clothes he had provided for her. Though they were not to her taste, she could not refuse his hospitality.

Much to Corwyn's annoyance, shortly after this unpleasant incident Du Joles declared that he feared for her health. In order to protect herself from the tropical heat, she should take a cool bath during the afternoon, the hottest part of the day. When she tried to ignore his recommendation, he grew angry, ordering her to her room. She would do herself no service, he informed her curtly, if she became ill. She was his guest and she must trust him in these matters.

So, per his wishes, she bathed once each day with the help of her lady's maid. In the highly humid environment of Port Royal, she might well have chosen to take baths with great frequency, but she could not understand why Du Joles had ordained the specific times that she retire to her room. Why should he care when she took a bath? Could it be that even this small activity had to fit into the rigid schedule he imposed on his home?

The shy Dora attended her each afternoon, pouring water along her back, helping her wash the masses of black hair. Corwyn was unused to personal attendants. She had kept none at Chase manor, and she had asked Christina not to provide her with one at the Wakefield townhouse. Even Margaret had been more of a traveling companion than a maid. To be forced to accept Dora's careful ministration made Corwyn very uncomfortable. Yet when she had approached Du Joles regarding this preference he had made his wishes clear. A young woman of her station required a maid. So Dora remained, serving as Corwyn's personal attendant regardless of her wishes.

Shortly after Corwyn began bathing every day, she noticed that when she was not with Dora or Du Joles, another servant always stood near by. When she looked out a first floor window or strayed near a door that led to the outside world, her attendant would move closer to her, as if afraid she might try to escape. Wherever Corwyn might find herself, whether in the garden, or reading in the ornate lounge, she was always watched.

She also realized that she rarely heard the servants, over a dozen of them, exchange even a word in her presence. There was none of the spirited conversation and laughter between staff members that had marked every home she had ever been in. What was even more startling was that they rejected her attempts to engage them in conversation.

She doubted, after repeated attempts to converse with Adam, that he could speak at all. The other servants would sometimes respond with a single word in reply to a direct question, but Adam would only shake his head. Even with Du Joles he seemed to communicate using a system of hand movements.

On the few occasions when Corwyn tried to breach the wall of silence between herself and Dora, she sent the girl almost into hysterics. The slave's movements grew more agitated as Corwyn spoke until finally she would leave the room in a panic.

When Corwyn had been in Du Joles home for almost ten weeks, she allowed herself to think the unthinkable. She had simply exchanged one cage for another. It was no longer possible to believe that Du Joles had forwarded her letter. If Ben had been contacted he would have paid the messenger, or another if necessary, to deliver an immediate reply. The trip to Virginia from Port Royal was surely no more than three or four weeks in length, even allowing for bad weather.

What, then, could Du Joles have in mind for her? If he did not plan to return her to her brother, what did he intend? Did he plan to make her his mistress? He had never approached her in this fashion and Corwyn found it difficult to believe that this was his aim. After all, why should he have waited so long?

Perhaps her unwillingness to discuss her capture piqued his curiosity, and he meant to wait for her confession. Perhaps he thought he could collect more from whomever she was escaping than he could from her family. At the very least, negotiating with someone in Port Royal would involve less risk than the same transaction with an officer in the English Navy.

It was time to take matters into her own hands, Corwyn found herself thinking as she regarded herself in the mirror in the walnut armoire. At Du Joles' request, she was wearing a pale blue gown that made her eyes seem greener, her skin more vibrant, and caught the color in her hair. This was the first time he had taken it upon himself to dictate exactly what she wore and it marked a disturbing trend.

If she permitted this to continue, she had no idea where it might lead. She had not come to him for new clothes, a pleasant room, or even sustenance. She had come to him for aid in returning to her brother. She would not sit quietly by waiting to discover what his plans for her might be.

Her first step must be to contact Ben. After her many experiences with blackguards and knaves, Corwyn could not bear to return to the streets. She had no illusions left. She knew she would find herself in a brothel, or on the block, or perhaps dead if she tried to escape the protection Du Joles offered. This time she would wait to be rescued if at all possible.

Without knowing how she might deliver the message, Corwyn took up a quill and paper, and penned a short, concise letter to Ben outlining her location and her concerns about her protector. Sealing the letter with candle wax, she directed it to Benjamin Chase sailing from English Naval base in Virginia. She could not believe that Ben would have given her up for lost. Surely he must sense that she lived still.

When Dora came to collect Corwyn for the evening meal, Corwyn took the girl by the arm and led her to the window. Whispering, lest someone be standing outside the door, she said "You must help me-"

The young maid pulled away, looking about as though she too feared that someone might have heard them. She shook her head violently.

"Please, I know you are frightened, but you must help-" Corwyn began again.

Without waiting for Corwyn to finish, the girl turned and ran from the room as though the devil himself pursued her.

Corwyn followed her into the hall through the open door. She saw no one. Why had Dora run away? Mystified, Corwyn had no choice but to join Du Joles for dinner as he had requested.

Du Joles dinner guest turned out to be an English planter, Edward Jacobs. He came from one of the Southern colonies where the primary crops were tobacco and indigo. He was wealthy enough, as Corwyn ascertained early on, to have traveled throughout the colonies and much of Europe. Though during the meal they discussed London and the weather in order to make small talk. After dinner Corwyn took the opportunity to ask him about Virginia. Perhaps she could use him to carry a message to Ben.

"A prosperous colony," the planter allowed. "Of course their weather is cooler than ours and their crops tend to be smaller." His blue eyes reflected his surprise at her interest.

"I am told they have a sizable military establishment," Corwyn said, toying with the stem of her wine glass. She wondered if Du Joles would allow her to ask the man to contact her brother.

"Army as well as Navy," the planter replied. He took a moment to push himself away from the table, making more room for his ample girth. "You see, in the colonies we are in need of constant protection."

"So I have heard," Corwyn replied congenially. "My brother has explained that the natives in your area are usually pacific, however pirates and the encroachments of foreign powers inhibit trade." She noted, as she spoke, that the planter's eyes fell to the swell of her bosom above the bodice of her dress. Despite herself, she felt the blood rush into her face. Were all men so forward here?

"Your brother is correct," the planter admitted, apparently unaware of her discomfort. Reaching for his glass, he turned to Du Joles. "Of course, these military agencies are not always benevolent. There are times when they obstruct the natural trade between colonies, or even between the colonies and other European nations, almost as much as the pirates. It is a most difficult arrangement."

"Indeed," responded Du Joles who appeared to take little interest in the conversation as he finished his wine.

"As I am sure Lord Du Joles has told you, I was abducted by pirates on the way to join my brother in Virginia," Corwyn offered, watching Du Joles to see what effect this declaration might have on him.

"He has told me of your misfortune," the planter replied, turning toward her curiously. He seemed to be rather startled that she should bring this matter up.

"In fact, I am waiting for my brother, Benjamin Chase, to come for me," Corwyn noted that Du Joles still appeared to take little interest in their conversation.

"You must have been very frightened," said the planter, as though he had not heard her last statement. "I have heard that pirates are not kind to their women. It is a miracle you survived."

"I was fortunate that I was placed in the hold and remained unmolested for the short duration of the voyage," Corwyn lied coolly. "I was, therefore, spared their brutality."

The planter looked incredulous and looked to Du Joles for confirmation. Du Joles shrugged his shoulders and looked away.

"You mean to say they did not lay a hand on you?" the planter asked. His disbelief was apparent. "Surely it is the first occurrence I have ever heard-"

"I was indeed fortunate," said Corwyn rising. "As you might guess, discussing the topic makes me uncomfortable, so I believe shall leave you men to your port."

Retiring to her room, Corwyn tried to make sense of the odd evening. Rather than being interested in any business he might have conducted with Du Joles, the planter seemed to care only for her. Why had he asked all those questions about her abduction? It had been quite improper for him to bring up the matter of her virtue. She found it impossible to believe that mores differed so much between England and its colonies.

At the appointed time, Dora came to help her undress for the evening. Standing behind her mistress she undid the tiny buttons at the back of the gown and slipped it off over her mistress's head. Then she took away the underskirt, the crinolines, stockings and shoes and finally the chemise. It took Dora a moment to find the lawn nightdress that Corwyn preferred, but when it was presented she helped to slip it over Corwyn's head.

She did not give Corwyn the opportunity to speak with her, slipping away once her mistress was in bed.

Turning down the lamp, Corwyn wondered why Du Joles had asked her to dine with his guest? Why would not Dora speak to her? She felt as though she was the only member of the household left out of a most important secret. It was a disturbing impression.

In the middle of the night, Corwyn was shaken awake. A hand was pressed over her mouth so she could not makeasound. It took her a moment to realize who was in the room with her, and when she did, her heart skipped a beat.

"You mus' never talk ta' me when he is here," Dora whispered, drawing her hand away. Her accent made understanding her difficult.

"Du Joles?" Corwyn asked. In the darkness she saw that the girl sat at the foot of her bed.

"He hide in the mirro'," Dora said, pointing at the silvered mirror of the armoire. "He see us talk. Hear everythin"'

Corywn looked at the mirror, its surface black in the dark room. What did she mean? Du Joles hid in the mirror? How could that be? "I do not understand," she whispered. "You mean he hides in a room behind the mirror and watches me?"

Dora nodded. "They all watch," she whispered in a frightened voice. "All the ones they bring to see you-" and she stopped as though she heard a sound in the hall.

For a moment they were both silent, eyes flickering between the mirror and the door. When the sound did not come again, Dora continued. "What you say befo'?"

Shaken, Corwyn could not remember what she had tried to say to the girl earlier in the day. Surely Du Joles could not be showing her body to strangers. That was too ridiculous to contemplate. Why would he do such a thing? Putting the thought aside for a moment, she slipped from the bed and crept across the floor. Reaching her small desk, she found the note she had penned and handed it to Dora.

"Give this to any honest sea captain in port. If my brother only knows where to look for me, I am sure he will come-"

"I be killed," said Dora, standing. Refusing to take the note, she regarded Corwyn. "If I be catched, they kill me."

"If you deliver this note, we will both be rescued," Corwyn replied, careful to keep her voice very low. "If you do not deliver it, I am afraid neither one of us will ever escape."

Dora glanced at the note and then at Corwyn as if wondering what to believe. Then, with a furtive motion, she took the piece of paper and folded it into a square. "I give," she whispered, "to the first honest captain I meet. I tell him he get gold for taking to Virginia."

Corwyn slipped back into bed, her heart pounding in her chest. If Dora got caught delivering the note, they might both be killed. "Thank you," she whispered, reaching out to take Dora's hand for just a moment.

The other girl smiled, eyes luminous in the darkness, and then she was gone.

Alone, Corwyn considered Dora's revelation. Du Joles watched her bathe and dress in the mirror. Furthermore, he invited his guests to watch her. The thought made her skin crawl. Why would he do such a thing?

And then she understood. What a fool she had been! Du Joles was a slave trader. He meant to sell her. Why had she not realized this before? The men who came here were buyers. This one must have been very interested because Du Joles had permitted him to speak to her.

The horror of her situation washed over her. If Ben did not discover her quickly, she would be sold into slavery.

Elizabeth stirred as Black left the bed. Auburn curls spilling in every direction, she opened her eyes and looked around in panic, as though fearing that he would leave without saying farewell.

"Is it morning, already?" she asked, sitting up to look out the window at the pre-dawn sky. "It seems we just went to sleep."

"We did," Black replied. She was such a beautiful woman, red hair, green eyes, and pale, translucent skin. Perhaps most important, she had a good heart. Since the day he had purchased her on the auction block and immediately set her free, she had been devoted to him. Until now, he had never found her lacking.

"Why must you sail so early?" she demanded with a smile. "What difference does it make to the sea if you sail with morning or the evening tide? Men are so foolish this way."

Black returned her smile as he pulled on his boots. "You will never make a sailor Liza," he replied. "You should never waste the daylight."

Elizabeth made no reply, her smile fading as he finished dressing. Wrapping her arms about her shoulders, her insecurity was clear. "Are you coming back?" she asked.

"I intend to," Black responded, as though he did not understand the import of her question. He knew she was asking about more than his attempt to deliver a message to Benjamin Chase, or his commander in Virginia. This was a mission involving some danger, since his ship was a known pirate vessel and if he was taken he would certainly be hung no matter what his objectives were.

"To me?" She had felt the distance between them, had been aware of its cause. She had steeled herself to lose him once and had seen his return as a reprieve. It would hurt to lose him again.

"No," said Black without looking at her. He did not want her waiting about for him. He had made his decision. When he found Corwyn, nothing would compel him to let her go. He could not bear to lose her. He knew that now.

"What if you do not find her?" Elizabeth asked. Ever the pragmatist, she wanted to know exactly where she stood.

Black picked up his bag and placed it upon the bed. Drawing it closed, he shook his head. He could not imagine what his life would be like if he did not find her.

"Liza, do not wait for me. You are a beautiful woman, and you deserve better than to have a rogue like me who is too foolish to open his eyes and see the treasure before him."

Elizabeth made no response, and when Black looked up she was crying, silent tears pouring down her face.

Unable to offer any comfort, Black hefted his bag onto his shoulder and left the room. When he returned in a few weeks, having alerted Chase that his sister was in Port Royal, perhaps he would have divined something he might tell Elizabeth. There was no doubt that he cared for her. There was also no doubt that he wanted Corwyn, and only Corwyn, in his bed.

Stepping into the cold morning, Black shook his head. What madness this was! He planned to sail right into a British strong hold, deliver a personal note to a naval commander, and then sail right out again. With luck he could be home in under a month. Without it, he could be dead in just under a fortnight.

Chapter Seventeen

Corwyn stared into the mirror, examining her appearance as though it were her only interest in the world. Behind the mask of her face, her thoughts whirled. Where on earth was Dora?

She had been in attendance the day after Corwyn had given her the note, but since then she had been missing. In the two days since her disappearance, another maid had been assigned to help her dress and undress. This one refused to meet her eyes or speak a word no matter how Corwyn tried to communicate.

At the sound of a chime, Corwyn rose to her feet and walked to the door. Du Joles expected her to appear promptly at his dinner table each evening.

As she entered the private dining room she felt him watching her, following every move she made until she sat across from him at the small table.

She wore a gray gown, probably the most discreet of those in her closet. Despite the high neckline, the form fitting waist and the tight bodice left little to the imagination. As she ate, Du Joles continued to watch her. She could not control the color that rushed to her face.

"You are distracted this eve," observed Du Joles, pale eyes examining her heightened color with interest. Dressed in well-tailored dove britches, and an ivory waistcoat embroidered with silver thread, he appeared every inch the fashionable gentleman dressed for fine company. "What can disturb you so?"

"I fear my brother dead," Corwyn lied, having conceived of an excuse for her strange mood earlier in the day. "What will happen if he cannot rescue me? I do not know what I will do."

"You will stay here," Du Joles said, as though her concern surprised him. "Could you have considered me so cold as to return you to the streets?"

"I cannot accept your hospitality forever," said Corwyn. Did her voice betray her fear that he would never let her escape? "I think perhaps I should leave you and try to make my way to England." Try as she might, she could not bring her eyes to meet his.

"But that is ridiculous," said Du Joles. "You must not even think of such a thing." Placing his linen napkin upon the table he rose and moved to the door. "You need my protection and I am more than prepared to provide it to you."

"But I cannot stay here indefinitely," said Corwyn, "It is too much to ask."

Du Joles turned, brow furrowing as though she had said something puzzling. "Can you believe that a gentleman would let you wander about this uncivilized island?" When she made no reply, he continued. "Rest assured. You will have a home here until your brother arrives or other arrangements are made."

Corwyn remained silent as he left the room, wondering what other arrangements he might have in mind. How could he pretend such concern when his intentions were so base?

Hours later, Corwyn could stand the prison of her bed no longer. When she judged it to be past midnight, she slipped out from under the blankets to pace.

Where was Dora? Surely she should have returned by now. If she had come in, she would want to speak to Corwyn, tell her what had happened. What would she do if the girl had been hurt while on her errand? Corwyn knew she would never outlive her guilt for putting the girl at risk.

A knock on Corwyn's door startled her into turning around. Despite her lack of response, she saw the handle twist and the door fall open. Du Joles stood in the doorway wearing a silk dressing gown, a lamp in his hand. "Good evening," he said, voice level, "Since you are awake, come join us below."

"I ... I am weary," said Corwyn, backing away. "I think I will just go back to bed-"

"Do not make things more difficult, Mademoiselle," replied Du Joles. Moving into the chamber, he caught her by the arm.

Unable to muster strength for a struggle, Corwyn allowed herself to be led from the room. He ushered her down the dark stairs, through the main hall, past the dining room, into his study, the only room alight at this dark hour. Corwyn could hardly force herself to walk through the door.

Dora lay on the floor, her eyes wide and staring.

Horrified, Corwyn pressed her hands to her mouth. What had she done? Her eyes took in the ribbons of flesh and the blood that covered Dora's back, the long wound that went from ear the ear. She started to wretch. She rose, turned toward the door and saw Adam blocking her path. She spun to face Du Joles.

"I see you recognize your maid," said Du Joles. Having placed his lamp upon a table, he moved to stand before her.

Corwyn said nothing. She found it difficult to hear his words through her fear and grief.

"I expect she was on an errand for you when she slipped away. Perhaps you would like to tell me about it." Du Joles appeared to be unaffected by the still body or the distraught girl before him.

"Murderer!" Corwyn managed. "How could you do such a thing?"

Du Joles rose to approach her. He delivered an open handed blow her face. "Tell me where you sent her," he said in French.

Hand against her burning face, Corwyn wondered what she should say. If he did not know about the note that Dora had carried then the girl had obviously completed her mission. Could it do any harm if she told him the truth? "I gave her a note to give to any honest captain in Port Royal," said Corwyn, barely able to speak for her fear and anger.

"You will tell me who note was for and what it said." Du Joles still stood within striking distance of her. When Corwyn made no reply, he answered for her, his tone showing his annoyance. "Another note for your brother," he said tersely. "You did not believe I sent the first letter as you requested. I can assure you that I did."

"I do not believe you," said Corwyn. "If Ben knew where to find me, he would have been here by now, or sent word."

"Perhaps he is at sea, or dead, or not as fond of you as he should be," said Du Joles, apparently content with her answer. He moved toward Dora's body, then reached down to pick up a thin, bload-soaked whip. "I know only that he is not here to claim you and that I am tired of waiting for him to arrive."

"So you plan to sell me." Corwyn felt the blood drain from her face. Did he mean to beat her now?

"Yes," replied Du Joles. Letting the whip uncoil, he watched her expression.

"You are contemptible," she spat.

Du Joles watched her. "Perhaps. If, however, I were not able to get such a high price for you, you would have shared your servant's fate. I do not tolerate disobedience or deception in my slaves."

Corwyn made no response.

"Now, you will begin by telling me who captained the ship you came here in." The whip snapped in the air, making Corwyn jump.

"I do not know," she lied. If she told the truth he might well kill her.

"You will make this more difficult?" Du Joles inquired.

"I have told you that I do not know," said Corwyn. Should she tell him? Would he return her to Devon Black or to the man he had sold her to? But Ben would look for her here. And if she told Du Joles about Devon Black, maybe he would kill her for lying to him. He would know she was no virgin, that she would not fetch a high price anymore.

"And his ship?" inquired Du Joles thoughtfully, "That had a name?"

"I do not know," Corwyn repeated. Meeting his eyes, she spoke again, "If I knew, I would tell you. Why should I lie?"

Du Joles did not reply for a moment. "I have wondered that. This is something I would very much like to know." Taking a deep breath he returned to his questions, "The man he sold you to," said Du Joles. "What was his name?"

"I never knew it. I escaped before I found out," said Corwyn, "I do not know anything about him." That at least was true.

"Let us begin then," said Du Joles, his French spilling across her like the whispers of a snake. "Adam and I shall find out if you are telling the truth." He nodded at Adam.

Corwyn, when she was permitted at last to stumble up the stairs to her bed, bore a dozen welts from Du Joles' whip. But her secrets remained untold. She was fortunate, Du Joles had informed her curtly, that an English woman was worth more without scars.

Hours later, racked by pain, Corwyn heard her bedroom door open. In too much pain to turn her head, she prayed that it was not Du Joles. She did not think she could bear another assault. Pretending to be asleep, she heard the door close and a moment later felt her bloodied nightdress lifted away from her skin. She heard the sound of a knife ripping through her gown and then felt the cool air upon her skin.

Then someone gently smoothed a foul smelling unguent upon her skin. The relief was so intense that she started to cry. By the time the procedure was complete she was fast asleep.

The next morning she discovered a crude metal container that held more of the ointment. As she applied it, she wondered who her benefactor could be.

"Wear the blue gown," Du Joles ordered, "as I asked you to. The man is not seeking a matron but a beautiful young wife upon which to sire a dynasty." Seated at his desk he scowled at Corwyn, "Yellow makes your skin look like candle wax."

"Thank you," said Corwyn, "you are kind to say so." Once again in his study, just minutes before one of his guests was to arrive, she modeled the yellow gown.

"I think," said Du Joles as he stood, "that you suffer under the misapprehension that I will not lose my temper with you. When you become obstinate, your value to me lessens. When your value lessens there is no reason to hold my temper in check. Have I made myself clear?" His French was terse, biting, indicating his irritation.

Before Corwyn could make a reply, Adam entered the room. His face was impassive as he admitted the muscular, middle- aged Spaniard.

"Senor Lucas," said Du Joles coming around the table to take the square hand offered by the sugar plantation owner, "I trust your business in port went well today." Speaking in English, Du Joles ushered his guest to a chair.

"Es posible," replied the gray-haired man, his brown eyes flickering to Corwyn, reviewing her obvious assets. "The auctions have always the highest prices, I prefer to buy slaves by the boat full. It cost less," his English too was awkward, indicating his unfamiliarity with the language.

"I trust you will be happy with this afternoon's selection," replied Du Joles. Seating himself in a chair across from his guest, he gestured at Corwyn. "May I present Corwyn Tyler Chase, an English Lady who fell into the hands of pirates some months ago. I have taken it upon myself to provide her with a new home."

"Pirates are hard on their women," remarked Senior Lucas, his eyes narrowing. His contemplation of Corwyn had not ceased since his arrival.

"Not to those they mean to ransom," replied Du Joles. Offering his guest a cheroot, he too contemplated the girl before them.

"How do I know she is an English Lady," queried Senior Lucas suspiciously, "You could dress any woman so."

Nodding his assent, Du Joles ordered Corwyn to pour their guest some wine. His eyes were cold and iron hard as they dared her to refuse.

Corwyn, heart beating wildly in her chest, moved to the silver tray on a nearby table. She poured a large amount of the ruby liquid into the crystal glass. Demur, eyes lowered, she moved toward the obviously skeptical purchaser. Without a word she threw the wine in his face.

Senior Lucas leapt to his feet, livid with rage, wine crawling down his face to nestle in the cream colored collar of his fine shirt.

"Corwyn" said Du Joles in French, "You will apologize to Senor Lucas."

Corwyn spun to face him, emerald eyes flashing with defiance. "You can go to hell!" she spat. In a moment she was gone, fleeing up the stairs and into her room.

Soon thereafter Adam broke through her door. Without a word he dragged her from the bed where she sat fully dressed. Using a long, curved blade he sliced the yellow gown from neck to hem. He ripped the dress from her and locked her arms behind her back. When she could have knelt to cover his nakedness, he forced her to stand upright and face the mirror.

Too frightened to scream, Corwyn looked at herself in the mirror. Humiliation made her flush from head to toe.

After what seemed a very great length of time, Du Joles opened the door of her bedroom. With a gesture he indicated that Adam should free her and leave the room.

"You made quite an impression. Senior Lucas has offered the most outrageous sum. Your offended dignity was most appealing," Du Joles made no effort to hide his amusement. "He finds it easy to believe you are a virgin."

"You are contemptible," said Corwyn. She lay where she had fallen, face buried in the counterpane of the bed. Exhausted, angry, afraid, she wished Du Joles would go away.

Du Joles moved to sit beside her on the bed. "Beautiful," he said softly, "I sometimes wish . . ." And he stopped, his thought left unfinished. When he spoke again, his voice was hard, "You will not disobey me again."

Corwyn brought her head up to look at him. "Go to hell."

"Your obstinacy will cause me to punish you," he informed her. "Sometimes when I begin, I cannot stop. This is how Dora died. You understand?"

Corwyn turned away.

"You think you are safe because I will not touch you. If I took you, you might become pregnant and thus worthless to me. If I beat you, you command a lower price. You believe you have the advantage of me." He smiled. "I think I must teach you a lesson. Today you wore clothes that displeased me. From now on you have no clothes to wear."

"What?" Corwyn demanded?

"Since you know about the mirror, I think we shall do away with this artifice. The men will come, you will present yourself to them."

"I will not!"

"You will not eat until you agree."

"I would rather die."

"Perhaps you have never been hungry before." Du Joles rose, a smile on his face. "Perhaps you will be glad to serve Senor Lucas when next he returns."

Chapter Eighteen

"I have seen the most beautiful woman today," said Senor Lucas. Using a long serving fork, he reached for yet another slice of the roast beef while shaking his head in disbelief. "I did not know they still made women so spirited. Such fire!" Dribbling juice from the meat upon a slice of bread on his plate, he turned to his host.

Andre only cocked an eyebrow, content to watch his guest devour the meal secure in the knowledge that the profit from the slaves he had sold would cover its price a thousand times over.

"She had coal black hair, like the natives," said Senor Lucas, placing a fork full of meat into his mouth. "And her figure was. . . perfecto!" and he kissed his fingers to indicate his satisfaction.

"Did you purchase her?" Andre inquired politely. Entertaining his business associates was rarely a pleasure. For the most part he found Spanish farmers ill-mannered and loud. The alcalde owned a sugar plantation on the coast of the Spanish colonies. He represented the Spanish government in his region, reporting only to the governor, and then only rarely. As one of the early colonists he considered himself something of an aristocrat. Andre found his pretensions irritating.

"I made an offer. Quite a ridiculous offer," and here he took a sip of the rich red wine, "Francois says he will accept no other bidders. If I return with the other thousand, she is mine."

"The other thousand?" Andre asked, his interest suddenly piqued. "How much did this prize cost you?"

"Four thousand. It is an exceptional price but she will father many fine sons," Senor Lucas continued in Spanish. "You know that suitable women are rare. If I wish to have a proud family, I must find a proud wife."

Andre nodded his assent. It was difficult to find European women who would choose to live in the Spanish colonies. Lodgings were primitive, work was hard, pestilence, disease and a complete lack of contact with family and friends made it difficult to attract cultured wives. Still, four thousand pounds was more money than he could lay his hands to if he liquidated his entire stock of slaves and all his working capital. Senor Lucas must be wealthy indeed. "I am sure you will be very happy."

"I must hurry and return with the money or she will not be mine," and he pushed his plate away. "She is a fine English Lady and I believe there are others who would pay even more."

Andre found that hard to believe, but made no comment. There were madmen who would pay ridiculous prices for stones in the street as well.

Senor Lucas stood. "So, though I would love to stay and enjoy your company, I must leave on the evening tide. I will be back in six weeks to collect my new bride and to pay off my debts."

Andre rose too. "I will look forward to your return, and I hope to meet this spirited young woman which is worth such a price." Leading him out of the room, he tried to imagine what such a girl would look like.

"Oh no!" laughed Senor Lucas, his hand against his belly. "I know your penchant for green eyes and she . . . she has eyes the color of emeralds. I shall certainly not introduce her to you!" And then he was out the door, walking toward Andre's carriage.

Andre closed the door and leaned against it. An English Lady with coal black hair, an unbelievable figure, emerald green eyes and a terrible temper. He might have known the young spitfire would cause him trouble yet again.

Returning to his study, he penned a letter to that cur Du Joles. Though he could not match Senor Lucas' price alone, he hoped he could pay the man to wait long enough for Black to return from his trip to the English colonies. Perhaps together they could raise that much.

If all had gone well, Devon should arrive in just a few weeks. Surely they would have enough time to complete the transaction before Senor Lucas returned.

"This letter is over a month old, is unsigned, and gives no proof that the girl is still alive. Surely you do not wish to pursue this matter any further," Admiral Brooke made no attempt to conceal his irritation.

"It says she is alive." Benjamin Chase, captain of Her Majesty's Ship the Verity, fought his urge to strangle the skeletal officer with his bare hands. Balding, with protruding blue eyes, he looked as if he had never cared for anyone in his long life.

"Captain," Admiral Brook's voice rose. "We have made every accommodation for your grief. For six weeks we gave you no assignment at all, lest she turn up and need your care. Now, after a single assignment, a short one at that, you mean to take your ship and crew on a wild goose chase because someone who could not bother to give his name says he saw your sister once."

He stood up. "There are not two dozen men in the colonies who do not know your sister's name and there are not five who would not lie to you in order to receive the reward you are offering. Do you really believe that this is anything other than an attempt to extort ransom from you?"

"I cannot afford to take the chance that she is in some ruffian's hands in Port Royal." Ben stood up, unable to control himself any longer. "I will move heaven and earth if I have to. If she is still alive, no matter where she is, I mean to find her!"

"Do you know what the likelihood of a letter reaching this post from that stronghold of vermin is?" The Admiral inquired. "How could such a letter be real?"

"I must investigate-" Ben began.

"You must not investigate," the Admiral stood up, pale face now red with fury. "You will not take a naval vessel into Port Royal in search of your sister."

Ben was silent, pondering his alternatives. He had enough money to procure a small ship. He was sure he could find a crew in the busy Virginian port. He would only need about thirty men. "Sir, I resign my commission," he said without preamble. He stripped off his weapon, pulled the insignia off his uniform.

"Be sensible!" The Admiral pounded the table. "You are acting like a child."

Ben did not take time to reply. Without another word he dropped the abandoned symbols of his rank on the desk and left the room. It would not take long for him to acquire a ship and crew and make sail. He only hoped that the delay would not cost Corwyn her life.

Admiral Brooke stared at the pile on his desk and permitted himself an expletive. He had destroyed the other two messages he had received from those claiming to have found the girl, but someone had managed to deliver this note directly to Captain Chase.

Damn the man! Why could he not see that his public search for the girl had encouraged the unscrupulous to pray on his hope. The girl was dead, lying at the bottom of the sea with the crew of the Albatross. If the Albatross had been taken by Pirates, she would still be at the bottom of the sea. Pirates threw their women overboard when they were through with them.

He picked up a pen, dipped it in an inkwell, and applied it to a blank page. Captain Benjamin Chase had been a well-respected master, already marked for higher rank by his associates in the Navy. It would be very hard to explain his abrupt resignation. But he could not be expected to make allowances indefinitely.

Chapter Nineteen

Black examined the house from the street, ordering Andre's coachman to pause before moving onto the long graveled drive. She was in there, he could feel it. He had looked long and hard to find her, imagining the worst, and at last he knew where she was.

Four thousand pounds, the figure echoed over and over in his mind. No matter how he added the figures, he simply could not afford to pay four thousand pounds to purchase her. And he did not have much time to work on the problem. He had been detained in Virginia, hiding from a Navy ship that took too much interest in the Wraith. Upon his arrival Andre had told him that Lucas was a week over due already.

If he sold his ship, and accepted Andre's substantial loan, he might just be able to make her price. But he would not be able to leave the island and he would have lost the means to support himself and his crew. Perhaps if he had more time, he might be able to acquire the funds from a variety of sources. But he did not have six weeks, he did not have six days, he wasn't even sure he had six hours before the transaction was complete.

He had toyed with the idea of stealing the girl from Senor Lucas as he moved her through the town, or perhaps even taking her on the open seas. But he might not have much opportunity to kill him in Port Royal, and the man's ship was very well armed.

Black shook his head to clear it. He had absolutely no idea how he was going to get her back. But it was wonderful to know she was alive and that he would finally see her again.

He rapped on the floor of the carriage with his cane, letting the driver know he wanted to continue. When the carriage came to a stop before the marbled steps, two liveried slaves came to attention. Posted in the afternoon sun to welcome Du Joles' guest, they looked extremely uncomfortable in their heavy clothes. While they opened the door so he could step out upon the graveled drive, Black recalled his time on a slaver. He had never lost his loathing for trade in human flesh. It went against everything he believed. And yet, in the West Indies and the Southern Colonies, slavery was a way of life. To argue against it, even with close business associates, was to risk making enemies.

As he mounted the steps to the front door, he saw it open, and the diminutive Francois Du Joles admitted him.

"Lord Black," said Du Joles, leading him through the foyer into a white and gold study, "Andre tells me you are in the market for a woman."

"Not a woman, the woman you have here," said Devon, keeping his manner light. If he learned that this little martinet had harmed one hair on Corwyn's head, he would certainly kill the little wretch with his bare hands. Of course, that would mean that he could never return to Port Royal, but that would be a small price to pay.

"I do not see how this could be. She was taken on a ship, thrown in a hold, and never saw her abductor. I cannot believe that you would treat a Lady so," said Du Joles, slipping behind his desk while offering Black a seat.

"If you will bring her in, I am sure we can establish ownership easily enough," said Devon curtly. What was the point of discussing the matter? If the girl were here, he wanted to see her.

"Ownership has been established," said Du Joles. "I own her. Shortly, unless you have a great deal of money, Senor Lucas will own her." Leaning forward, he met Black's eyes. "I am sure we understand one another."

Black only nodded, unwilling to discuss the matter further until he could see Corwyn. "Where is the girl?"

"I shall have her brought to us," said Du Joles. Rising, he crossed to the pair of doors leading back to the foyer. Speaking to the largest man Black had ever seen, he gestured at the staircase. In a moment he was back at his desk.

"Corwyn?" Devon asked. He stood up when she entered the room. She was so pale, and her gown fairly hung on her frame. Her eyes were sunken, downcast. She had changed so much!

She looked up then, and he thought he saw surprise register in her eyes, but then she looked down as if she could not bear the sight of him.

"Lord Black wishes to buy you," Du Joles told her with a trace of a smile. "Can this be the faceless man from the nameless ship who abducted you?"

Corwyn made no reply.

"Have you nothing to say?" Du Joles inquired. "He seems determined to have you whatever the cost." He turned to Black. "I almost feel I should charge you an extra fee for putting a civil tongue in her head."

"I've seen her," said Black. "That is enough. Send her away." He could not bear to see her this way, beaten and afraid.

He did not want her to hear them barter for her like a mare or a side of beef.

"As you wish," and with a nod Du Joles dismissed her. "So, do you have the money with you?" he inquired.

"No," Black replied, "but I can get it."

"Well go fetch it then. Senor Lucas will be here any day now. I will have to give her to him unless you have her price," and Du Joles shook his head, "You would not want that to happen I am sure."

"If you can wait a month, I will give you an extra thousand for your trouble," said Black, keeping his tone level. He had no idea how he would come up with such an amount of money in so short a time. It galled him to think of the thousands of pounds he had held before he had gone to England. Was ever money worse spent? Elizabeth was right, revenge was never worth the price.

Du Joles pretended to consider the offer, and then gave his answer. "I am afraid not. Senor Lucas is an important man, he gave me a great deal of money to hold her and I told him I would not accept any other offers. I would not want to offend him unnecessarily."

Black held his tongue, biting back the words he wanted to say. Why alert the man that he was prepared to kill to get her back. He stood up instead. "I will be back," he said firmly, "and I will have the money you want." Or, he added silently, I will simply end your miserable life and the consequences be damned.

"Do not come back," Du Joles said, "unless you have the money with you."

Devon was escorted from the house by Du Joles' huge body guard. It was rare, he reflected as the slave loaded him into his carriage, that he met a man he knew he could not defeat. This slave was such a man. As Devon closed the door, he dropped his cane and the black man bent down to pick it up. As he handed it back, Devon took his chance.

"Meet me outside the gate as soon as Du Joles leaves. I've a proposition for you." The words were said so quickly that he feared the slave might not have understood him. To his relief, Adam gave him a curt nod and then gestured for the driver to pull away.

Going down the road just a quarter of a mile, Devon jumped out. He had ordered Andre's servant to take the carriage home and ignore his unusual departure. Once out of the coach, he moved into the foliage along side the road. Making himself comfortable, he prepared for a long wait.

Corwyn watched Black's coach roll away. Had he abandoned her yet again? She had expected him to pay her price, no matter how high it was. How foolish she had been.

"Come away from the window," Du Joles ordered.

Corwyn turned to find him standing in the doorway. His face was white with anger.

"I will overlook, for the moment, that you lied to me," he said, moving into the room. "That you are not a virgin is something that you will have to explain to Senor Lucas when he owns you."

Corwyn made no reply. That was an aspect of this transaction she had not considered.

"But I want you to know that Lord Black has not purchased you. If he should try to speak with you or take you away, I want you to know that I will kill him. Is that clear?" Du Joles studied her, waiting for her to betray herself with hope or fear.

"I will arm Adam. He will have orders to kill Black if he sees him again. You should make no attempt to see him if you want his life spared," Du Joles continued.

Corwyn's heart began to pound. Once she had wanted to see Black dead, now she knew she would rather die herself. She saw Dora's face every night in her dreams. The idea that she might see Black die brought her to the edge of madness. "I understand," she managed, hoping Du Joles would say nothing more.

"I hope you do," and then Du Joles left her alone.

"Tell me, are you ready to escape?" Black inquired, remembering the feel of her hair as it passed through his fingers. The stiff back, so prim and proud, the graceful way in which she sat, her emerald eyes, nothing had changed.

Of course, that wasn't true, he thought as he watched her. The woman he had known would never sit so still. She had not been emotionless, cold, but full of passion. This strange creature before him simply wore Corwyn's face.

"Escape?" Corwyn asked, refusing to face him. "With you?"

"Do you like it here? Do you want to go with Lucas?" Black asked. Lord, they did not have time for a discussion. He had forgotten how difficult she could be. She had to rise now, and move to the door, as though it were the most natural thing in the world. He did not want to alarm the servants.

"What I like and dislike has mattered very little since I met you," she replied. "As for this, what should I dislike? Am I not to be married to a very rich man who is willing to pay a great deal to have me? Does it matter what kind of a cage I live in?"

"A prison is a prison, I suppose," Black replied, moving to stand before her. He raised her chin until she met his eyes. "You look terrible," he offered. Why would she not stand, slip into his arms and make everything easy for them both.

"Why thank you," Corwyn jerked away from him. "You have such a special way with women."

"Not with women," Black responded. "Just with you." He watched her rise, turn away and move toward the house. What made her walk so stiffly, so gracelessly. Why was she so thin? If, he thought with silent irritation, the silly chit had simply remained with Andre, she might even now be home, safely cuckolding an unfortunate husband. "We must leave now."

"I am sure Francois will return momentarily," Corwyn said in a remote voice. "Please go," she gestured mechanically toward the French doors.

"I would like you to come with me," Black insisted. He took her arm to prevent her from walking away again. "We must leave now."

"No," replied Corwyn, defiance just audible in her voice. Adam was about, somewhere near by. She would not play a part in Black's murder.

"Then I will be off," returned Black. Did she really wish to marry Lucas? Why should she pretend that she did? Perhaps he had made a terrible mistake. "I am sorry that I have disturbed you on your wedding day. I hope you will be very..." and here he paused for a moment, "happy." He brushed past her and walked toward the house.

Corwyn watched him go with a mixture of despair and relief. She had not allowed him to rescue her, had not pleaded with him to stay, and yet every bone in her body wanted him to stop, to turn, to hold her in his arms once more. She had saved his life, she knew. Even if Adam had not killed him, Du Joles and

Lucas would have tracked him through the city. She doubted that they would have been able to reach the wharf.

Drawing a shaky breath, she turned to follow him into the house.

Approaching the French doors she saw Adam holding Black, and Du Joles issuing orders. Senor Lucas stood beside the strange trio, his face purple with rage. Before she could make sense of the scene, Du Joles was walking out of the house toward her.

"I warned you!" he said, delivering a blow to her head before she could open her mouth.

Corwyn fell to the ground, aware of Black's shout. She opened her eyes to see Senor Lucas walk back toward the front door. Obviously he would not be buying her today.

Du Joles kicked her once, and then again, knocking the breath out of her body. She felt something in her chest give way. She could not breathe!

A loud report sounded and blood seemed to rain from the sky. Managing to open her eyes, she saw Du Joles spiraling toward her, blood pouring from his chest, his eyes wide and angry still. Not sure what might be real and what a dream, Corwyn thought she saw Black give orders to Adam, the giant black man bending only slightly to listen. Corwyn tried to clear away the cobwebs that were filling her mind, was forced to close her eyes when the world began to spin. When she managed to open them again, Black was kneeling beside her.

"Well, there is another one for you," he said as he moved the hair from her face. "One man dead in England, a whole ship full on the Atlantic, and now this. I will not be welcome anywhere soon." His hands explored her torso, making her gasp. "Is <u>any</u> of this blood yours?" he asked.

Corwyn turned her face away. Her head pounded, her chest hurt, and she thought she might be sick if she did not close her eyes.

"Pick her up," ordered Black.

Corwyn felt herself lifted an impossible distance from the ground, cradled against a broad chest. She opened her eyes to see that Adam had her in his arms.

"No!" gasped Corwyn, beginning to struggle despite the pain. "Leave me alone. Leave me alone!"

"Be still, Corwyn," ordered Black. "If you move again I will have to clout you myself. In your present state, that would probably kill you."

And, despite Corwyn's objections, Black and Adam left the garden, moved into the house, and then into the carriage Du Joles had just departed from. Once Corwyn lay inside, cradled in Devon's arms, Adam climbed atop the coach and they set off across the rough white stones. The pain drove Corwyn to unconsciousness almost immediately.

Chapter Twenty

Ben watched the ship in the harbor being unloaded and cursed his luck. Lucas had a fast ship, but even with a day's delay he had managed to catch up. To his surprise, his crew had utterly refused to attack the vessel, pointing out that they were out gunned three to one. Instead they had insisted that they drop back and follow the Spanish ship until it made port.

So they had followed Senor Lucas at a distance, shadowing him until his ship moored at a private landing hidden among the marshes and swamps of the Spanish colonial mainland.

Ben ordered a dingy put into the water upon his arrival. The men had drawn lots to see who would accompany him. Now five men crouched with him in the reeds watching half-dressed Indians and Negroes unload crates and barrels onto the wharf. Sunset painted the scene in red and amber.

"Lucas has left the ship," said Ben, He slipped back and let the reeds fall back into place. He turned to find his landing party, muddy and wide-eyed, behind him. "He will have taken Corwyn to his house. He will not expect anyone to rescue her. It should not be difficult to reach his home undetected-"

"Beggin' yer pardon sor," said one of the men, a thin dark-haired man with no front teeth. "The span'ard keeps cane, and slaves to cut it. He 'll have guardst' mind 'em."

"I am sure we can slip past them-"

"Pardon, sor," the man interrupted. "I an' the rest dinna' sign to fight, but to sail."

"This is mutiny!" Ben looked at each man in turn.

"Nay sor, this be dry land. We ha' come this far from respect, but nay more."

"You will not help me? Not one man among you will help me?" Ben felt his face grow hot. "I tell you this before God. Were it the wife, daughter or sister of any man here I would not serve him so!"

"Ay, an' we know it. An' so we have come so far." The man looked around at his compatriots. "An' we c'n stay the night here. If ye c'n bring 'er this far, we will die to keep 'er t' the ship."

"And if I cannot bring her this far by morning? What then?"

"We make for home." All the men nodded their assent.

Ben studied their faces carefully and saw he had no quarter. They would not risk their lives to help him. If he meant to effect a rescue he would have to do it alone.

"Wait here until noon tomorrow. If I do not return, you may have my ship since you will have already taken my life." Ben made no attempt to keep his contempt concealed.

"Dawn if ye please, sor," said the spokesman. "We leave at dawn."

After three hours of creeping through tall grass and sugar cane, Ben found himself near the dozen or more structures that comprised the Alcalde's plantation. It was clear, now that he could see it for himself, why his crew had refused to come with him. Dogs prowled the cleared earth around the buildings, while men sat watch around campfires.

A sprawling house, the only structure he suspected a regional governor might occupy, was five hundred yards away, on the far side of the clearing. It would be hard to approach it undetected.

Ben kept his blade raised as he crept from the dense cane to the nearest structure. Once there he put his back against the wall of crude earthen bricks, listened hard for some sound that might indicate that he had been detected. He almost leapt out of his skin when he heard someone from inside the building call out. When nothing followed the call, he moved to peer around the corner at the front of the structure. There he found a dozen half-height doors barred with thick stalks of cane. He heard the voice again, this time followed by a wracking cough.

These must be the slave quarters, he thought grimly, and someone inside the nearest cell must be ill. When his pulse slowed somewhat, he realized that a solution to his problem stood before him. He slipped around the corner and in a matter of seconds had unbarred the all the doors.

When the first head emerged from a half-open door, he could not credit it as human. It was a ball of matted hair that seemed entirely without a face. The head was followed by a body so emaciated as to be no more than a loose sack of skin and bones. The creature, for he found hard to call it a man, was pale in the moonlight, the body bare save for a crude loin cloth covering its sex.

In seconds, another face emerged. This one was black as night, skin striped with the white scars of countless whippings. Then other bodies poured swiftly, silently from cells that looked too small for a single man. The smell that came with them made him want to retch.

Some of men ran toward the fields as though the devil himself was at their heels, others turned toward the remaining barracks. Doors were flying open at two other structures when the Ben heard the first shouts of alarm from the guards. When he turned toward them he could see strong, well-fed men leaping to their feet.

Content that there would be enough distraction to cover his movements, Ben slipped back into the darkness, determined to follow the perimeter of the buildings until he reached the largest house.

Ben saw a pair of doors thrown open on the second floor of the two story, U-shaped plantation house. The doors opened onto a balcony that faced the rest of the compound, now in pandemonium. Vines led from the ground up to the balcony making a convenient entrance to the house.

He slipped through the doors and found himself in a dark bedroom. In the moonlight he could make out a man hunched over the shape of a woman, body coiling and uncoiling at an uneven tempo. When he heard the woman cry out, he lost all reason, crossed the room in three strides and jerked the man from the bed onto the floor.

He put his blade to the man's throat.

"Quien es?" The man demanded, not the least worried by the weapon. "Voy a matarte!"

"Where is Lucas," Ben barked in English. "Tell me or I will kill you!"

"I am Lucas! How dare you come to me like this!" The man was heavy, but strong, a soldier gone to seed. Ben could see his eyes shift in the silver moonlight, planning an attack.

"Where is my sister!" Ben looked toward the bed, saw the huddled shape. "Corwyn? Is that you?"

The girl sat up. Her hair was black, her skin white, but she was older than Corwyn, had an older, longer face. Ben's heart sank.

As Ben turned back, Lucas threw a meaty foot into his knee. The crack of bone breaking sounded like gunfire and Ben felt his body strike the smooth wood floor through a white haze of pain.

"Who sent you to kill me!" Lucas had rolled to his feet. To emphasize his demand for information he kicked Ben in the stomach.

"Where is my sister!" Fear and loss overrode Ben's pain. "You bought her, damn you! Where is she?"

"What are you talking about?" Lucas stepped back into the darkness.

"Du Joles! You bought my sister from Francois Du Joles!" Ben struggled into a lopsided crouch, aware his knee would not hold his weight. "Where is my sister, you bastard!"

There was silence for a moment, then a sharp laugh. "You want the English puta," he paused as if amused. "You are her brother? Jesu Cristo! What a stupid people you are!"

"Where is she?" Ben demanded again.

"Du Joles killed her I think." Lucas said. After a moment's thought, he continued. "If I would have married her, you and I would be brothers." He laughed again. Stepping back into the moonlight pouring through the open door, Lucas kicked him in the head. "Too bad for you she is dead, eh English?"

Chapter Twenty-One

At long last Corwyn awoke to find herself alone, in a cool bed, somehow away from the twisting movement of the sea and the constant murmur of the crew as they drove the ship through the water.

She lay in a simple, clean bedroom, covered in cool, clean sheets, lost in a down mattress. Light poured into the room through an arched window. The late afternoon sun was red with the last heat of the day.

Corwyn stared at the shadows running across the wall before her, touching the silver mirror, the dark wood of the vanity, the smooth finish of the floor. Before too much time had passed, she fell asleep again.

A young Indian woman was bathing her head when she woke next, her brown eyes gentle, expression concerned.

Mustering her resources Corwyn managed to smile. How wonderful it was to have someone to care for her.

Her nurse returned the smile. She took up a clay bowl sitting on the bedside table and offered Corwyn a spoonful of broth. Corwyn took it uncertainly, wondering if she were hungry.

To her surprise she was famished. She struggled to sit up until a sharp pain in her chest made her stop.

The woman put the bowl down, then carefully propped Corwyn up with pillows. Once she was comfortable, the woman picked up the bowl again and fed her spoonful after spoonful of the clear chicken soup. When Corwyn could eat no more, she put the bowl down with a satisfied smile. She helped Corwyn lie flat again, and covered her with the warm blankets.

Corwyn was asleep before she left the room, dreaming of a home half a world away.

For several days, Corwyn could not exchange many pleasantries with her nurse, nor did she find herself seeking many answers. It was enough that she was no longer being tortured and this kind woman had come to take care of her. Though she found eating difficult, the woman insisted, gently encouraging her to finish everything she was given.

One day she woke to find a stack of leather bound volumes awaiting her attention. Careful not to turn her body lest her ribs protest, she selected one of the books. It was, she noted with a smile, the Tempest. It was that clever play about a king stranded on a magical island with his beautiful daughter. She had read it many times before and she found the first few pages very comforting.

Later that afternoon her nurse appeared with a heavy tray. Entering the room, she seemed delighted that Corwyn had finally taken an interest in the world around her.

"Buenos Dias!" the woman said. She placed the tray on the table and moved a chair from the corner of the room closer to the bed. "Que milagro!" Realizing that the young girl had not understood, she spoke in stumbling English, "I am surprised you live. For so long you sleep." Picking up the bowl of broth, she continued, "We worry foryou. Maybe you never wake up."

"I do not remember very much," said Corwyn. "I do not know how I came here."

"Some day you remember," the dark woman replied, bringing a spoonful of broth to her patient's lips, "Now you eat and soon you better."

Corwyn reluctantly took the spoonful of broth the woman offered. Suddenly she felt ill at ease being waited on so completely. "I think if you will give me the bowl, I can eat by myself," she offered.

"But of course!" laughed the small woman. "I feed you as a child and talk to you as a woman." Placing the bowl on the table she moved Corwyn into a more comfortable position. A moment later Corwyn was feeding herself for the first time in days, or was it weeks? How long had she been ill? It was impossible to remember.

"What is your name?" Corwyn asked as she ate.

The woman's face lost its radiance, sadness touching her eyes. "The fathers call me Maria," she said.

"Is that what you call yourself?" Corwyn asked.

"You can not say my true name even if I say it," the woman said. "It an Indian name. Only Indian say it. You call me Maria like the others." Smoothing her skirts, she changed the subject. "What your name?"

"Corwyn Chase," Corwyn replied, still wondering how a name could make the woman sad. "You must think me quite strange. Staying in bed and allowing you to nurse me. I apologize."

"No, you too sick," said the older woman. "He tell me," she said, gesturing at the door, "that you very hurt but very brave. I want help you."

"I do not know how to thank you," said Corwyn.

"Now that you awake, I go home. My man tired of his own food," the woman smiled again. "But, when you well, you visit me. I see you then."

"I shall visit as soon as I am able," said Corwyn, surprised to find tears in her eyes. She must be very weak indeed if such a simple thing could make her cry.

"You tired now," said the woman. "Sleep, and soon you strong again." She took the bowl from Corwyn's hands and helped her to lie flat. In another minute she was gone and Corwyn slipped into a troubled sleep.

When a young dark skinned maid came to bring her a tray the next afternoon, Corwyn asked that a bath be brought as well. The girl declined at first, but Corwyn was firm. She could not remember the last time she had had a bath, and she felt sure her bones would ache less after a long soak in warm water. When the girl left, she was not certain her request would be fulfilled. After all, she had little power to force the issue.

She was rather surprised when a pair of boys rolled a large wooden tub into the room, then returned to fill it with several buckets of steaming water. The young maid came again to give her soap, a nightgown and a yard of linen to use as a towel. She left a moment later, obviously uncertain that she had done the right thing.

Corwyn struggled into a sitting position and carefully unwrapped the ribbons of bandage that wound about her body. Her chest groaned at the sudden loss of support. With the help of the bedside table and a nearby chair, she managed to make her way to the tub. Once in the water she took some time to examine the bruises that flowered across her right side. It was a wonder she had survived Du Joles beating.

As the water cooled, she began the laborious process of washing her hair.

"You are a fool," said Black, entering her room unannounced just as she finished.

"Get out," said Corwyn. "Even a dog can expect privacy in its kennel."

"Well," Black's eyes contemplated the discoloration of her flesh though the clear water, "You are one dog I have taped together with my own hands. I rescued you from that hell hole, and with the dubious aide of a ship's doctor I saved your life. I reserve the right to keep you alive even against your better notions."

"Please leave me alone," said Corwyn, covering her face with wet hands. She was tired and cold and she did not want to argue.

"Stand up," said Black. When she did not comply, he lifted her from the water. He carried her to the bed and arranged her limbs to make her lie flat upon the cool sheets.

His hands carefully explored the black and magenta blooms that flowered across her chest. He seemed unaware of Corwyn's discomfort and embarrassment as he prodded here and there, stopping only when she cried out.

"Animal," he said as if speaking to himself, "I am glad he is dead." Turning his attention to her, his expression became stern. "Listen," he said as he pulled her into a sitting position. "I am going to bandage you up again. If you remove these bandages in under a fortnight, I shall have to return to reapply them." When she did not look at him, he reached forward to turn her head. Do you understand?" he asked her.

Accepting Corwyn's curt nod as an appropriate reply, he scooped up the strips of cloth from the floor, where she had dropped them, and began to wind them about her body. His touch was impersonal, as though she were nothing more than an unfortunate cabin boy who had taken a nasty fall. When he had finished his task he helped her lie down again, and covered her with a sheet. A moment later the boys appeared to remove the bath water.

"Read," he said sternly, placing a book in her hands. "Do not walk, do not sit. Stay in bed. You have two broken ribs. Shift about too much and they will poke you in a lung. You will then die. Do you understand?" When she nodded, he followed the servants from the room.

Corwyn obeyed Black's orders rather from her own inclination than any fear of him. She did not really believe that he would hurt her, having gone to so much trouble to find her and bring her here. In any case, she reasoned, what more could she suffer from a man?

She occupied her afternoons for the next week with the books at her bedside. She consumed one a day because she had nothing else to do. Her appetite returned as time passed, and her strength ebbed back a little at a time.

When her ribs became less painful, she explored her room and finally found herself standing before the window, staring out at a sunlit sea. Black's home was a tall Spanish fort that sat on the ragged edge of a cliff. Her window overlooked a lagoon protected by tall cliff walls. In the morning the tiny bay was lost in deep blue shadow. In the afternoon it was bathed in golden sun.

When ten days had passed since Black had reapplied the bandage, Corwyn carefully unwound the strips from about her ribs. Thankfully, though still tender, they did not scream with pain as they once had.

From a small chest at the foot of the bed she removed one of three gowns. There were no crinolines, not even a chemise, just three white dresses that laced up the front. Donning one, she found it acceptable, if somewhat too large. Without another thought, Corwyn opened her door, and exited into the chill darkness of the stone hall.

It took some time to leave the house. Stairs leading to the first floor were easy enough to find, but an exit from the domicile proved a challenge. In a long hall that faced away from the afternoon sun, Corwyn found a great oak door. She pulled it open to reveal a tropical garden. There was a lush lawn and beautiful roses covered in blooming vines. A number of geese milled about, squawking as she approached.

Down the long hill she saw Black's ship moored in a tiny walled bay. Men moved about the vessel, some aloft and some on deck. They seemed to be making repairs. She watched them for a time, then returned to her exploration of the area around the fort. She followed the edge of the building and then made her way down to the lagoon following steps cut into the cliff.

Before long she stood on the tiny beach that she could see from her window.

The sand of the small beach was so white it hurt her eyes, and it burned her feet as she made her way across it. She found the sea warm as bath water and it took her only a moment to pull off her gown and slip beneath the waves.

Corwyn took two days to explore every nook and cranny of her small haven. The walls around the bay and the great boulder that had fallen from the cliff into the water offered a great number of surprises. Tiny crabs and strange new fish peered at her curiously as she followed them around. She discovered that the flat plane of the boulder served well as a sunning rock, and that the walls around her radiated heat as the day progressed. She found herself laughing at what Mattie might have said about lying about desert islands in the nude. Since her childhood, Mattie had been telling her to put on a hat.

Black watched her from the top of the cliff, seeing how the sun and water had strengthened her body. She was incomprehensibly beautiful and he doubted that he could leave her alone until was completely recovered.

Once she was safe aboard his ship he had discovered her broken ribs and despaired for her life. There was no way to stop internal bleeding or to repair a damaged heart or lung. She had been delirious for a couple of days, crying out for her brother. Lost in her nightmares she had told him over and over again that she did not want to die. All he could do was hold her hand and promise her that she would not, all the while praying that it was true.

Of course she had also told him how much she hated him, hated him for stealing her, hated him for making love to her, hated him for letting her fall into Du Joles' hands. She told him how she would see him swing one day, and then, unaccountably, began to cry.

And, through it all, one thing became clear. He could not give her up. He did not care how much she hated him, he did not care that it was cruel to keep her. He did not care that she wanted to go home.

He could not bear to part with her. She would be his mistress just as he had told Elizabeth the last time he had seen her. He could not, would not, live without her. Perhaps, in time, she would come to love him. They were not so different really.

On one golden day, Corwyn woke to feel a hand caressing the curve of her spine. With a gasp she pulled away and sat up. Black was lying naked beside her.

"Do not touch me!" she gasped.

"But you are so beautiful," Black offered. "Do you know," he continued in a strange quiet voice, "that I always imagined you here." He spoke as if to himself, "This is the most beautiful place in the world and you are the most beautiful woman in the world. I think you belong together." He moved a stray curl over her shoulder, fingertip brushing her collarbone.

Corwyn remained silent. She had wondered if he still found her attractive, wondered if the time they had lived together on the ship were a dream. It was hard to remember what it had been like to share passion with this giant. Then he had gone away, left her with a stranger. Could she ever really trust him?

"I do not want to hurt you," said Black, his fingertip moving to the delicate line of her jaw, following it up to caress the area under her ear. Then hand moved down, curving to touch where her pulse beat an unsteady tattoo at the base of her throat.

"Please -" Corwyn whispered as he moved forward. But she let him kiss her. As always, she reflected, it was perfect. He embodied the sun that poured down upon them, the warm water that beaded upon their bodies. His exploration of her mouth drove all thoughts away.

His hands were rough when they found the gentle mounds of her breasts, his caress knowing as he awoke the tender rose buds. His lips followed his hands, shaping her breasts with kisses, making her want to draw away even as she pulled him closer. "Am I hurting you?" he whispered.

"No," Corwyn let her head fall to his shoulder, seeking the smell of him, her own surrender.

He helped her to recline on the smooth heat of the stone again, his arm pillowed her head. His hand tickled the tender ribs, explored the shallow plane of her belly, rolled lower, as he kissed her, to part her thighs, reaching to flex one of her knees.

"Frightened?" asked Black, moving back to touch her nose with his.

"I am always frightened of you," said Corwyn. She wished that her words weren't true.

"I do not think you should be," said Black in a low voice. His free hand moved to explore lower, to rediscover secret places she had almost forgotten. His touch was sure, thorough, cautious. He kissed her gently over and over again while he continued. He stopped when a cry of passion escaped her lips.

"I want you to ride me," Black said, "I am afraid I will snap those ribs I've so carefully repaired."

Corwyn laughed, burying her head in his shoulder again.

"I am quite serious," he said. He moved away and Corwyn sighed with loss.

"Come," whispered Black, rolling onto his back. "Astride me, girl." He tugged upon her arm to draw her atop him.

Corwyn complied, her eyes opening only enough to move her body over his. She could not look at him. Black helped her position herself so that he could enter her. He pulled her down, ever so gently, upon his desire. His gasp echoed hers.

"Slowly," he whispered, as he began to move.

He established a rhythm with her, and Corwyn found herself arching into the sun. He guided her movements, drove her ever higher and yet denied her the peculiar satisfaction she sought.

As the end drew inexorably near, her lips found his. Her breath became more uneven as the passion mounted.

When the conclusion tumbled across them she cried out, pleased to find her voice echoed by his rough call. She fell forward to hold her heart against his.

"I have never had a woman," said Black, speaking so softly that Corwyn could hardly make out the words, "who drove me to such extremes of anger, error, and desire."

"You will surely tear me apart," she said quietly.

"I probably already have," said Black in a more normal voice. He rolled her away from him, onto her back. Then he rose on one elbow and ran his fingers along the bones of her chest. "How are your ribs holding up?"

"They ache," Corwyn replied. How could two people be so intimate and yet so very far apart. "I should probably go to bed and recover." She thought of the cool sheets and an escape from the sun.

"I am afraid my bed will offer you little time to rest."

Corwyn turned to regard him with curious eyes. She found him smiling. "The best laid plans . . ." he told her and kissed her nose. "Still, this world offers little enough pleasure to its inmates. Why make the terms of confinement more difficult?"

Corwyn wrapped her arms about his neck. One day she would hate herself for this weakness, but now she just wanted him to carry her up to his room.

Chapter Twenty-Two

The pale dawn had only just touched the sky when Corwyn awoke to find Black dressing. Her eyes reviewed the unfamiliar contours of his room, larger than hers, its furnishings more luxurious, more masculine. She sat up despite the slight resistance her ribs offered, found words, "Where are you going?"

"The world does not stop because we make love, My Lady," Black smiled, teeth white in the semi-darkness. "I am refitting my ship for my next encounter with the Spanish, or," he added, tightening a cord attached to his knife's sheath, "whoever else happens along."

"I want to come with you," said Corwyn. She threw off the heavy coverings, moved to slide off the bed.

"You weren't invited," Black pointed out, struggling into his boots. "You will stay here, sleep, read, perhaps even swim. I will come back."

"When?" Corwyn asked. She stared at her hands, uncomfortable with him again. How could such intimacy fade so quickly?

"This afternoon," he told her. "In a few days, I will give the crew a holiday, and I will take you to explore my island." He pulled on a rough jerkin and gave her another smile, "You will like that."

"Your island," mused Corwyn out loud. "Does it have a name?" she asked, wondering if she might have seen it on those maps so long ago.

"Not really," Black replied. "Or, as is more commonly the case in these parts, it has many."

"May I know some of them?" Corwyn asked. Surely she could do him no harm with a name.

"You ask too many questions," Black noted. He raised her chin so he could look her in the eye. His warning was unmistakable. She should not press the issue unless she was interested in an argument. He gave her another kiss. A rap on the door interrupted more extensive explorations.

"Cover up," he ordered, moving to the door. When she was once again in bed, under the sheet, he opened it to reveal Adam. He was naked to the waist, barefoot, as silent and inscrutable as ever.

"What is he doing here?" Corwyn demanded, suddenly frightened. She thought she had dreamed that Adam had taken orders from Black, that he had carried her from the house. When she had woken up she had been unable to believe that Du Jole's faithful servant had betrayed him. Could that strange dream have been a memory?

"Momentarily, he is serving as third mate on my brig," Black's voice was cold. "Today, in particular, he will supervise the tarring of the hold. I hope these arrangements meet with your satisfaction." His tone clearly implied that he cared little for her manner.

Corwyn made no response. How could she bear to see Adam every day?

"Do you want to meet me at the lagoon?" Black waited to hear her reply.

Corwyn nodded. When would she understand him? He was angry with her one minute, tolerant of her the next.

Corwyn, seated on the warm plane of the boulder, regarded the sea. A gentle afternoon wind caressed her damp skin. Could this be the trade wind that blew ships around the world? She wondered if she would ever see home again. It was hard to believe she would never return.

Why had she agreed to share his bed again? Though she could not deny her desire for him, it was sheer folly to surrender. Sooner or later she would regret her decision, wish that she had forced herself to turn him away.

"What are you thinking?" His low voice interrupted her thoughts. "How can you be so solemn on such a beautiful day?" Black pulled himself out of the water to sit beside her.

Corwyn turned to watch him. The sun had burnt him brown and he seemed happy now, at peace somehow. "I am thinking," she said, "that nothing has changed."

"I would like to think," said Black, falling away to lie with this head beside her seated form, "that everything has changed. This must be something of a step up from your previous . . . arrangement." His raven hair, damp with sea water, curled as it began to dry.

"Perhaps," Corwyn replied. "But a prison, is a prison, is a prison." She knew he understood what she was trying to say.

"Prisons are subject to a wide diversity in conditions," His eyes were closed, face impassive. "I've seen a good number of jail cells and I can assure you that this is a particularly attractive one."

"Why do you keep me here? You cannot still wish to punish me. Surely I've enough scars to make up for any you have acquired. Just take me home." Corwyn watched him, wondering what he would tell her now. "Are you really going to keep me away from my family, from everyone who loves me for the rest of my life?"

Black did not respond for a time. "If I told you that I would send you home when I tired of you, you would become obstinate and unpleasant. If I told you that you were never going home, you would become disconsolate and distant. So, I shall say that I do not know what I am going to do with you, so you will take care to please me."

"Hope," said Corwyn. She fell back and unfolded her legs into the sun. Her head came even with his thigh, and she found herself looking at the fine hair that covered it. In a moment she moved to touch his leg with her lips, revealing in the warmth of his skin. A moment later she rolled on to her side, moving to press her lips against the heat of his stomach. She trailed her kisses lower, flowering across his desire, until he gasped and caught her head in his hands.

"Ah, my sweet, whatever are you doing?" he asked. He rolled her atop him and covered her face with kisses.

"I have nothing left to lose by pleasing myself," said Corwyn, shaking her head. She moved to sit astride him and trailed her hands across his chest. "When there are so few pleasures in the world, why abandon one more?"

Black brought his hands to her slender hips, pulled her up, and then brought her down gently upon his passion.

Corwyn buried her head in his chest and gave herself to pleasure.

That evening over dinner, Black marveled over the change in his captive. Suddenly she was calm, as though she were content to wait forever for him to send her home. All her defenses were gone. It was as though they had been together for a hundred years with nary an argument.

Black could hardly bring himself to question this calm, this peace so unlike all the time they had shared together. And yet, this was not what he might have expected from his spirited guest. He finally broke the companionable silence, "Alright, out with it. Why are you acting so oddly?"

"Oddly?" the girl asked.

Black said nothing, waiting for her to answer his question.

She sighed, pushed her chair away from the table. In one of his more expensive dressing gowns, she came to stand before him.

"I just cannot bear to fight anymore. Maybe one day I will have to pick up the gauntlet again, and you and I will once again stand toe to toe. But for now, I just cannot bring myself to battle you day after day." She placed a small hand on his shoulder. "If I were you, I would enjoy the calm before the storm."

Black wondered why her words should disturb him so. He had recommended this course of action from the beginning. "Agreed," said Black. "For the moment, we have a truce. Lord knows we can use the respite. It has been a busy year." He pulled her into his lap. "Whatever shall we talk about if we aren't going to fight," he asked, then he nuzzled her hair.

"I would like you to tell me about yourself." said Corwyn. "I do not know who you are."

She might as well suggest that he climb back into the pit of hell. For the first time in months he had a grip on his emotions, had plans for the future. Thinking of all he had lost might drive him mad again. "You first. My story is more unpleasant, and I do not want to darken our peace so soon."

"Talking about the past will make me melancholy," she put her head on his shoulder. "I should have to tell you that I am an orphan. My parents died when I was nine. My brother is my only sibling and he took care of me until I came to London. I would have to explain that I love him very much and that I miss him. I should have to explain that his heart will be broken because he believes me dead." she stopped.

"Let's see," said Black, at pains to turn the conversation to a more comfortable topic. "Why do we not talk about the York ball, where we met."

"I remember it was my first ball," she said, eyes luminous with the memory. "I remember wondering why all the men were being so pleasant. I remember Thomas Brougham and his ridiculous story about hunting. Henry came and tried to force me into accepting a boating invitation. I am afraid I was more than a little rude. So was he." She shook her head. "I am glad he is dead," she said fiercely. After a pause, she continued. "I remember Ben introducing me to the tallest, most attractive man I had ever met. I remember thinking you were like a statue, a greek god changed from stone to flesh. And we danced ..."

"I remember wishing I could whisk you off into a corner and teach you to kiss. You were an incredibly appealing woman even then," said Black. He could see her standing before him now, startled by her first brush with passion, trusting him. "Things have gone wildly astray, have they not Milady?"

Corwyn nodded.

"I do not think the past is the best topic for us," said Black with a sigh. "And I am willing to wager the future would prove even more awkward. Our conversation is going to be a bit difficult."

At that moment, Adam entered the room, presenting Devon with a scrap of paper.

The girl tensed, hid her face in his chest.

"Tell him to proceed in the morning. I never intended for you all to work this late." He gave the paperback. "You should find your bed too. I am not running a slave ship."

Adam nodded, disappearing from the room.

"We can discuss that," said Black. He pushed her away. "Why are you afraid of him?"

"You do not know what he did to me," said Corwyn. "You have no idea."

"What he did? Or Du Joles did?" asked Black. "I will warrant he never laid an ungentle hand upon you. In fact, I rather think he tried to protect you when he could."

"He did not stop Du Joles ..." Corwyn protested.

"What should he have done?" Black replied. "Killed Du Joles? Do you know what happens to renegade slaves in Port Royal?"

He could remember the hundreds of men he had seen tortured in years past.

"He could have let me escape," said Corwyn softly. "You do not know..."

"He would have been killed for his pains. Besides, you would just have ended up on an auction block. Is that so much better than what happened?" Black asked.

"I do not want to argue," she surrendered the battle. "I do not want to talk anymore."

Black stood up. He could still remember searching for her, knowing that whoever had her would want to keep her. She could have been raped, murdered. She was almost sold to planter old enough to be her father. Were it not for him she would be servicing him now. As it was, she had almost died. He could never let her go again, never let her out of his sight. So she was still a prisoner after all.

As he carried her to his room, he felt despair wash over him. How long could he bear to keep her against her will?

Chapter Twenty-Three

In the next few weeks, Corwyn became stronger, her skin growing golden as it captured the sunlight. She made a conscious effort not to think past the moment. What difference would it make if she fought her fate? She might rave at Devon, and drive him to hate her, but what would she gain? He would not let her go no matter what she said. So nothing mattered anymore. As he had suggested so long ago, she was learning to accept the few pleasures that life afforded and to stop thinking about the sacrifices she had made.

From the large window in Black's room she could watch the activity aboard his ship. She saw the men strip the ship from stem to stern, working to prepare her for the next voyage. Corwyn watched Black, discernable even at this great distance, scale the rigging. She watched him lower the long sheets to the deck for repair, check the masts, and refit the running lines. She saw his men hurry to obey his instructions, removing every object on the ship so it could be piled on the wide stone wharf. Watching him move made her yearn to join him.

At night he would order the men off the ship and into the houses that surrounded the wharf. Corwyn could see women going out to meet the men sometimes, like the women of her village had come to meet their fishermen when they returned from the sea. Sometimes she watched young children playing in the yard behind the barracks. Black had created a tiny town here, a sanctuary for his crew.

One day, after hours of reflection, Corwyn decided the time was long past to visit Maria. Two of the children, she knew from her long hours at the window watching them play, belonged to the woman. It would be a pleasure to meet them.

As she walked down the long hill Corwyn wondered what she would say. Could she explain why it had taken her so long to visit? Would Maria wonder that she lived with Black so openly? Perhaps Black had kept other women here and thus Maria would understand her position. That thought, strangely upsetting since she knew she could not permit herself to care for Devon, made her feel uncomfortable. As she walked past the five children and the dozen or more chickens that played in the fenced area, Corwyn looked up to see Devon watching her from the ship.

"Can I help you?" he asked.

It took Corwyn a moment to reply. Would he always make her heart skip a beat? How long would it be before she was immune to his charms. "I've come to thank Maria for caring for me," she called back.

"A nice gesture," said Black. Then he turned back to his work.

Summarily dismissed, Corwyn turned to the dozen or more little houses, each with its own window, door, and chimney. They were clean, well kept homes, some had flowers planted out front.

Before she could make up her mind which door to knock upon, she heard voices coming down the path. Turning she saw nine women appear, each with a basket of damp laundry upon her head or in her arms. Maria was among them."Buenos Dias! I wait for you to come," Maria said. She placed her basket upon the ground. "I tell my friends how beautiful you are."

Corwyn blushed. She had not expected to see so many women, or to be viewed with such obvious curiosity. "I wanted to thank you for taking care of me," she said as she tried to master her discomfort. Surely she could not find a gaggle of such welcoming faces frightening.

"It nothing," said Maria. He smile softened "Come sit while I cook."

The other women went on to a cleared area behind the houses where rope had been hung to support the laundry. Setting the baskets down, the women began to hang the damp clothes, their voices coming back to life. One came back to collect Maria's basket with a shy smile.

As she entered the house, Corwyn saw that it was a narrow room. She saw two cots where the boys slept, a table and a kitchen fire, and then a curtained area where she could just make out a bed. Obviously Maria and her husband slept there.

Indicating that Corwyn should take a seat at the table, she moved to a cupboard where she removed flour, butter and a large bowl. Sitting these on the table near Corwyn, she brought a few more ingredients and began mixing them together. "I glad to see you," said Maria, glancing up to give Corwyn a smile. "We worry you still sick."

"I am much better," said Corwyn, watching the rhythmic movements of the woman's hands as she kneaded the pliant dough.

"You brown and strong. I glad see this," said Maria. While Corwyn watched, Maria moved a large iron sheet into the oven, then she moved to bring a large flat stone to sit upon the table.

Corwyn thought of her long afternoons with Black, the swimming and passionate games they played. Was the change in her so obvious? To avoid further discussion, she gestured at the palettes. "You have children?"

"Yes," said Maria with a smile. "Moro, he . . ." and she paused as if searching for words, "four. Miguel six."

"I have seen them playing," confessed Corwyn. "They look like wonderful boys."

"They like their father," said Maria, obviously pleased. "He very strong, very proud."

"How did you meet him?" Corwyn asked, suddenly eager to know more of Maria's past. How had she come to this place?

Maria's face became somber, and she avoided meeting Corwyn's eyes as she replied. "He save me from . . . fathers. They force me . . . and he stop them. He take me here." Her words were obviously painful.

"He must love you very much," said Corwyn. She had been unkind to ask such a personal question.

Maria's features softened again as she turned toward the fire. "I cannot say, but I think so," she said. After wrapping cloths around her hands, she stooped to lift the hot iron out of the fire. She placed the flat piece of metal upon the stone, then flattened her pieces of dough into large, thin patties which she then pressed onto the iron. She had a dozen flat cakes on the make-shift griddle before she began turning them over using her finger tips.

"What are you making?" Corwyn asked, mesmerized by her movements.

"You English have no name," said Maria with a smile. Pulling one off the metal plate, she handed it to Corwyn. "It very old. My mother taught me."

The strange flat bread was wonderful, practically melting in Corwyn's mouth. Before she had finished it, she had asked to make one herself. With a laugh, Maria agreed to teach her.

When Black came to collect her, an hour later, she had her own small stack of warm tortillas. Presenting one to Devon, she jealously guarded the rest, declaring that they would share them at dinner. On their way out the door she met Miguel, happy to see the warmth in his brown eyes as he watched his wife laughing over Corwyn's efforts. Behind him trailed his two children, each clapping their hands as their mother gave them a warm tortilla to eat before dinner.

"I should let you mingle with the other women more often. It seems to please you," offered Black as they walked toward the castle at the top of the hill.

"Can you tell me about Maria?" asked Corwyn. "She seems so sad sometimes and so happy at others."

Black took his time in replying, lifting a branch so she could step under it without ducking. "Her family was killed by Spanish soldiers. She was taken, along with the five other children that survived the massacre of her village, to one of the missions. When Miguel found her, she was tied up and one of the fathers was raping her. Apparently it was not uncommon to use the young Indian women to sire half caste children."

"He rescued her?" asked Corwyn.

"He killed the friar and brought her away. A year later he signed onto my crew and we brought her here," Black smiled. "I do not think I ever saw two people more in love."

Corwyn was silent as they entered the house. Following Black to the dining hall, her tortillas still warm in the cloth Maria had given her, she wondered at his words. How horrible it would be to watch your family die! And yet Maria seemed happy now, with two fine sons, and a good husband.

Setting her bundle upon the table, Corwyn shook her head. Would she ever forget the past enough to feel that way?

Chapter Twenty-Four

Ben watched the overseer shove the native girl down into the mud between the forest of head-high cane. For the most part women did not serve in the fields, they were too weak to till the soil or to cut the cane. In fact, female slaves did not last long even when they were kept out of the fields. They usually died from rape and repeated beatings within days of their arrival. This particular overseer seemed to enjoy having women brought to him in the fields, as though the sound of their cries were music to the men around him.

As the six-foot blond brute fumbled with his britches, Ben stepped closer, then crouched. The girl was kneeling, a hank of her hair held in a hairy white hand. Turning his machete on its side, Ben slid it through three feet of cane, jabbing the girl in the thigh. She looked down and jumped back as if stung. The overseer took her movement as defiance and clouted her across the head. Ben saw that she fell toward the blade.

The worn band of a braided whip cut deeply into Ben's shoulder. Instinctively his hands flew to his head, warding off another blow.

"Get up, lazy English, or I feed you balls to the dogs!" Manny, one of the many Spanish guards who marched the slaves through fields and oversaw their work, put another burning stripe across his back to emphasize his order.

Ben made a show of favouring his bad knee as he rose. Manny was not as bad as some of the guards, so he had took his time. He had given Ben some extra food once for showing his crew how to keep the cut cane on the carts without using rope.

On another occasion he had allowed Ben to set another slave's broken arm.

Ben turned his head as he stood up, tried to see how matters stood with the girl. The overseer had his sex near the girl's mouth. He saw that she had the blade gripped in hands white with tension. It was poised between the man's legs.

Once on his feet, Ben kept his back turned to Manny so he would not notice that his blade was missing.

The howl to his right cut off Manny's next insult.

"Snake" Ben shouted, stepping through the grass toward the screaming man. "Serpent!" he added for good measure. The tropical cane fields were filled with a viper the local Indians called the two-step snake. It killed so quickly that there was rarely time for man to do more than call out before he was dead. The snakes would actively search for other victims after a bite, striking through the stalks at legs that came too close. He could hear the cane around him explode as slaves and guards alike fled the area.

A moment later he was crouched over the dying overseer. The slice through the man's thigh had cut through an artery and blood pulsed onto the ground with every heartbeat. The girl held the machete up as if toward him off, eyes scared but determined.

"Correle!" he whispered. "Vaya a su gente!" He pointed away from the plantation and toward the jungle westward.

Wide-eyed, she dropped the blade. She followed the direction of his hand and gasped. Then she darted into the stalks, brown legs flashing in the uneven light.

Ben retrieved his weapon and set off to the north where he knew the plantation landing to be. Dressed in rags, hair and beard matted into dark clumps, he knew he had little chance of remaining unrecognized as a slave. There was still less hope that he would happen to find a ship at the dock. Senor Lucas came and went freely from his plantation.

On the other hand, being killed on the run was better than spending another night in that hell hole with four men even more desperate than he was. His leg, and the sharp cough he had inherited from a fellow prisoner, would make progress slow, but he was determined to escape if he could.

They caught him before he was a mile away. He heard the dogs barking first, saw the cane wave as the animals raced through it like rats. Human voices echoed the dogs. They came toward him from every part of the field, guided first by the hounds, then by his own frantic movements. As was always the case with an escaped slave, the dogs brought him down before the men arrived. He killed a few using his machete, but more followed. Their teeth tore into his arms and legs, dragging at chunks of skin as though they meant to pull him apart.

Manny reached him first. "English? English? Are you under all this blood?" He sent the dogs away with some well placed kicks, then dragged Ben to his feet. "Why you try to run? You no like it here?"

Hard as it was, Ben mastered enough strength to spit in Manny's face.

Manny back handed him by way of response, then hauled him to his feet again. "You my special friend English. You smart.

Kill the man, then call out snake. I like that." He prodded Ben into movement with the tip of his machete. "I got new job English. Now I the cane boss." He laughed and shoved Ben forward when he stumbled. "You my lucky Englishman. I keep you with me if you live."

When they cleared the field, Manny used a whip to drive him into a limping run back to the barracks. Every step he took jarred his damaged leg, and he fell several times only to be jerked once again to his feet by the laughing Spaniard.

When they returned to camp, Manny shoved him into a half buried wood box that sat near the middle of the plantation. Manny stuck his round face into the box just before he closed the lid. Ben recoiled from his fetid breath and broken teeth. "If you live three days English, you be my special friend. So you try hard not to die, eh?"

Three days without food and water, trapped in box exposed to the searing sun, drove Ben to the limits of his sanity. He screamed for hours the second day, begging for death and throwing his body over and over again against the wood of his tiny prison. How many men had died here? He could smell them in the heat, their sweat was trapped in the wood forever. On the third day, mute, thirsty beyond description, pain itself kept him alive, preventing him from sinking into sleep and perhaps into death. When the lid to the box was opened, he lifted his eyes to find Manny hovering above him.

"You alive English? You want out of the box?" He used the handle of his whip to push a lock of sweaty hair of out his eyes.

Ben managed a weak nod.

"You never run away again, right?"

Ben nodded again.

"I let you live English. You remember. I no kill you because you lucky for me. You got me new job. Now I make you lucky."

Ben nodded once more. He would do or say anything to leave this living grave behind, would sell his soul for a sip of water.

"Out you go English." Manny hefted him out of the box with one arm, his stubby hands biting into the festering dog bites. He dragged Ben across the compound into one of the small rooms reserved for guards and dropped him onto a pallet of hay covered with a worn cotton cloth. "I bring someone to take care of you. You keep her if you like." He closed the wooden door behind him, leaving Ben in utter darkness.

When he returned he had a had an Indian girl by the arm and carried a candle that gave off less illumination than smoke. He placed the candle on the floor then shoved the girl forward. She held a chunk of old bread and an earthen container in her hands.

After surveying the scene, Manny kicked him in the foot. "Remember English, I do you favor. Next time you go in box, you not come out." Then he was gone.

For a moment, no one moved. Ben was too tired and too ill to sit up, and the girl seemed so frightened that she would not look at him. Finally, Ben managed a croak. He was trying to ask for water, but his tongue was too swollen to frame words.

The girl raised her eyes to his.

It was the Indian girl he had tried to help. When she recognized him she dropped to her knees at his side. With shaking hands she poured water on his lips, then as his mouth opened wider, onto his tongue. Her dark hair spilled around them like a curtain, and her soft hands felt his forehead. When he had consumed half the water in the jug, she made him stop. She took bread and dipped it in the water, then placed it on his tongue. Soft as it was he could hardly swallow it.

In under an hour, Ben felt well enough to attempt conversation. "Thank you," he croaked. At her confused look, he said it again in Spanish. To this she nodded.

There were so many things he wanted to ask her. Why had she not escaped? How had they caught her? But he did not know even enough Spanish to ask the questions, much less understand her answers. He would have to settle for something less ambitious.

"What is your name?" he said, struggling to speak above a whisper.

She shook her head.

With an effort he raised his hand to his chest, tapped it. "Ben," he said.

She patted her own chest and said, "Mea."

He wondered if that were her Indian name or some appellation the men in the camp had applied. He hoped he lived long enough to find out.

Mea made him drink more of the water, and eat most of the remaining bread. Then she rose and collected the candle and brought it closer to the cot. She examined the dog bites with great care. Using a corner of the thin blanket that covered him, she bathed the wounds, then washed his face. Just as he was dropping off to sleep, he felt her lie down at his side.

Manny visited Ben often as he recovered. Sometimes he brought food or wine, often he brought items like more candles or worn blankets. After about a week, when Ben was capable of sitting up unaided, he brought other things.

"How are you my lucky English? You look better." He dropped new clothes, a whip and a knife onto the floor by the pallet. "When you think you ready for work?"

Too startled to speak, Ben said nothing.

"Now you be a jefe. You not be a slave." He picked up the whip and caressed its coiled braid with broad hands. "You beat the slave, make him work."

Ben stared at the weapon with revulsion.

Manny sat back on his heels, pensive. "You a smart man English, but you stupid. There only two sides to the whip. You take handle or you take sting. Which you want?" He held it out again.

Ben forced himself to take the handle.

"Good. You jefe now. You drink, you eat, you keep your woman. No more slave."

"Can I leave?" Ben asked, knowing the answer before he heard it.

Manny's broad face flushed red, dark eyes becoming beady. "Why you want to leave, English? I give you everything. I make you lucky and now you want to leave?"

"I will stay," said Ben with a sigh. "You are a good friend to me. I will stay with you."

Manny smiled, face relaxing with satisfaction. "In two days you go to work, English." He patted Ben on the leg. "You smart English, so you make me smart. You help me. I help you."

Ben nodded, manufactured a smile. It seemed that he had just jumped from a prisoner in hell to one of its chief administrators.

Chapter Twenty-Five

One day, not long after Corwyn began visiting Maria and the other women that lived at the foot of the hill, Black took a day off to show her the island. First he woke her in the blue pre-dawn by making love to her, movements urgent, wordless, then they dressed, prepared a lunch and set off just as the sun rose.

Corwyn followed him down the long hill, and then onto a track that led onto a narrow strip of beach between the island foliage and the sea. The water in this area was shallow, the sea floor visible beneath the low waves.

"How did you find this place?" asked Corwyn. She hoped his decision not to tell her the island's name would not interfere with her knowing its history.

"Actually," said Black with a laugh, "quite by mistake. We had just managed to slip away from an English man-of-war, we were taking on water and the foremast was broken. It was late at night, there was no moon, and this island appeared to rise out of the water. We almost ran aground. At the time I considered its timely appearance nothing short of a miracle. The harbor was deep, the fortress in fair repair, and there was a fresh water well. I decided to adopt it permanently. I paid the men for the private use of the house, since, by right they could have claimed a share of it."

"How long have you lived here?" Corwyn asked, following him along the curve of the beach past a clearing where she could see a well house and a huge stone pool. This was obviously where the women did their washing.

"Eight years, on and off," replied Black, glancing at her.

They walked past a garden, no more than five acres, where vegetables and corn grew in long rows. A small shed housed a bull calf, two cows, several goats and a few dozen chickens. Corwyn noted that the stock animals showed evidence of good care. Their coats were well brushed and the manger before them was filled with fresh hay.

He then led her around a long flat lagoon filled with pools of shiny fish and alive with sea animals that swayed with each swirl of the tidal pool. The lagoon they shared, he informed her, was just around the curve in the island. He slipped into the warm water and struck out for the deep water with Corwyn right behind. The water was very deep here, sinking away under her feet and growing colder. She followed the wall of gray stone that climbed to Black's fort and was happy to find the seclusion of their bay. She joined him on the sunning rock, gasping for air.

They made love, then Black led her up the long path to the garden, and then down to a small graveyard lost among swaying reeds. There were only eleven graves here, some so old that their legends were unreadable. Others were new, shipmates and children that had died during Black's ownership of the small island.

"That's it then," said Black, after they spent time sitting near the stones and looking out over the water. "It is not very big, but I do believe it is the most beautiful place I've ever seen."

Corwyn considered his words. Certainly it was a beautiful place, magical and romantic. He had turned it into a home not only for himself, but for his crew. Why, she wondered, had Black ever left this paradise? She longed to ask him, but that would violate their silent agreement not to discuss the past.

Corwyn recognized the change in her body immediately. Having shared Black's island and his bed for over four months, she should have expected the inevitable. And yet, when she finally missed her monthly courses, she was shocked.

The wave of emotions that washed over her stole her senses for a time. She knew, with a sense of resignation, that this would mean the end of their short peace. She wanted this baby with all her heart. Perhaps this was one part of Devon Black she would be permitted to hold onto, a part of him that would grow into the man he might have become.

Black sensed the change in her almost from the start. "What is wrong with you?" he demanded over a late dinner in the garden one evening. Under a dark sky filled with an uncountable number of brilliant stars, they shared a candlelit supper.

Corwyn made no reply. Instead she stared up at the sky, a half smile playing across her face.

"This is the most successful ploy yet," he said. "Anything that makes you this happy is bound to irritate me."

Corwyn turned to look at him, "I do not know what you are talking about." Her smile had disappeared.

"What are you keeping from me?" asked Black. He could feel the gulf between them appearing again, pushing them farther apart second by second.

She said nothing, and he decided to let the matter drop. Christ, he cared for her too much. He had to remember he could not keep her. Someday, somehow, she would have to go home. He owed her that. He would not own a slave and he would not have her be one. And yet, to consider her departure was to stand at the edge of an abyss.

The feeling would fade away, he assured himself, as she watched him pour him another glass of wine. Love, infatuation, desire, lust, all words for the same fleeting passion. She did not love him, and someday he would stop wanting her.

He would take her home then, home to her family and friends. That he had stolen her, that her every moment with him was a violation, troubled him when he permitted it to occupy his thoughts. But, he could ignore his misgivings until his passion was sated.

Suddenly, consumed by the desire to understand her, he breached their agreement to abandon the past, "Tell me about home."

Corwyn, still staring at the sky, smiled again. "I had believed it the most beautiful place in the world until I came here." Turning her head to meet Black's eyes, she granted him a smile. "Now, I am not so sure."

Black raised his glass at the compliment. Cornwall, close to his father's lands in Devon, had always been beyond his reach. He had heard of its mysterious coastline, dark with hundreds of ships lost in the rough waters. Tin mines and fairy circles, witchcraft and magic, he could only imagine what a striking place it must be.

"I come from a place near Land's End," Corwyn said after a time. "It is a small town. There are not very many people, and those that live there make their living from the sea. My brother inherited Chase Manor when my parents died. It is a beautiful house, made of native stone. Strangely enough," she turned to regard Black with distant eyes, "the legend is that one of my forefathers was a pirate, or a smuggler, who purchased respectability. He married a lord's daughter, and he built her the house. Some say they died in each others' arms."

"Poetic," Black offered uncomfortably. He wanted to know more, and yet, the more he knew about her, the more terrible his crime seemed. Lord, why did he care for her so?

"Storms come up suddenly, sweeping in off the sea with the fury of the devil himself," Corwyn continued. "A sunny afternoon can fade into a violent night, thunder and lightening filling the sky, wind driving the waves into huge peaks that sweep fishing boats right out of the harbors." Corwyn trailed off. When she spoke again, her voice was unsteady. "I do not think I should talk about this any more."

Black did not reply. She was quite right. With her every word she longed for home, she begged him to take her there. He could not surrender her yet, would not let her go. He had no future if she left him. The days would stretch forward into a gray, meaningless eternity. Why could not he demand some happiness from the world when it had demanded so much of him?

Corwyn lay in the cradle of Black's arms, fighting off the feeling of lethargy and satisfaction that was the legacy of their love making. While he slept, she pondered her future, wondering what was to become of her in the months ahead.

Pregnant, she knew she had to leave Black, leave his island and make the long journey home. She was determined to bear her child at Chase manor, in a place where those he grew up with would love him as much as she did.

It seemed that fate had already taken a hand in her affairs. Black had announced, in a brusque way he affected when he expected an argument, that he would be setting sail for New England in less than a week. He had even offered to take a letter to her brother, though she had been forced to promise that it would contain no mention of him, or of the island, only that she was well and content for the time being.

Corwyn had accepted his proposal, penning the letter with tears in her eyes. She could only imagine what Ben would think when he saw it. He would believe that she had returned from the dead. She finished the missive with the line, "I hope that we may meet at Chase in the nearest future. I cannot bear to be apart from you."

Black had scowled at this, his features darkening. "He may believe you home, or on your way there, if you end this way," he pointed out.

"Am I not on my way home, My Lord?" Corwyn asked innocently. "I thought I had something to hope for."

Black had responded by kissing her fiercely. "Home, Milady? Not for some time yet I fear."

Now, lost in the smell of him, the feel of her flesh against his, Corwyn wondered how she would manage to sail with his ship.

She could stow away when the provisions were loaded, but it would be difficult to remain undiscovered on board the ship without an accomplice.

Nevertheless, when Black made port to deliver her letter, she would escape. It would be simple to leave the ship without being seen.

Black, seeming to sense her thoughts, shifted in his sleep, pulling her closer. A moment later, Corwyn knew he was awake, listening to the sound of her breathing.

"What is wrong?" he asked, voice almost a whisper.

"Nothing," said Corwyn, her voice, like his, barely audible. "I cannot sleep."

"Something is wrong," Black told her.

"I am thinking about home," said Corwyn softly, "About the rain, and the moor, and a bay a few miles from my house. I am remembering my bedroom, and the way sun would pour into it in the morning. I am recalling-"

"Quiet," said Black, his voice, though still a whisper, carried a command.

Corwyn sighed.

"Do not try to wile me with memories and sympathy. I am a monster. What matters to me is that you share my bed."

Corwyn sat up, the moon bathing her flesh with silver light. "Honestly," she said in a normal voice, "what can have made you into such a beast?" Slipping out of bed to stand on the moonlit floor she turned to face him. "You can be almost human at times, and then you will say something so terrible..."

"What? Is this some show of life in my kitten?" Black asked, propping his head up with his hand. "I had almost forgotten that you had a temper."

"Once you promised me that you would tell me about your past. I think I have a right to know who holds me prisoner," said Corwyn, disregarding his words. She moved to sit away from him, upon the cold wood floor, her eyes wide in the darkness.

"You have no rights," said Black. Then, with a guarded look, he went on. "Do not impute any great meaning to my past, My Lady. It is not entirely responsible for who I am."

"Tell me," Corwyn prompted. One day she would relate this tale to her child, to Black's child.

"My uncle, sensibly enough, found the order of his birth an inconvenience. He arranged to have my father and mother killed. He wanted me dead as well. Unfortunately, the man assigned to murder me found it more lucrative to sell me into indenture than provide my uncle with a head on a pike," Black paused here, regarding Corwyn with stony eyes. "I served time as cabin boy on a trader, then after an argument with the captain my indenture was sold to a cane plantation. I grew up there, under the lash like every other slave." He stopped as if remembering something terrible. "I spent six months on a navy ship, then skipped ship to a slaver. I served as third mate, then first. When my last captain became too much of an inconvenience I led a mutiny." He stopped, lost in thought. When he continued, his words were clipped. "When I had enough money, I returned to London, I murdered my uncle, and tried to regain my lands. You know the rest of the story." He regarded her almost defiantly, waiting for her judgment.

"Poor boy," said Corwyn remotely, imagining a terrified child on a foul, rat infested ship bound for the New World.

"That 'poor boy' has kept you in chains, has he not? Perhaps my uncle too had his history. Or are you ready to forgive we murderers one and all?" asked Black, irritated. "Enough soul searching, back to bed."

Obediently Corwyn crawled under the covers, curling her now chilled body around him. "I understand you better now. It all makes so much sense," she murmured, her head curling into his neck.

"Christ!" He sat up. "I am not an ill-treated animal that has become vicious. I am the man that I am because that is who I want to be. I would not have it any other way," said Black. "Do not make excuses for me."

"And the way you hurt me," said Corwyn softly, "and that you keep me here though you know it is wrong. Is that the man you want to be?"

Black sat stared at her with obsidian eyes. "You belong to me."

Corwyn, eyes wide in the darkness, said nothing for a short time. Then, she slipped out of bed and onto her feet in one lithe movement. "I think" she said slowly, "That you are wrong. I think your past has made you exactly who you are."

"I would rather have your hate than your pity," said Black.

"Then the current state of affairs should suit you admirably," said Corwyn. In a moment she was out of the room and racing down the stairs. Once outside she instinctively stumbled down the path to the lagoon that she and Black had shared since her arrival.

In the darkness, the cliff walls were sinister, frightening, towering over her as she moved onto the narrow strip of sand that comprised the beach. Wading out into the cool water, she climbed the rock that she and Black had shared that first day of their new relationship. In the darkness it was cold, uninviting, half submerged since the tide was in. Perhaps, Corwyn found herself thinking, this darkness and chill, this is the truth, and the golden days were just a dream.

Chapter Twenty-Six

Corwyn assiduously avoided Black for the few days before his departure, appearing only for meals and to share his bed. In the interim she lost herself in books and sat in the garden. She spoke as little as possible, not wanting to divulge her condition, or her plans, by some misspoken word.

As she had realized from the start, she could not operate alone. Choosing her accomplice had been less of a decision than an acceptance of fact. Adam, once her chief gaoler, now something more uncertain, was her only hope. She confronted him, the day before Black's departure. He had passed by her as she gathered roses in the garden.

"I need your help," she announced as she turned to present him with a bright red blossom. The late afternoon heat had beaded the sweat upon her brow, and she wiped her damp forehead on the sleeve of her dress.

Adam, shirt matted to his chest, wiped his own brow and looked down toward the ship in the bay.

"Exactly," said Corwyn. Now that the moment had come, she found she was calm. He had to agree, he would agree, she could not imagine what she would do if he refused her. "I am to bear a child. I wish to go home to my family and those who love me. You must help me to escape."

Adam said nothing for a moment, and Corwyn wondered if he might be thinking of what could happen if his aid to her were discovered. When he turned his eyes to look at her, she saw pity. He nodded.

Corwyn moved to place her hand upon his arm, tried to find words to express her thanks. So much she did not know about him, so much he could never say, the sorrow washed over her. He was willing to risk everything to help her escape. What an enigma this man was! "I hope," she said softly, "that I can do something to repay you one day."

Adam waved as if to indicate there was no debt owing. He then looked back down at the ship, obviously watching Devon as he oversaw the loading of the boat. He shook his head as he walked away.

On the evening before Black was due to depart, he made love to her gently, caressing the length of her body, exploring the waves of hair that cascaded everywhere. Wordlessly, with a feeling of betrayal, Corwyn allowed herself to respond to his touch, to revel in the heat of his sun kissed skin.

The next morning he was up before dawn. Shaking her awake when he was fully dressed, he bent to bid her farewell.

"Good bye," said Corwyn, curled up in the remains of the warmth he had left behind.

"Good bye sounds far too serious," Black whispered. "You will be here when I get back," He kissed her on the forehead.

Rather than argue the matter or lie, Corwyn turned away. "I will miss you," she said honestly.

"I thought you hated me," he said, obviously thinking of the last few days.

"Hate, pity," Corwyn said, "What should I feel? You are a monster to keep me here, away from those I love, just because it pleases you to do so."

Black seemed startled. He waited, as if he thought she might say something else, then finally left the room without another word.

The moment Black was gone, Corwyn flew from the bed and struggled into the britches and shirt she had filched from an old trunk of clothes. Fortunately, though large, they did not swallow her with fabric the way Black's cut down clothing always had.

Black's two trunks were stacked at the foot of the bed, waiting for someone to collect them. Corwyn, exited into the hall and darted into the room next door. She retrieved a cask Adam had procured for her last night. Though it was small, she had already tried the fit, and she knew she could stowaway in it until she was safely in the hold. A mallet waited inside, so she would require no help getting out. Rolling the cask into the hall, and then into Black's room, Corwyn stumbled into Adam, obviously concerned that she wasn't there to meet him.

He helped her into the cask and tapped the lid loosely into place. He made sure that the two air holes bored in the top were unobstructed, lest she suffocate during the trip to the ship. Then, Corwyn heard him pick up the first trunk. In a moment he was gone. He returned for the second trunk, and then after a long wait, he came to collect her.

Unable to see anything from the cask, Corwyn knew she was in a wooden wagon on her way to the bay where the ship stood ready to sail on the next tide. The swaying movement of the conveyance, and the heat from the cobalt sky she could see through the holes in the top of the cask, served to make her nauseous. In time she heard voices and the sound of the sea, the she was hefted with no ceremony into a net. Hoisted to the deck along with the rest of Black's possessions, she remained top-side for over a quarter of an hour while fresh water was taken on board.

She could hear Black's voice bellowing orders to the crew from every corner of the ship. Her heart was beating so loud was sure that she would hear it. When at last she felt herself lifted onto someone's shoulders, she breathed a sigh of relief. Someone, probably Adam, carried her down into the dark hold. She was placed on the planking, and her bearer departed.

When silence had reigned for a few moments, Corwyn used her mallet to free the cap on her cask. She could not take the chance that someone would place something atop her and seal her in. She resealed the cask then darted deeper into the darkness, hiding near crates of fresh fruit.

Corwyn sequestered herself in the darkness near the rafters of the hold, obscured from sight by fabric, crates of porcelain and food. She fell asleep, and awoke only when she felt the ship shudder as it left the dock. At last, she thought sadly, I am free.

Chapter Twenty-Seven

Mea knelt before the cook fire, knees brushing the uneven stones that surrounded the pit, dark hair swinging dangerously close to the flames that licked the hanging cook pot. She ladled a stew of rice, beans, corn and salt pork out of the pot and onto the pair of trenchers that waited by the fire. Then she slid the pot to the side of the pit. She used a stick to expose a broad, flat rock lying under the red coals. A wooden bowl to her right contained a flour, water and fat mixture. Taking a piece of the sticky dough she dabbed at the rock, removing dirt and soot from its surface. Moments later she was cooking flat cakes by pressing the dough into the hot stone. When she had finished the task, she piled more wood onto the fire so it would burn until morning.

Ben marveled at her expertise. She was so young, and yet she managed the preparation of the meal as if she had cooked a thousand meals in this fashion. He could never have been so proficient with the limited tools at their disposal.

She brought his plate to where he sat, back against the door of his quarters. The rest of the guards shared dinner, rum and women at a common cook fire but he and Mea always ate apart.

"How did you learn to cook this way?" he asked as she sat down beside him.

"This is how we cook," she said after a moment. She spoke slowly, choosing her English words carefully.

"Your family you mean?"

She nodded, then used one of the cakes to collect a mouthful of food from the plate. She dropped the wad of food into her mouth. Then she waited for Ben to take a bite.

"How do you cook?" she asked. "This is only way I know."

Ben was at a loss to explain the concept of a kitchen or a stove to her, much less acres of white linen or china plates. Obviously leavening bread with yeast, baking foods in an oven, even the use of eating utensils would be foreign concepts. He finally smiled. "It is not important," he said.

She nodded, as if content with his dismissal. For a time they ate in silence, watching the sky fade from red and blue to black. When they were done eating she collected his trencher and placed it near the fire, then came to sit beside him again.

"Do you want to teach me English?" she asked as she settled beside him. "I practice today."

Ben looked down, noting that the firelight colored her dusky skin red, that her eyes sparkled with its light. She was quick, incredibly so, and already spoke English as well as any man on the plantation. He nodded.

"I have a mother and a father. I have three brothers. I have five sisters. I am a girl. I wear a dress. I eat food. I run fast." She turned to him for confirmation.

"Very good," he said. "What do you want to know today?" Yesterday they had discussed their families. She had learned about his parents and Corwyn. He had learned about her family. She had been captured on the coast as she was fishing for her family several months past. He had explained that he had been captured while searching for his sister.

"Tell me more about your land," she said, putting her head against his shoulder.

"What do you want to know?" Ben asked. It was always so difficult to explain things to her. Things were different here, incomprehensibly different. His stories might have been in ancient Greek for all the sense they must have made to her. But still she wanted to hear them.

"About the women," she said with a sigh. "Do they look like you?"

"Well," said Ben, "they have white skin and pale hair like me, but the rest looks like you."

"Do they have hair on their faces?" she asked.

Ben laughed. "No, their skin is smooth, like yours." He could still remember how she marveled at his facial hair. Her people had none, and when he had used his knife to cut his beard and trim his hair she had marveled that his skin was like hers beneath it all.

"Do they wear clothes like me?" she asked, gesturing at the dirty cotton dress she wore. It came only to her knees and it was just possible to detect symbols drawn upon it.

Ben smiled. "They wear clothes a little like you. They wear dresses that go to their feet. The dresses are very large around the bottom."

"What?" she looked utterly bemused.

He leaned forward to draw a picture in the dirt with his finger.

She cocked her head to one side as she examined the crude image.

"How do they walk?" she asked.

"Slowly," he replied with a laugh. "They do not run as you do."

She was silent, then spoke again. "Are they... pretty?"

"Some of them." Ben felt his pulse leap. They had lived together for several weeks, and he had never touched her. He could remember the overseer, could picture what she had endured before she was given to him. He did not want to be one of the human animals to whom she submitted herself, did not want to do anything that might result in his child being born here, a slave.

"Am ... I pretty?" She lifted her eyes to his.

"Yes," replied. "You are very pretty." He did not know what else to say.

She nodded as if affirming his words. They sat in silence for some time until they saw Manny emerging from the darkness. Without appearing to hurry, Mea rose and entered the cabin.

"English," said Manny as he approached, "You smart. Today the work went well. We work fast with less men." He had put on more weight with his new position, calves becoming as thick as tree trunks, arms growing more massive every day. He was stronger too, often competing with other guards in wrestling matches that lasted hours.

"I thought so," said Ben. It was no surprise that with a malnourished and sickly workforce, a day or two of rest each week would result in increased productivity.

"You tell Hans to move the men. You tell me why." Manny threw himself down onto the ground at Ben's side.

"I wanted to put the sick ones together," said Ben. He had thought long and hard about this decision, aware that he was effectively signing a death warrant for those who were ill. Sick men sharing such tiny quarters were guaranteed to share contamination. On the other hand, it would give the men who were well a better chance at survival. He had noticed that the coughing sickness seemed to leap to any man that shared quarters with someone who had it. "The others will not get sick so quickly. They will live to work for more time."

"Clever English!" said Manny. "And we no feed the sick ones!"

Ben felt a jolt of fury, worked hard to master it before he spoke. "No," he said, "we feed them and make them work less."

"No," said Manny, wrinkling his brow.

"If we feed them, and they get better, we get another strong worker." Ben spoke slowly, though he thought his reasoning should be obvious to the most stupid of men. "It costs less to make them well than to buy new ones when they die."

"When they get sick, we feed them and do not make them work?" Manny shook his head. "You crazy, English."

"Like horses," Ben said through gritted teeth. It was hard to believe that common livestock were treated better than men here. Livestock cost more. After all, there were always more Indians to be captured, and a half-dozen Negroes cost less than a good horse.

"We try," said Manny, struggling to his feet. "It no work, but we try." When he was standing, he gave Ben a proprietary look. "You smart man English. Weak, but smart." Then he strode away into the night, walking toward the common fire closest to his little house.

Ben rose and entered his own cabin. He walked a tight rope here, unwillingly responsible for slaves whose condition he found abominable. On one level he was their advocate and their benefactor, on another he was a conspirator participating in their imprisonment. Sooner or later he would be put in a position where he would have to sacrifice either his comfortable position here or his own humanity.

He removed his shirt and lifted the thin blanket that covered Mea. She was nude, long body and well-formed limbs brown against the cotton sheet. Her eyes were open, watching him.

Ben felt his pulse race as he examined her figure, the small breasts, slender hips. He wanted her, wanted to descend into the heaven of her body and never emerge. He had never wanted a woman so much. He dropped the blanket and stepped away.

Mea watched him.

"No," he said, meeting her eyes. "I do not want this." She was silent, still watching him.

"I like you. You are pretty. We are friends." He continued. "But I will not touch you this way." He realized that his voice was harsh, saw that tears were running down her face. He knelt. "It is not safe," he said.

Mea looked confused.

He held his arms as if cradling a child and shook his head. He saw comprehension come into her eyes, watched her tears stop.

He lay down on the hard floor beside her, reached under the thin blanket and took her hand. How hard it was not to tell her that he loved her, not to prove it with his body. Only the knowledge that neither of them had a future here could prevent him.

Chapter Twenty-Eight

Corwyn stood on the deck of the Elizabeth Jane dressed, for the first time in many weeks, like a respectable woman. The undergarments, crinolines and heavy dress felt awkward after so many months spent wearing practically nothing at all. Like everything else she had experienced since her escape from Black, her clothes were going to take some adjustment.

The first jarring note had come when she met with Ben's commanding officer at the military outpost in Virginia. She stood before the hawk-nosed man dressed in one of the loose fitting gowns Black had provided to her months ago and filthy from living weeks in the hold,

"You asked to see me." Admiral Brooke did not offer her a chair.

"I am Corwyn Tyler Chase, and you are my brother's commanding officer." Corwyn kept her back straight and looked him in the eye.

"Your brother is no longer in Her Majesty's navy. He left in search of you several months ago in response to a note delivered here."

"He is searching forme?" Corwyn could not believe her ears!

"So it would seem." The Admiral folded his hands. "If I may inquire, where have you been so many months?"

Corwyn had anticipated this question, and now concentrated on delivering her story without a flaw. "The Albatross was captured by pirates. I was taken captive and the captain of the pirate vessel sank the Albatross with all hands." She paused, leaving him to imagine her fate aboard the pirate vessel. "I was sold to a slave trader in Port Royal, who sold me to a pirate from Barbados."

"And the names of these pirates you spent so many months with?" Admiral Brooke dipped his quill in ink.

"The captain who took the Albatross was James Fitch. The second, who purchased me, was Edward Jacobs."

"Those names are unfamiliar. Can you describe these men for me?"

"Yes." Corwyn described two of the men who had visited her when she had been held captive by Du Joles. Maybe their names and a description would not result in their hanging, but it was a chance at revenge she would not pass by.

"Well you can remain here while we book passage for you on a passenger ship-"

"If you please, sir," Corwyn steeled herself to say the words, "I would like to take the first ship home. I am carrying a child and would be with my family at this time."

"A child?" The admiral's disgust was apparent.

"You understand my urgency."

"Miss Chase, you cannot expect us to send you home at a moment's notice-"

"My father was a very popular man, as you may recall, and my family is not entirely without influence. I am sure they can and do expect you to treat me with all the dignity and compassion I have every right to expect from an officer in Her Majesty's navy." She took a step toward the desk, "If you do not send me home immediately I assure you that you will come to regret your decision."

After some reflection, Admiral Brooke did made the arrangements for her passage, even going so far as to have his wife make up a trunk of decent clothing for her to wear during the voyage. His contempt for her was obvious in his refusal to meet with her again, and his wife made it evident that she would have died before she submitted to rape and slavery.

Nevertheless, Corwyn had little to complain about. In less than forty-eight hours she was aboard the Elizabeth Jane, sharing her passage on the military vessel with wives and daughters making their way home from the colonies. She allowed herself a grim smile of satisfaction. After so many months in the company of men like Devon Black and Francois Du Joles, Admiral Brooke was an easy victory.

Corwyn sent word to Christina immediately after the ship made port in London. In under an hour her cousin appeared, an impressive retinue in tow. A doctor, a maid, two footmen and a groom ushered her into the carriage, where Christina folded her into her arms. Home at last, Corwyn started to cry.

Hours later she was back in the room she had stayed in more than a year ago. Servants had bathed her, brushed her hair and put her to bed like a child. Now, Christina sat on the edge of the bed, almost as if she were afraid that Corwyn would disappear again if she left the room.

"So, you are to have a child."

"I am sorry to have brought yet another scandal upon you," said Corwyn. She took her cousin's hand. "I will leave tomorrow morning and no one need ever know I was here."

"Perhaps in Cornwall servants and sailors have no tongues." Christina said with a little smile. "I can assure you that by now half of London knows you are here and the rest will find out in the morning."

"I did not know-"

"Its alright my dear. No one will hold me to ill account for providing you a place to stay, and I should not care if they did."

"I do not know what to say. You have been so kind to me and I've been nothing but trouble to you."

"Do not be a goose." Christina patted her leg through the coverlet. "You seem well..."

"I am. I want this baby more than anything in the world." Corwyn said the words without thinking, then added, "I mean, I am glad to be here. I've been through so much. And I cannot help loving my child."

"Of course you cannot. Is it Devon Black's?" Christina asked the question as though it were a matter of course.

"No! What gave you that idea?" Corwyn's blood ran cold. How could Christina have guessed such a thing?

"Just curiosity. He wasn't seen in London after his escape from Newgate, and rumors have it that he was a sea captain who kept a ship in the Pool. You can be sure I will not be the only one jumping to that conclusion."

"He is not the father. The father, should anyone care, is Edward Jacobs, though I have no idea why anyone <u>should</u> care. After all, I am quite beyond the pale of respectability now. Is it just idle curiosity?"

"Perhaps," said Christina. "But we can take on the world in the morning. Until a few hours ago I thought you dead. Now that I know you are safe I think I will have my first good night's sleep in almost a year." She stood up and shook the folds from her gown. She leaned down to kiss her cousin and to embrace her for several minutes. "I am very glad to have you home."

Chapter Twenty-Nine

Who could possibly be calling upon her less than twenty-four hours after her arrival in London? Roused from a sound sleep, Corwyn learned that a guest sat in the front parlor, unwilling to leave until he spoke with her. Could it be Devon? How could he have followed her here so quickly?

With the help of the maid she dressed in one of the gowns the Admiral's wife had loaned her. It stretched tight across her breasts and did little to hide her swelling figure, but it would have to do for the time being.

She entered the parlor with the maid in tow. If Devon had somehow managed to follow her here, she did not want to be alone with him.

"Lady Chase. I cannot tell you how surprise I am to see you again." Henry Norfolk said as she entered the room. He was fashionably dressed in a pearl gray suit, his pale hair was pulled back into a queue.

Corwyn could not believe her eyes. She stumbled back to collapse into a chair. "I thought you were dead," she finally managed.

"Then how happy you must be to see me!" Henry moved across the room and sat in a chair a few feet from hers. "My uncle told the world I was dead after Black slipped away from Newgate. I was in no position to defend myself, you understand. In a few days, when no services were held, he had to let everyone in on the ruse. But by then I was faraway, and so, might I add, were you."

Corwn struggled to her feet. "I do not ever want to see you again."

"My dear, I think we are past that. You will stay here and we will have our first..." he paused as if in thought, "real conversation. With all the trouble we have caused one another, I believe we can avoid falling into old habits. I shan't attack you. You shan't try to run away."

"Why should I want to speak with you?" Corwyn remained standing.

"You have so much to lose if you do not. Now be a good girl and send for something to eat. I am here at daybreak you know. I thought you might try to slip away when you heard I was in town."

Corwyn sank back into the chair and nodded to the maid. A moment later she and Henry were alone.

"Shall I show you my momento of our last encounter?" He untied his cravat to show her a mass of scar tissue on his throat that was as big as her hand. "It festered you know. They had to bleed me for weeks on end, draining the infection from me drop by drop. It is impressive, isn't it? They say I should have died."

Corwyn nodded, staring at the tortured flesh. Yes, he should have died. She was quite certain of that.

A maid returned with pots of chocolate, rolls, butter, cheese and jam. Henry ordered the girl to set a table between them and then to see that they remained undisturbed.

"Shall I tell you how it is to be?" He buttered a roll and handed it to her.

"I am not afraid of you any more." Corwyn put the bread down. "You cannot frighten me as you did before."

"I would venture to say sharing a man's bed holds few surprises for you. What have you to be afraid of? I am just another man, am I not?" He ate his roll and poured chocolate into their cups. "Still, you know I am unlikely to forget our unfortunate past. In fact, I am determined to find you and kill you if you try to run away again. I could kill you now with hardly a qualm. You know that, do you not?" He looked up to meet her eyes.

Corwyn nodded.

"But, I have more pleasant things in mind for us. You will return to that shabby home of yours in the West Country and I will stay at one of my properties near by. You shall have your child and we shall pack it off to someone we need never hear from again. Then we can marry."

"What!"

"I confess I am obsessed with you. Who do you suppose I thought of all those months in silent agony? I thought of you. I dreamed of you. I cannot say all of my fantasies have been pleasant ones, but I can assure you that you have featured in every one. Surely you see that I am in love. We will take our wedding vows and live together until death do us part. Best of all, you have already proved yourself fertile. I am sure you can bear my children as well as Black's-"

"What are you talking about?" The words were out before Corwyn could stop them.

Norfolk leaned forward as though he were sharing a confidence with her. "I knew a great deal about the Black Earl even before you left. I know more now. He kept a ship in the pool of London for weeks before he disappeared and just before our unfortunate altercation, he was making plans to set sail. One way or another you ended up on that ship. I know it in my very bones. I also know that you carry his child in your belly. Tell me I am wrong and perhaps I will believe you."

His gray eyes took in her every move.

"This is not Devon Black's child. I will not marry you. You now know what you came to find out. Let me tell you one thing you might not know. I will not let you bully me anymore." Corwyn wished she felt as confident as she sounded.

Henry laughed and clapped his hands as if she had told an amusing story. "Quite a performance! Of course I am quite determined to make your life miserable in every conceivable way unless you agree to marry me. You have no one left to defend you, and if you did I would hack my way through them just in order to have you."

"What gives you the right-"

"Do not be ridiculous, I have the right because you are in no position to stop me." He brushed crumbs from his clothes onto the floor and stood up. "I assume you will be leaving town directly. You can expect to receive me at your home in a week or so. By the look of things," his eyes dropped to her swollen belly, "we won't have long to reach an understanding."

Lord Norfolk left the house with a spring in his step. Once in his carriage he took a pinch of snuff and contemplated his future.

It was hard to believe the girl had returned to England, and surprising at best to see her heavy with child. He had no doubt that Lord Black was the father of the babe. The Earl had a ship, was known to have property in the colonies, had disappeared just prior to Corwyn's abrupt departure. It did not take great imagination to believe that he and she had conspired to depart London, and that their affair had progressed to its natural conclusion.

Marrying her would be a bold move, but it was the best way to insure he would have his chance at Lord Black. Sooner or later the man would show up, and when he did Henry intended to have his revenge. Weeks at the brink of death, months of pain, Lord Black had a sizeable debt to repay and Norfolk meant to collect it in blood.

After Black was dead, or if he never came to claim his soiled lover, Norfolk would simply arrange for his young wife to have an accident. He would not be the first husband, or the last, to be swiftly widowed by mischance.

Chapter Thirty

When Corwyn arrived at Chase manor, Mattie bustled about her as if she might die without another cup of tea or another log on the fire. A stout woman, as devoted to her bairns as she had been to their mother, she forced Corwyn to eat three times a day or more whether she wanted to or not. "Else it is yer own teeth thy babe will have to build his bones," she warned.

"And thee will not be ridin' out as thy did before thee left. Thy babe has no use for a fall," she said whenever Corwyn approached the door. "A girl in thy way should stay within."

So Corwyn wandered to and fro about the house and gardens in an endless search for something to occupy her mind and keep her thoughts off Henry and what might have become of her brother and Devon Black. Sometimes she did venture into the stables to feed Hercules a ration of carrots or apples. The huge black stallion would press its head against hers, sidling up hard against the gate that kept them apart. She knew he wondered why they could not go for a long ride along a beach or a race across the fields towards Lands End.

At night she let Mattie put her to bed only to rise again a few hours later so she could wander about the house. She would sit in the library looking at Ben's old letters or trying to find a book she had not read a hundred times. Sometimes she would pour over maps, looking for the island she had shared with Devon, remembering the sunlight and the water and the way he had touched her. Long after midnight she would drag herself up the stairs to bed, there to toss and turn until dawn finally came.

A fortnight after she returned home, Henry appeared in her library. He wore black riding clothes and it was the first time she had ever seen him in something that did not look rather girlish. Now he looked sinister.

"As you see, I have come to call." He folded himself into a chair before the fire and tapped his boots with his riding quirt, knocking mud onto the floor.

"Get out," Corwyn did not look up from her book.

"Or what? Will you send that housekeeper of yours after me? I would like to teach her some manners. Perhaps I will when we are married."

"I will never marry you." Corwyn closed her book, stood up. "I do not even want to speak to you."

"I think you will marry me eventually. You have so much to lose if you do not and I have so much to gain if you do." He looked at her curiously. "I also think you have filled out a bit since I saw you last. Strange how women change when they breed. I have had a mistress or two swell over the years, but I never lingered to see what became of them."

"Get out of my house or I will call some of the groomsmen to put you out." Corwyn tried to remember if either Tom or Jack were in the stables today. Mattie sent them to town twice a week to buy flour, sugar and other necessities the manor could not provide. Was this one of those days?

"I do not wonder that Black discarded you. You have quite an evil temper."

Corwyn could not stand it any more and turned toward the door. Surely she would be able to find someone to throw this madman out of her house.

Before she could reach it, he was in front of her. "I did not say you could leave."

"Get away from me!" Corywn took a step back and was startled to find he followed the motion. She had forgotten how quickly he could move.

"You must stop running from me. Look where it has got you." He tilted her chin up so she would look at him. "Besides, it is no use at all since I mean to have you."

"Please-" He was so close she could hear him breathe. "Please stop."

"How can you ask that of me?" Norfolk ran a finger along her cheek. "I have waited so long for you to return, and have been so patient with your . . . condition. You should thank me for wanting to marry you now that the Earl has cast you off." He smiled. "I have quite a reputation for being ruthless. There are those who would be amazed by my restraint." He brushed his lips across hers. "I will marry you. I guarantee it."

"Go away! Go away! Go away!" Corwyn shouted. She pushed past him to the door and fled the room as though the devil himself were after her. She was at the top of the stairs leading to her bedroom when he caught up to her.

"One more thing, my precious. Be careful what you tell that little general of yours and all her little soldiers. You can trust me to be quite ruthless if you erect any barriers between us. I will destroy anyone that gets in my way." He brushed his lips across hers again, apparently unaware of her recoil. Then he bounded down the stairs. "I will visit again soon." he called as he left the house.

"And who is yon rogue who thrusts himself into thy house as if he owned thee?" Mattie's five foot full figured frame shook with anger. "He did push me into a closet and put a chair under the handle. Thee will send him packing."

"He is a friend," Corwyn said wearily. "Next time he comes, just fetch me. I will make sure he does not hurt you." All she wanted to do was lie down in her warm bed and go to sleep.

"He is no friend of thine! A rogue and a villain, he is, and I would sooner leave thee with a mad dog-"

"Please, just let me know if he comes again." Corwyn began to undo the long row of buttons down the front of her dress.

"Tis hardly tea-time and thee is fallin' in bed like it were the crack of midnight. Thee is white as a sheet. Thee has had a shock of some kind and devil take me if thy friend be not the cause of it." Mattie took over the buttons, and helped her step out of the dress when it fell to the ground.

"If thy brother were here I warrant he would chase the scoundrel away. I will not be doing less for thee-"

"Ben is not here. I am here. I will handle it." Corwyn slipped into bed, folded her body around the baby growing inside her and closed her eyes.

"Why will ye not let me help thee?" Mattie, hands folded across her substantial bosom, waited for a reply.

"You will help me most by doing as I ask," said Corwyn with her eyes closed. Why had she ever come home?

"Beggin' yor pardon, M'lady," said the weathered little man, "I come about yer brother, Cap'n Chase." He had appeared at the door just at sunset the next day.

"What about him?" asked Corwyn. She had been summoned to the front parlor to meet with someone who claimed to have word of her brother. Now that he stood before her she could hardly contain her excitement. "Do you have a letter from him? Can you tell me where he is? We have been so worried-" What if Ben were to be home in time to see the baby arrive? Would not that be wonderful! Together they could decide what to do about Norfolk. It would be wonderful to have someone she could completely trust.

"The others thought I should come because I saw 'im at the end when 'e went looking fer ye-"

The end? Corwyn felt her heart sink. "I know he went looking for me in Port Royal. He gave up his commission, hired a new crew. But surely he discovered that I was not there anymore."

"'e were told yer were bought by a Spaniard, Senor Lucas. We lit out after him and found 'islands. Yer brother left the ship to find ye." He licked his lips, then continued. "We waited for 'im but 'e never-" He stopped, as if not knowing what to say. "When we made London, we 'eard ye were alive and they sent me to tell ye." While he talked he screwed his hat around in his hands, twisting it first one way then another.

Corwyn said nothing, unable to take in what he was telling her. Ben, dead? He could not be! It wasn't possible. He died trying to find her? She did not believe it. She would not believe it. She would <u>never</u> believe he was dead. As the darkness clouded her vision and she felt her legs give way beneath her, she promised herself it wasn't true. Ben had to be alive.

Chapter Thirty-One

Ben watched the struggling Negro thrown into the box with a sense of resignation. He had known it would come to this. For months he had wiled, connived and sometimes pleaded to keep from having to make this decision, but the day had finally come when he could put it off no longer. He could not live with himself, would not be able to live with the monster he became, if he did not find a way to avert this disaster.

The slaves were healthier now, they worked longer hours and got more work done. They lived longer, and occasionally they even recovered from illnesses that seemed to strike far less frequently. He had made a real improvement in the lives of the men he considered to be under his charge.

But with improved health had come more ambition. Like men anywhere, they wanted to be free. Two men had escaped in the last month, and now a man who would have been the third lay in the coffin Ben had all but died in. Manny would not agree to release him, and Ben would not watch a man die there for attempting to regain what should never have been taken from him.

Ben turned away, moving toward his cabin now that the interment was over. He only had a few hours to arrange matters before he would have to take the black man's place.

Manny caught up with him before he could enter, thick legs stumping the earth so loudly that he sounded like a galloping bull. "Where you go English? Time to work."

"I know," said Ben without stopping. "I want to eat."

"You come to fields and eat later," Manny said, breathing hard as he strode beside Ben.

"I am hungry now," said Ben tersely. "I eat now."

Manny grabbed his shoulder with a hand the size of a fist and spun him around. "Later English. You eat later. You come to the fields now."

Ben let himself be held. "I did not eat yesterday because we searched for the black." he said. "I did not eat last night because we talked." He had spent hours trying to convince Manny that the box should be abolished as a punishment for trying to escape. "I will get sick again if I do not eat."

Manny pondered this.

Ben turned back toward his cabin, but Manny stopped him again. "You smart English. But you weak. You come to the fields with me today because you make big mistake if you do not."

Ben appeared to consider his words, then said, "Can I have the girl bring me food?"

Manny looked relieved. "She bring food. I wait for you to tell her." He crossed his massive arms in a caricature of patience.

Ben completed his walk to the cabin, opened the door to find Mea sweeping the floor with a branch.

"I must work today. Make me some food and bring it to me in the east field," he said. "I am hungry, so come soon."

"Yes, Ben," she said. "I will come before the sun is high."

He took a moment to look at her, to study how her body had changed in the time they had shared. She seemed more beautiful somehow, more confident and stronger. He loved her more with every passing day. He left the cabin and walked back to Manny. They set off for the fields.

True to her word, Mea appeared before noon. She had tied the food into a piece of cotton that she carried like a bag. As soon as she appeared he walked her away from the crew he was supposed to be watching, moving to a distance that would let them speak freely.

"Today you must leave," he said without preamble. "You have food, and you will have a long head start. You go back to your people."

"I want to stay with you!" she said, her face betraying her horror at the idea of leaving him.

"I am leaving too," he lied. "Tonight I leave for home, and you cannot come with me. It is not safe for you."

"Take me with you!" Tears welled in her eyes.

"I cannot. I want you to be safe. If I am gone and you are alone here you know what will happen." He wished it were not necessary to remind her of her first days on the sugar plantation, but he saw no alternative. "Go now, please."

She studied him, then said, "Do you really want this?"

He took her hand and pulled her to him. When she was inches away, he brought his lips down to brush against hers, caressed her cheek with careful fingers. When she opened her mouth he deepened the kiss, explored her warmth slowly, savoring the feel of her in his arms. Then he broke the kiss and said. "I want you to go home where you will be safe, where your children will be safe. This is no place for you when I am gone."

She brushed her head against his chest, then took a deep breath. A moment later she was standing tall before him. Without a word she disappeared into the waving cane.

"I warn you English," said Manny. "I say you be my friend and you live. You betray me and you die."

Ben turned his head to the wall of the box. He no longer had to play the fool for this animal. He had the freedom to ignore him now.

"We catch the Negro soon, we put him back in the box after you are dead. You win nothing," said Manny. "You weak English, and you stupid."

Ben still did not speak.

"You beg me to kill you English. You strong this time and you take long time to die." Manny closed the lid and Ben heard the lock close. Once again trapped in a living hell, Ben prayed that Manny was wrong.

Chapter Thirty-Two

Black had them load Chase's body into the wagon though he doubted the man would last the five miles to where his ship waited. Curse Andre for a fool I Why had he told Ben that Lucas purchased his sister? Had not they done enough to the girl without killing her brother?

Of course, Ben had not shown the best judgment in storming right into the Alcalde's house and demanding the girl. There was no love lost between the British and Spanish in these waters. A less direct approach would probably have yielded better results. In fact, they could hardly have yielded worse.

Black shuddered at what Chase must have endured. From the scars on his back it looked as if Ben had not become one of the Alcalde's slaves willingly. But who would choose to break his back day after day in the cane fields? And he had spent days in that box before Black had been able to rescue him. What inspired a man to sacrifice himself so completely?

Corwyn, of course. Who could imagine the girl bedding that old man, bearing his children, wondering if she would ever see home again, without wanting to save her? Black felt the familiar ache in his chest, a return of the old sickness. Best to think of something else.

"Give him some water," he ordered one of the men in the wagon. "Find a way to keep him cool."

He was not going to think about Corwyn. That madness was past now and he would not bring it back again. He did not love her, he did not hate her. He did not hope for her forgiveness or fear for her safety anymore. In fact, he did not feel anything for anyone, and he meant to keep it that way.

The weeks after he had discovered Corwyn's disappearance had pushed him once again to the limit of his sanity. He had almost taken out after her, determined to capture her before she reached London and demand an explanation. Had not she loved him? He knew women, he had seen it in her eyes a hundred times. She loved him and yet she had gone away. She owed him a reason for her betrayal. She had not even bothered to leave him a note.

But her words echoed in his ears, and he had come to accept them. He was indeed the man his past had made him, and he really was something than less than human. There was no redemption at this late date, with so much blood on his hands.

At first the realization filled his head with hundreds of actions he now wished he had never taken, so many that his days became a waking nightmare of remorse. In a single-minded determination to revenge his parents' murder, he had not cared how many had suffered. How many ships had he sent to the bottom of the sea? How many men had he killed? And when he was denied his victory by a mere slip of a girl wearing her first party dress, he had hunted her down, raped her, held her captive and carelessly let her be abused by strangers. He wasn't sure he could live with himself any longer.

After weeks of misery, he had decided that he did not care if he lived or died anymore, and with surrender had come relief. He had lived in this world of his own making for many years before he had met the girl and now he took some comfort that she, at least, had escaped.

When Andre mentioned that he had sent Corwyn's brother to his death, Black had felt a flicker of regret. Yet another death on his conscience? He could not bear it. And so, here he was dragging Chase's broken body through the jungle so the man could die a free man rather than a slave. Pity he had not gotten here a week or two earlier when there might have been some hope.

They reached the clearing and the dinghy. Ben did not stir as they moved him into the bobbing conveyance, nor when they brought him on board the Wraith. He seemed determined to die. Black had Ben placed in his cabin and called for that worthless whoreson who claimed to be a surgeon. Of course, what Chase needed was a miracle not a doctor. With a start, Devon realized he could provide one.

"Chase!" Black shook him. "Can you hear me?" Ben did not stir. "Wake up, damn you!" Black shook him again. "Wake up! Your sister is alive and I am taking you to her." Black had to repeat the words several times before Ben cracked open his eyes. "Yes, that's right, you are going home and she is there to meet you." He made his voice harsh. "Is seeing her worth living for?"

Ben managed a nod, then closed his eyes again.

Black left the cabin and climbed back up on deck. He gave the order to set sail for England and with some surprise he heard his men cheer. They were probably hoping someone would hang him when they arrived. He had dragged them half way around the world twice in one year.

Well, he would put Ben off the ship in Cornwall, far from London and close to home. He would make no attempt to see Corwyn. God forbid. He wished he could forget that he had ever met her. He would just drop Lord Chase off and set sail for France. Smuggling, privateering, there was always treasure for the taking in France.

Chapter Thirty-Three

"That little martinet told me your brother died. Is it true?" Norfolk trailed after her, poking plants with his walking stick as they walked around the garden.

"I do not know," said Corwyn. She felt bone weary and sick to her stomach.

"So, it appears I am now marrying an heiress," said Norfolk.

"Really? Who?" Corwyn inquired.

"You, my dear. Now that you have your brother's estates, you area woman of substance. Of course, with your rather dubious history you are still no prize. Nevertheless, this turn of events does go someway toward compensating me for all the trouble I have endured."

"Do you not have anything better to do?" Corwyn lumbered around to face him. "You know I have no intention of marrying you. All things considered, I think I would rather hang."

"Now there is an intriguing alternative," said Henry, pausing as if to consider the thought. "Unfortunately, I am afraid it is quite impossible. In a few weeks we will be married. Your estates will be sold and we will move to London. I am afraid we must break the news to my mother gently-"

Corwyn gave up and turned back toward the house. She had no idea why he tormented her this way. She had no doubt that it served some deeper purpose than merely amusing him. She just could not imagine what it was.

"She holds you quite responsible for my recent brush with death," he said as he followed her up the gravel drive. "Which is quite sensible since your betrayal almost led to my death. Nevertheless, she will come to accept you as my wife, and you can spend the rest of your days proving to her that you love me."

Corwyn felt the first pain convulse her body as she stepped through the front door. It started at the top of her thighs and radiated up, into her belly like a knife. She gasped and clutched at the door handle. When the pain subsided, she found Henry watching her.

"Well, I suppose I will find that little housekeeper and send her to you on my way out. It seems you are about to deliver yet another bastard into the world already filled with them. I will drop by in exactly one week and shortly thereafter I will make you Lady Norfolk." Then he was gone, striding toward the kitchens as if he owned the house already.

Mattie appeared shortly after Norfolk's departure. With agitated efficiency she helped Corwyn up the stairs, holding her steady when a contraction doubled her over. Once upstairs she helped Corwyn undress and slipped a loose linen gown over her head.

"How long will this go on?" Corwyn gasped at the end of the next contraction.

Mattie, having summoned maids to strip the bed down to its sheets, patted her on the shoulder. "Ye'll find the sun up before the child's born, like as not," she said.

"So long?" How could she ever bear it?

"A fine strong lass like yerself? Ye'll not be a whimpering, will ye?" Mattie gave her a stern look. "Tis labor they call it, and labor ye will. But ye'll live, and ye'll have a babe in yer arms soon enough."

Corwyn took a deep breath as she felt the next pain start, held it until it passed. Somehow it was better when one steeled oneself for the pains, rather than merely submitting to them when they came.

Mattie smiled, "Ay, that's the way of it. Some say ye'll have an easier time of it if ye stay on yer feet as long as ye can stand."

At that point the midwife arrived and Mattie bustled away. Against all the woman's protestations, Mattie forced her to wash her hands with strong lye soap and boiled water, and to change into a freshly laundered apron. "Me ma were a midwife" she whispered to Corwyn, "an' I'll have the best in the way of care for ye."

Over time, the pains came faster and lasted longer. Corwyn held onto the bedpost as they rippled through her. After her water broke, they came even harder, until she could not stand.

Mattie helped her onto the bed, put her back against the headboard. When the first urge to push came she was surprised. Even more surprising was that pushing provided a moment's respite from the pain.

In what seemed like no time at all, she had her son in her arms. Dawn was just creeping into her window.

He had black hair and steel gray eyes. His hand curled around her finger when she touched his palm. As she put her child to her breast for the first time, her heart ached for Devon Black. Where was he now? Could he not have learned to love his child?

Nearly a week after her son's birth, Corwyn sat in the library before a blazing fire. Rain lashed the windows and a rising wind blew the branches of the trees outside the window to and fro. Having lived a lifetime in Cornwall, Corwyn recognized the signs of a gale blowing up and prayed for any ships that might be off the coast.

This kind of weather often caused shipwrecks and on more than one occasion she had watched vessels dashed to pieces off the rocks near Lands End. Any ships that had not made port already were in for a very rough night. They would not sail into any of the harbors for fear they would be blown into a breakwater or onto the shoals, and they could not stay in the channel for fear of capsizing in the rough waves and furious winds.

In her hand she held a letter from Norfolk. He promised to arrive in the next day or so, and warned her to be prepared to marry him.

Corwyn watched her baby sleep and wondered how she rid herself of Norfolk once and for all. She pulled her feet up under her dressing gown and rested her head on her knees. One thing was certain, she was through trying to appease him.

Devon Black examined the fallen tree blocked the road in front of him. Under normal circumstances he would have driven around such an obstruction, but the ground on either side of the road was a mire of mud and water several feet deep and chances were good that the old cart would sink up to its axles if he left the path.

"Are you sure this is the right way?" Devon asked Chase for the third time in the last hour. Pray God the man did not die a few furlongs from home.

"Another two miles down this road," Ben said. He shivered uncontrollably even though he was wrapped in several layers of oilskin.

Devon jumped down from the seat. He moved to unhitch the horse from the wagon. "Has it occurred to you that you have extremely bad luck?" he called back to Ben. "It seems like something unfortunate is always happening to you."

"I met you did I not?" Chase laughed a little until a cough took over and left him gasping for breath.

"Yes, and now *I* have bad luck, too. Do you think you can ride? We do not have a saddle-"

"I can ride," said Ben, sliding to the edge of the cart. "I am not an invalid."

Devon moved the ancient animal closer to make mounting easier. "That is probably for the best because I doubt this horse will carry you the entire two miles and you will have to walk the final bit alone." Once Ben was astride, he picked up the flickering lamp that provided the only source of illumination on this wretched night.

"Will not you reconsider? Stay with us a few days. I want a chance to thank you properly." A hacking cough interrupted him. When he continued, his voice rasped. "If I tell Corwyn to trust you, she will. I will explain how Norfolk used you."

Devon winced. It had been hard to come up with the host of lies required to answer Ben's questions in the last weeks. He was sure, in fact, that Ben would see through them himself if he ever had his wits entirely about him. It was all too fortuitous that he had just happened to be buying rum from Lucas when he heard about an English man being executed and decided, for no apparent reason, to save him. And Ben seemed to entirely have forgotten Corwyn's state of undress on the night Norfolk was killed. How else to explain his acceptance of Black's story that Norfolk had tricked them into what looked like a compromising situation. No, it was a pack of lies that only a man who had hung on the brink of death for weeks would believe.

"I insist you stay," said Ben thickly.

"No, no. I can feel the rope around my neck already. I will get you within sight of home and then I will head back to my ship, assuming I still have a ship." He had meant to leave Ben in Penzance, but there wasn't a room to be had. Crews from a dozen ships had filled every inn from here to Mousehole. He could not leave the man shivering out in the cold. In his weakened state he would have been dead by morning. So, here he was, delivering Chase to his door in the middle of the night, even though a chance encounter with his sister would be the end of him.

Devon led the horse around the tree and in the process found himself up to his knees in mud. It took him fifteen minutes to struggle back onto the gravel only to find Chase slipping off the horse again. He caught him in time to prevent a fall, and shook him awake. "If I can slog about in this mud, you can manage to stay on the horse. Do you hear me?"

Ben mumbled something Devon had to take as agreement, and they set off once more. The gravel was slick and the horse lost its footing with some regularity. Each time the horse stumbled, Ben would pitch forward, then start to slide off. Before long, Devon was trying to walk and hold him on. It was with some relief that he saw the windows of a manor house ahead.

"Is that it?" he asked, nudging Ben to bring him around.

Ben stirred, lifted his head slowly and peered through the darkness and rain. "I do not know. It is so dark."

"You can make the rest of the journey alone, can you not?" Devon tried to put more conviction into his words than he felt.

"I ... I think so," said Ben. "I am just a little dizzy." And with that he fell off the horse into the mud.

Devon sighed. He heaved Chase over his shoulder and made for the lights. The damned horse would have to fend for itself. It painfully obvious that Ben was falling prey to the fever that had plagued him on and off throughout the voyage and there was no point trying to convince either of them otherwise. The sooner he got the man out of the rain, the better off they would both be.

When he finally stood on the wide porch, his back felt like it would break, and his heart was pounding in his chest like a cannon. If only Corwyn were asleep, or in London, or anywhere other than answering a stranger's knock on her front door in the middle of the night. It really wasn't too much to ask. He would simply deposit her brother with some humble servant and then he would disappear. He could not bear to see her again, to see her and not have her. Just one look and it would all come back to him, all the madness and sorrow he had finally purged from himself. Mustering his courage, he pounded on the door loud enough to be heard over the storm.

In just a few seconds, the door fell open and he felt as if he were looking into the sun.

She was in a dressing gown with lace at the neck and wrists. Her eyes were wide, dark pools and her face was as white as a sheet. He tried to say something but she drew away from the door as if the devil himself stood there. He followed her into the house, wanting to explain, to banish her fear. But he found himself mute. What could he say?

After a moment, he remembered why he had traveled so far. With great care, he turned and let Ben slip from his shoulder to fall with his back against the door. Devon saw her eyes fly to Ben's face, then back to his. Without a word, she fainted.

Chapter Thirty-Four

When Corwyn awoke she was in her bedroom and she could hear Mattie ordering men about in the hall. She sat up in bed, eyes flickering around the room until they found what they were searching for.

Devon Black sat in one of the armchairs before the hearth, his child a bundle of white in his arms. Father and son stared at one another as though she had never existed, a picture of perfect harmony in the dying light of the fire.

"Devon?" Corwyn could not quite believe her eyes.

"Is this my son?" he asked, without looking at her. "I mean to say, is this our son?"

Corwyn nodded, though Devon wasn't looking at her.

"To think I might never have seen him." "You brought Ben home."

"I stumbled across him and thought you might like to have him back."

"I do not know how to thank you-"

"Please do not. To be honest, he may not survive the night, and if he does he will never be the man he was. He is very ill, and he has been badly abused over a period of months. You must not be shocked when you see him."

Corwyn sat in silence for a moment. In the morning Lord Norfolk would arrive. He would find Ben alive, and would discover who had brought him here. He would also learn that her child had been born.

Quite suddenly his determination to remain at her side made sense. It was not for love of her that he hung about, rather a desire for revenge. He had expected Devon to return for her.

"You must leave right away." She announced.

"No." Devon did not look up.

"You are going to take your child and leave my house tonight. You are never going to come back." Corwyn heard herself say the words and felt the emptiness in her chest that went with them.

"I do not understand." He looked around.

"I do not want you near me and I do not want the baby. I do not want either of you in my house. Get out!" Once they were out of the house, safely away from Norfolk and his twisted scheme, she could rest easy. In fact, now that she had seen Devon with his son, she knew the child would be safe, would grow up loved and happy.

And, she could dispose of Norfolk herself. Of course she would hang because she was about to kill him in cold blood, but that seemed a reasonable trade. It was better than living without her son and without Devon, surviving in a loveless marriage with a man that hated her. In fact, she doubted that Norfolk would let her live long after Devon was dead. He hated them both.

"I cannot believe what I am hearing." Devon's face was tight, his eyes like black pits in the dark room.

"Get out of my house." Corwyn felt her heart breaking as she spoke. It was all so clear.

Devon stood up, his child in his arms. "You are a most unnatural woman."

"Get out."

She heard him leave the room, heard his footsteps in the hall. She fell back onto the bed, heart pounding with uncertainty. She could run to him, could catch him, could beg him to take him with her. But what of Ben? Norfolk was still alive, still determined to punish her. If she were gone, who would Norfolk punish in her stead?

She heard the front door open and close. It was over. They were safely out in the clear night left by the rain. It was a few short miles to Penzance, where Devon could surely find a wet nurse, then onto his ship where he would be outside Norfolk's reach.

She studied the firelight flickering on the ceiling. After a time she found she did not feel like crying or running after them anymore. Her chest felt hollow, her mind felt vacant, but the fear she had lived with for so long was finally gone. It was strange how her problems had been solved so unexpectedly.

"Where is thy bairn?"

Mattie was shaking her. Had she fallen asleep? She had watched the dawn fill the sky in an idle search for peace. Then, just as she had finally decided to rise and dress for the day, she must have drifted off.

"Where is thy child?" Mattie was shouting at her, panic evident.

"With his father." Corwyn struggled to sit up and found that her breasts were sore.

"What?" Mattie took her by the shoulders and shook her hard. "What hast thou done?"

"I sent him away with his father. It was my decision-"

"Thou sent thy babby with that... that Pirate?"

"Devon loved him. I could see that." Corwyn felt anger stir. She had been through so much in the last weeks, and now Mattie was attacking her. Well, she would not stand for it. "Get out of my room."

Mattie slapped her hard across the face. "I curse the day I ever saw ye. Better ye had never been born, thou cruel, thoughtless, chit." She strode from the room.

Corwyn sat in the drawing room at the appointed hour. She had loaded a pair of Ben's pistols and they hid in the folds of her dress. She held a book in her hands, but instead of reading it, she watched the fire flicker. Where was Devon? The sky was overcast but the rain had stopped. He must have reached his ship by now. What would her son think of her when he grew up? She had held him for such a short time, he would never remember her. He would think that she did not love him.

She heard a rap at the door, and a moment later Mattie ushered Norfolk into the room. "Thy friend, milady," she said, then she disappeared, leaving the door wide open.

"So, you are safely delivered. Where is your son?" Norfolk looked about the room as if expecting to see the child in some corner.

"I sent him away as you instructed."

"I did not instruct you to send him away. I said we would find a place for him." Norfolk's voice rose sharply.

"I have already found a place for him," said Corywn. "He is with his father."

"I will kill you, you bitch!"

She brought both guns up as he took a step toward her, and she saw his face blanche.

"I can assure you she *will* pull the trigger." Corwyn heard Devon's voice and she turned to find him standing in the open door. He was dressed as he had been last night, in a lawn shirt, dark britches and muddy boots. The only difference was that this time his rapier was drawn. Her blood ran cold as she saw Henry turn toward him, saw his hands move toward his own weapon. She took careful aim at his head.

"Corywn, do *not* shoot him," Devon's voice was stern.

Corwyn pulled the trigger. In the small room the sound made her head feel as though it had been split open. She opened her eyes to find that Norfolk was substantially nearer the door, and Black was holding a blade to his throat.

She leveled the second pistol, and was surprised to see Devon step between Norfolk and the gun. "No."

Corwyn lowered the gun.

Then Devon turned his attention to Norfolk. "So, Henry, here we are. You have wanted me for along time, and now you have me. What shall I do with you?"

"Murder me and you, the girl and her brother will all hang."

"You mean, if I murder you, you will be dead and that is not at all part of your plan." Black smiled. "So, let us settle our differences like gentlemen." He took a step back. "Where do we fine gentlemen settle our disputes these days? I believe it is at the Oaks just outside London, isn't it?"

Norfolk straightened, his relief evident. "I see. We will meet there in a week."

"You will see me there in three days. We will leave now, and we will ride together, eat together, sleep together until I can kill you like the gentlemen I am supposed to be, before witnesses."

"Lord Black, this is none of your affair." Ben stood in the hall, dressed haphazardly and with a face as white as a sheet. "I will meet him at the Oaks-"

"No!" said Corwyn. She raised the second pistol and pointed it at Henry's heart.

"Corwyn, please put the gun down." Devon did not deign to look at her. "The situation is well in hand." He continued. "With respect, Lord Chase, you are in no condition to fight a duel with Lord Norfolk. He is said to be a competent swordsman, and as you are now he will kill you. You may serve as my second, if you wish."

"I cannot let you do this." Ben teetered, put his hand on the door frame to balance himself.

"Corwyn has just borne my child."

"What!"

"When all is said and done I think you will find you want to kill me far more than you want to kill Henry. Under the circumstances, I suggest you take on the loser."

Ben looked stricken, but managed to reply, "As you wish, Lord Black."

"So, Henry, are you up to defending yourself? Can you see us standing there, the fog clutching at the trees, toe to toe, cold steel singing for blood, its what you live for, is it not? Its not often you get a man like me who will give you a run for your money."

"I will have the girl after you are dead." "We shall see."

Black turned to Corwyn, eyes softening at her disheveled state, "We will leave in under an hour. Mattie already has you packed and our son, having rejected his nurse, is desperate for you."

She held out her pistol, butt first. "Why did you not let me kill him?"

"Because, my dear, if he died in this house, without witnesses, with you, your brother and I all in attendance, we really would have been hanged."

Chapter Thirty-Five

True to Black's word they left in under an hour. Black and Norfolk shared a coach driven by Adam and flanked by members of Black's crew. Corwyn, Ben, Mattie and the baby shared another coach. Holding her son in her arms again, Corwyn could not control her tears. His hands clutched at her breasts as she fed him, and his eyes grew wide as he searched her face. How could she have sent him away? She loved him so much.

That night they stopped at a bustling inn near Bodmin. Corwyn, Mattie and the baby shared one room, while Norfolk and Black shared another. Ben took a third. In the early hours of the morning, unable to sleep, Corwyn left her bed and descended to the taproom where she found Norfolk and Black playing cards. Adam stood with his back to the door.

When Black saw her, he stood up and ambled toward her. "Do you often frequent drinking establishments at two in the morning?"

"Why are you doing this?" Corwyn brought her hand to his lips. It was so hard to believe he was real.

"Norfolk's probably not much of a match. He is just a bully who has had his way for far too long. There are thousands of men like him in the islands. I've bested his kind before."

"I do not know how to repay you -"

"I am not asking you to repay me." Black brought a finger along her cheek.

"This is a touching little scene." Norfolk turned to lay his legs along the bench and put his back against the wall. "I cannot wait to see how things will play out when I've laid Lord Black and Lord Chase in their graves."

Black smiled. "Do not listen to him. He is a bit insane you know, and I am beating him rather badly at cards."

Corwyn's hand came to his chest, then slid up to his cheek, then curled into his hair. She pulled his head down until his lips met hers. Touching him, holding him, was like having heaven in her arms.

He broke the kiss, after a time, and took a step away. "Go to bed. It is late and we have a full day ahead."

The next day found Corwyn, Mattie, Ben and the baby jostling toward London. A light rain made the air uncomfortably damp, but the roads remained passable.

"Tell me how Lord Black came to father your child," said Ben. His face was flushed, as if he were again succumbing to fever.

"It is a long story-"

"You were aboard the Albatross, and then what happened."

Should she tell the truth? She would have to. She could not bear to lie to him after all he had been through. "He took me captive. In the weeks that followed I shared his bed. In Port

Royal I ran away and was captured by Du Joles. He was a slave trader-"

"Who tried to sell you to an Alcalde-"

"But Devon rescued me. I lived on his island and when I knew I was to have a child I found a way to come home-"

"I see." Ben closed his eyes. "I suffered the agonies of hell when I thought you were dead. And when I received the message-"

"My message about Du Joles?" Corwyn found herself remembering those dark days, how she had prayed for Ben to find her.

"I gave up my commission and I searched for you. I was told an Alcalde had purchased you. I went to him, demanded you, and became a . . . slave." The word seemed to trouble him. "I would have died if Devon . . . Lord Black had not rescued me." He spoke in a whisper.

"Aman, one of your crew, told us you were dead."

"I was, until I knew you were alive." Ben opened his eyes. "It is all his fault. He sought me out so he could see you again. All our misery is on his head."

"I do not think so-" said Corwyn, though it was hard not to argue that Devon was responsible for all Ben's misfortune.

"Do not defend him!" Ben sat up. "I know what he is. I know all about men like him. They see no reason not to take what they want, to force others to serve their will-"

"Please, please. I do not want to argue." Corwyn handed the baby to Mattie and reached forward to brush her hands across Ben's face. How hot he was, and how thin. This journey might well be the end of him. "Cannot you see it does not matter? You and I are together again and the past is behind us."

Ben buried his face in his hands. "It will never be behind me. You have no idea what I have seen."

"Why do you not tell me?" Corwyn asked. "Tell me what happened to you."

Ben turned his face to the wall.

Another day of travel brought Corwyn, Ben and Mattie to Christina's home in London. In a short time Ben was safely ensconced in a bed warmed with hot bricks, and Mattie was below stairs cooking a meal he might be compelled to eat.

Corywn was seated in the front parlor when a footman announced that she had a visitor. A moment later Devon entered the room.

"I hope you will forgive this intrusion. I wanted to see you-" he began.

"You are welcome. Please, sit down." Corwyn gestured at a chair. How handsome he looked, dressed almost as he had been the first time she had seen him so long ago. Black britches, waistcoat and greatcoat, snow white shirt and his hair tied back with a satin ribbon; he was the picture of an English Lord. It was hard to believe this tall, broad shouldered stranger had ever held her in his arms.

"Quite a shock isn't it?" He smiled. "It seems I am still a rich man because I did not quite manage to kill Henry the first time around."

"More is the pity," said Corwyn. How could he make light of their situation?

"I suppose there is no use prevailing upon you to stay home tomorrow." Devon met her eyes. "I cannot think you will find much joy in what you will see."

"I will be there," replied Corwyn.

Devon shrugged, surrendering without an argument.

"Where is Lord Norfolk?" Corwyn asked. "Is it safe to leave him alone?"

"When last I saw him he was announcing his intention to slit my throat to several members of his club. Since he has sworn to half of London that he will meet me at the Oaks, I am inclined to take him at his word. Henry acquits himself well on this particular field, so I expect he will show."

"Are you afraid?"

Devon shrugged. "I am rather good at killing. It seems to be the one trade I've mastered."

Corwyn said nothing, studying him. He seemed different some how, more relaxed than she had ever seen him.

"Can I see my son?"

"Of course," Corwyn leapt to her feet. She led him to the bassinet by the fire. "He is sleeping, I am afraid."

"No matter." With infinite care, Devon collected his son from his cot. "If he is like the men in my family, he will be very tall. It is hard to believe that we all start out little more than a handful."

"I told Ben about... the Albatross," said Corwyn.

"And about the rest of your journey I hope. He should know everything and I never knew how to tell him." Devon did not lift his eyes from his son's sleeping face. "I imagine that he is very angry."

"I believe so. He suffered terribly."

Devon nodded. "I imagine he did. I spent six years cutting cane on Barbados. It is the worst kind of slavery. Men are . . . destroyed."

"Six years," said Corwyn, wondering how anyone could survive for six years in the place Ben had described.

"To live that long you have to make a choice. You must either do what is right, or you must . . . participate in the crime." He put the child in its cot.

"Ben didn't." said Corwyn.

"Ben would have died," he said frankly. "Good men die there. Bad men thrive."

"Which are you?" asked Corwyn?

Devon smiled a little. "I do not know. I guess, given the same choice today, I would do what Ben did. The price is too high to do anything else."

"Too high?" Corwyn studied his face.

He smiled again. "You and your brother. It is hard not to admire you. No matter what the odds, you seem to know how important it is to keep your soul. I did not know I had one until I met you."

Corwyn couldn't believe her ears.

Devon brushed his hand across her cheek, then sighed. "I should be off. There are a surprising number of arrangements to make."

Corwyn followed him to the door. What if he died tomorrow? The thought was too horrifying to contemplate.

"Wait," she said.

He stopped and turned to face her.

"I ... just want to thank you," she said. "I do not know where I would be if you had not brought Ben to me, if you weren't here-"

"The question is where you might be if we had never met," replied Black. "I wonder if you would be happier than you are now." A moment later he was gone.

Devon sat in his solicitor's office reviewing a draft of his will. "It seems straight-forward enough. Is it likely to be challenged?"

The old man squinted at him, shook his head. "I cannot imagine who would have standing. If you were to die without making arrangements, I believe the property would revert to the crown for lack of an heir."

"As you warned my uncle repeatedly," said Devon, waving his hand to fend off the lecture.

"Indeed. And you are declaring that the child is of your body."

"Without any doubt at all." said Devon. "Should I make a record of some kind telling how he came to be conceived?"

The old man blushed, turned his blue lips into his hands and coughed politely. "I do not think that will be necessary."

"Are you sure?"

"If you and the mother affirm that the child is of your body, there is no bar to make. I trust she will do so."

"Yes," said Black, "I believe she will." He signed the document with a flourish, using the title that meant so little now. Who wanted to own an appellation that had so little to offer the world? If he survived, he would make sure it came to mean something remarkable.

"Well My Lord, your affairs are in order." The man gathered up the documents and placed them in wooden box with a stack of deeds and trusts tied to the Kettering house. "I look forward to a long and happy association."

"Nothing would please me more." Black said as he left the office. "Nothing at all."

Chapter Thirty-Six

Devon arrived shortly after sunrise, noting that more than a dozen carriages had surrounded the small glade. Though the grove known as the Oaks lay on the edge of the river, there was no fog this morning. The air was clear and cold and a slow breeze made the red and gold leaves above his head rustle.

He saw Lord Chase standing near Corwyn on the far side of the glade. His second seemed unable to stand up straight, and as Devon approached he could see that his eyes were hollow and his flesh was gray. Corwyn, on the other hand, stood poised as if it were she who would fight today.

"I think," said Corwyn, as he approached, "it would have been easier if you had just let me shoot him."

"For who? My Lady," Black replied. How he loved her! From the moment he had seen her, had seen his son, everything had become clear. He could not possess her, could not force her to love him. But nothing, nothing, could make him stop loving her. Given time to become the man he should have been, rather than the man the world had made him, he could find a way to contribute to her happiness. And that alone would be enough for him. He would start by making her safe and by protecting those she loved.

"For you," she said softly. "I cannot believe it has come to this-"

"Hush," Devon said. "There is no use arguing with destiny."

He turned his attention to Lord Chase, whose face was now flushed with anger. What could he say that would undo the misery of so many months? "There will be no trouble if Norfolk dies here?" he said by way of conversation.

"A man may settle his debts as he wills," said Ben, hand dropping to his own weapon. "If he chooses to meet, who is to gainsay him?"

A clatter came from behind him, and Black turned to find Norfolk emerging from a carriage. He was dressed with unusual simplicity, a red waistcoat, white shirt, black britches and riding boots. He looked rested, confident.

Devon turned back to Corwyn, "Kiss me," he said.

"What?" she took a step back.

"I am here defending your honor. It would look best if we appeared... associated in some way." Devon replied.

"She will appear a harlot." Ben's contempt was obvious. "You have-"

"Lord Chase, she is an unmarried woman with a child. She can hardly look more disreputable. We should at least make sure that Henry is not thought her savior."

Devon stepped toward Corwyn. He pulled her into his arms, and brushed his lips against hers, felt his blood sing at the touch. To his surprise she deepened the kiss, her body pressing against his, her hands coming to his cheek. He felt her breasts against his chest, her legs stirring beneath her gown. Christ, how he wanted her.

"Enough," he said, pushing her away. "I think that demonstration will be quite . . . sufficient." How beautiful she was, and how lucky he was to have had her.

It was hard to turn away and walk to where Norfolk waited for him, his steel blade already glinting in the sun.

"Shall we?" Devon asked as he drew his blade. It felt unfamiliar in his hand. How long since he had drawn it in anger? More than a year surely. It was hard to recall.

"As you will, Cur," Norfolk replied.

True to his reputation, Norfolk was fast and exceptionally well trained. His first parry caught Devon unprepared, the blade sliding along underneath his rapier searching for his chest. To counter Devon had to jump back and to the side.

Norfolk followed the move smoothly and a moment later Devon found himself forced to step back again to avoid a slashing strike to his neck. This time, however he managed a counter thrust that made Norfolk stumble back as well.

There was a pause as the two men, separated by more than a sword length, sized each other up.

Devon could feel a thrill of excitement, or was it fear, running through his veins. What he did not feel, which was quite surprising, was the bloodlust that usually came to him with the first thrust. Perhaps it was his hate and anger that had given him so many victories. Without that he might not be capable of killing. He shook his head to clear it. This was surely no time for self-doubt.

Norfolk made his next attack, his blade striking not for Devon's chest but for his sword arm. Steel met flesh and Devon felt a ribbon of burning pain cut through his forearm.

"You are not very good at this, are you," said Norfolk stepping away. "I had expected something more from the Black Earl."

Devon did not reply. Obviously Norfolk had decided to strike at secondary targets, opening up defenses until his blade could reach a critical target. That was very cunning. How distasteful it was to find one's opponent so much better than expected.

"Shall we proceed?" Norfolk stepped in again. His thrusts came thick and furious until Devon brought his rapier across the man's thigh. It was only a scratch, but it made Norfolk jump back.

Devon initiated the next series of attacks, striking hard to insure that Norfolk expended a great deal of strength parrying each blow. He struck repeatedly in the same area until Norfolk began turning his body to anticipate the blade. Then, when one of Norfolk's parries came just a little late, he brought his blade across the man's upper thigh again. Muscle was exposed, but his blade hadn't penetrated anywhere near the bone. Norfolk managed to respond with another, deeper strike to Devon's right forearm.

Both men fell back, breathing hard. Devon was the first to speak.

"Let us take a moment to bind our wounds before we proceed or you will faint before I can kill you."

"Done," said Norfolk. "I suggest you take a moment to say farewell to that tart and your son. You will not get another opportunity."

Devon walked toward his horse, his hand holding the wound on his arm closed. It was hard to grasp his weapon, hard to close his fist around the haft of the blade. He reached into his saddlebag for a length of linen. Always wise to be prepared, he thought as he pulled it out. He turned to find Corwyn standing beside him. She took the cloth away.

"Tell me what to do," she said.

"Get the dagger out of the bag. Slice away the shirt. Wrap my arm very, very tightly."

The pair of wounds, once exposed, were much worse than he expected. The second had gone clear to the bone, just missing an artery. It was bleeding a great deal. He watched Corwyn bite her lip. Without being told she started to fashion a tourniquet.

"I met with my solicitor," Devon said, "I have settled my estates on your son if I should die. To do that I had to acknowledge him as my son. The entail says I cannot leave the property to anyone else." Devon watched her tie off the bandage, already blood soaked.

"He is your son," she said. "You may tell anyone you like."

Devon saw that she was shivering from fear and shock. "I told you to stay home. This is no place for a woman."

"Its no place for anyone. How can men slice each other to bits like this-" she stopped, as if realizing that her words might hurt his performance.

"I may not get a chance to tell you, if I do not tell you now," said Devon. "I am very sorry. I hope you can forgive me. I have made so many mistakes, harmed you in so many ways-"

"Not now!" said Corwyn furiously, rubbing tears away from her eyes. "Do not ask my forgiveness now. I will not forgive you unless you live."

Devon laughed, and noted that the silent observers in the glen turned toward him. "Then I shall live, My Lady," he said.

He strode back to the center of the glen, noting how the grass was trampled and slippery with blood and dew. Norfolk's leg was bandaged, and he seemed more confident. Devon found that his right thumb and forefinger were numb. His blade wavered when he brought it up.

"Let us begin," said Norfolk, and he drove forward with a series of vicious thrusts. Black parried his strikes clumsily, making no attempt to counter attack. Norfolk was relentless, his blows coming closer and closer to Devon's chest.

Devon stumbled, dropped his blade, fell to one knee. Norfolk came in for the kill.

Devon, having picked up the blade in his left hand, drove it through Norfolk's belly and up into his chest. At Norfolk's surprised look, Devon said "I am as good with my left hand as I am with my right, you poor bastard."

Chapter Thirty-Seven

That evening, at his flat, Devon sat before his fire drinking Madiera. More than a year in his cellar had not harmed its flavor at all. In fact it was better.

The place was still musty, having been opened up less than twenty-four hours ago, and most of the furniture was still covered in sheets. He had not taken time to light any candles, preferring the solitude of darkness. His arm, stitched and rebandaged, ached unbearably. It seemed a good time to get drunk.

The knock at his door surprised him. It took him time to struggle to his feet, then to feel his way through the door and down the stairs. What he saw there was Benjamin Chase, holding a pistol pointed at his chest.

"I am not sure you should be out of bed," he said as he stepped back.

Ben made no reply, just used the pistol to gesture at the stairs.

Devon nodded and turned to obey his silent instruction. He heard Ben close the door and come slowly up after him.

Devon returned to his seat before the fire, and waved a hand at the opposite chair. "Please, make yourself at home."

"I have come to kill you," Ben said as he settled into the sheet-covered armchair.

"I will not try to stop you," said Devon. "If a man had done to me what I have done to you, I believe that I would want him dead." He took another sip of Madeira.

"But I believe my sister loves you. If I kill you she will hate me," Ben wiped the back of his hand across his face. "You have destroyed me."

Devon watched the fire burn in the hearth, wondering if Ben's words were true.

"How could you do this to her?" Ben sat forward.

"Well, early on I would have told you that I hated her because I had fought long and hard to come home and she had turned me into a castaway again. To lose everything twice in one life time seemed terribly unfair." He sighed. "But now I believe I loved her from the very start." said Devon. "When I lost everything, she was the one thing I would not give up." Devon took another drink, flexed his hand. Christ, his arm hurt. "I was an animal in a rage. I was very cruel."

"I looked for her for months!" said Ben, his struggle to control his emotions apparent. "You cannot know what I endured."

"Well that is not strictly true. She ran away in Port Royal. I searched and searched. It was a living hell. You really ought to shoot me for almost losing her there." Devon remembered the dark-haired girl he had come across, naked, beaten, raped. He drank again. "When I found her, she would not come with me. I think she was trying to protect me -" He stopped, contemplated the coals. "She almost died."

"I thought that bastard, Lucas, had her," said Ben.

"And he enslaved you." Devon gave himself another drink, "And that is the crux of the matter. I do not believe that I have destroyed you. I believe you are committed to destroying yourself."

"What!" Ben raised the pistol.

"You are going to shoot me for telling you the truth?" Devon shook his head in disbelief.

Ben was silent.

"I worked a slaver and I have cut cane. I know what you see when you close your eyes. I know how much you hate yourself for escaping rather than fighting to put things right. You want to die."

"I want revenge!" said Ben harshly.

"Then take it from me if you can," said Devon. "I hope it does you more good than it did me." He stared into the fire remembering all the years he had planned his revenge against his uncle, as if killing him would fix everything that had been broken inside.

Ben raised the pistol again, held it for a long time. Then let it fall. Then he buried his face in his hands.

Devon watched him for a while, then found himself speaking again. "My father was an unusual man," he said.

Ben looked up.

"They say he was a philanthropist. Founded charities, schools. He was as good as a man can be."

Ben stared at him.

"I have decided that the only way to have my revenge is to be like him. Otherwise all those bastards who made my life a living hell will have succeeded. They will have made me into a monster instead of the man I was meant to be." Devon smiled, "This sounds ridiculous, but I am committed to changing the world because I am tired of evil going unopposed."

"Hand me the bottle," said Ben, leaning forward. Taking it, he drank deep, then wiped his mouth on his sleeve. "I hope she will have you." His face looked haggard, but relieved some how.

Black smiled. "I hope so too. I certainly do not deserve her." He waited a moment, then continued. "By the way, I have never seen a man look so utterly miserable."

"I feel worse," Ben offered.

"Perhaps if you would just stay in bed for more than four hours at a time-"

Ben's head dropped onto his chest as if in reply, and Devon sighed. He levered himself out of his chair and walked unsteadily to Ben's side. Once again he was burning with fever, and his breath was shallow and ragged. Devon lifted him and carried him to bed. "There is a stubborn streak in your family," he told the sleeping man as his head hit the pillow, "and one day it will kill you all."

"Your cousin let me in," said Devon by way of apology. He closed the door to Corwyn's bedroom and moved to stand beside the bed. "She said you were awake."

"Your son has his morning meal with the sunrise," said Corwyn. She carefully pulled the baby away from her breast, and adjusted her clothing until she was decently covered. All things considered, she had little reason to pretend modesty with Devon Black.

"Do not let me interrupt you," said Devon. "I can leave-"

"He is finished for the time being," said Corwyn. "He cannot eat all the time though he seems inclined to try."

"I thought most gentlewomen engaged a wet nurse."

Corwyn felt the blood rush to her face. "One more word and we will have an argument. He is my child and I will feed him. I've heard quite enough from Mattie and Christina on the matter-"

"I quite agree," said Devon. "I have never understood the practice, I simply noticed that you had not adopted it."

Corwyn said nothing, somewhat surprised.

"At any rate, he belongs with his mother. That I am certain of."

"Why have you come?" she asked. "To see Ben?"

"I have seen Ben, thank you. He is at my flat, sleeping. I have had a pair of doctors in who have also seen him. The first was a blood-letting quack so I sent him packing. The second has some experience with tropical fevers and has some potions that seem effective." Devon rubbed his forehead as if it hurt, "What with one thing and another, He did not let me get much sleep last night."

"Was he angry?" Corywn asked.

"Furious," Devon replied. "He has his pistol at his bedside. I've removed the ball, however, so he will not shoot the doctor in a fit of delirium."

"So why have you come?" Corwyn asked. Her heart was pounding, and she could hear the blood in her ears.

"I was wondering if you would marry me, because I love you very, very much," said Devon.

"I-," said Corwyn, then stopped. She did not know what to say.

"When last we met you said I was the man my past had made me, and you were right." Devon stopped. He was looking at his hands. "I will not try to wash away those first weeks on the ship. I was unbelievably cruel, and what I did was wrong beyond words. But I can tell you that I loved you very much even then. I knew you would never forgive me, so I never asked you to."

Corwyn could not stop the tears from falling.

"I thought I would go mad when I lost you in Port Royal. I was trying to send you home, and you were so afraid of what I might do to you that you ran away," he looked up. "I looked for you everywhere. It was a waking nightmare. When I found you again, I knew I could never let you go. So I took you to my island and prayed that you would learn to love me. When you left, I knew you could not love a monster."

Black shook his head. His voice became unsteady. "And then I heard Andre had sent your brother to the Alcalde. I could not leave him there. So I found him and brought him back to you. I never meant to see you again. I wanted to let you go. But I fear I cannot live without you -"

"Yes," said Corwyn.

Black stopped. "What?" he asked.

"Yes, I will marry you. We will have a house full of children, and we will live happily ever after," said Corwyn, reaching for him. "Please do not <u>ever</u> let me go."

Epilogue

Corwyn absently rubbed her belly, soothing the child that kicked inside. "This one says you are a misguided mad man," she said as she read the newspaper. "A home for women and children only encourages husbands to abandon them."

"How informative," Devon replied without looking up. He dipped his quill in ink and added another entry to a column full of numbers. "At least it is better than last week. Then I was just trying to restore my unsalvageable honor."

"I thought that was the week before," Corwyn folded the yellow sheets and laid them on the table. She noted that her son was carrying the gray kitten about again. "Devon, put the cat down. He will not be much fun to play with if you choke him to death."

Devon released the cat, squealing with glee as it ran away. A moment later he had dropped to his hands and feet and was scrabbling after it across the carpet.

"I daresay I should pack. We will have to get an early start in the morning," Corwyn stood up.

"Cannot see why she's marrying the scoundrel," said Devon, turning to a new ledger. "She deserves better."

"The women in our family are experts at reforming scoundrels," said Corwyn, moving around the table to caress his shoulder.

"If that is a girl you are carrying," said Devon, "I do not want her to hear you talk that way." He put his pen down and shifted to put his head against her belly. "She should marry a good man, like your brother. A solid, trustworthy, kind and substantial man who will treat her well."

"That's exactly what a good scoundrel turns into, under the right kind of influence."

Devon pulled her into his lap, brushed his lips across the swelling mounds that pushed above her gown. "Care to influence me some more, My Lady?" he asked with a smile. "I feel quite the rogue just now."

THE END

FOR MORE BOOKS & AUDIO DRAMAS
BY ANDREYA STUART

VISIT

WWW.AMAZON.COM
WWW.MOBILELOVESTORIES.COM
OR DOWNLOAD THE DARK ROMANCE APP
FOR YOUR IPHONE, IPAD OR ANDROID DEVICE

Made in the USA
Las Vegas, NV
05 January 2023